THE LYING GAME

BRIGHTON BROTHERS
BOOK 1

SARA JANE WOODLEY

Cover character art by
YUMMY BOOK COVERS

ELEVENTH AVENUE
PUBLISHING

1

LACHLAN

It's all going down on a Thursday.

A *Thursday*. The most neutral, no-nonsense day of the week. Neither a low-energy slog like a Monday, nor the taste-of-freedom excitement of a Friday. If it were a color, Thursday would be gray.

Thursday is my favorite day.

Was my favorite day. Because right now, on this rainy, miserable Thursday, the very real crap is hitting the figurative fan.

"No comment!" I bark into the phone, hardly hearing a word from the person on the other end before punching *End Call*. I know what they're gonna say, what they're gonna ask. I've taken to answering the phone using the line we were trained to use during our media relations seminars. I might as well make it my voicemail outbox message.

I rifle through the papers on my desk, not that they can help anything or change what's happened. But having these papers to rifle through, to tear up and wrinkle and work between my hands makes me feel like I have some sort of control. Some say in what's going on outside of the glass walls of my office.

Through the far wall, I see Ariana stand from the front desk

1

kitty-corner to me. She begins click-clacking her way towards the mahogany door at the end of the hallway.

She's going to see Mike.

The meeting must finally be over.

My phone screen lights up again with an unknown number, and I ignore the call before scrolling in my contacts to my one and only, most trusted right-hand man. I hold the ringing phone to my ear with one hand while waving my other frantically at Ariana to get her attention through the glass.

She stops abruptly and blinks her huge hazel eyes at me.

The girl must've been one of those bug-eyed chihuahuas or something in a past life, I swear.

"Mike free?" I mouth to her.

She shrugs, all chihuahua-in-the-headlights. Then, she continues briskly towards the massive corner office belonging to our CEO.

I pinch the bridge of my nose, frustrated, irritated, and every other -ated you can possibly imagine. Not at Ariana necessarily, just at this whole *situation*.

Ariana's a new hire, fresh out of college. I try to put on a softer side around our new team members, but right now, I simply don't have the time or energy to seem "nice" or "pleasant" or "calm" or any of the other adjectives HR used to describe the impression I apparently *do not* give.

A "charm problem" is how they specifically described it. Which just sounds to me like a thinly veiled way to call me an a-hole.

Then again, I would bet that Mike hired me, has repeatedly promoted me, and continues to give me new projects *because* of that quality. There's a reason I've climbed the ranks so quickly at SparksFly, and I'd agree that "charm" is very much *not* something I concern myself with.

The ringing stops. There's a click, and then...

"This is Dee."

2

"Dee, finally!" I practically shout, my paper-rifling picking up ten-fold. "Listen, I need you to—"

"Thanks for calling. Leave your name and number, and I'll get right back to you."

There's a long beep, and I take a very slow, very patient, very *calm* breath in. "Hi, Dee. Not sure where you are, but I'm in a bit of a bind over here. If you could give me a call back as soon as you are able, that would be lovely."

I say this nicely. Patiently. Calmly.

It's potentially the hardest thing I've had to do all day.

Not that Dee would necessarily mind me barking at her over voicemail—we've worked together for a couple years now and have been through enough together that she knows not to take my briskness to heart.

The minute I end the voicemail, my ringtone blares out yet again, but the "unknown name, unknown number" clearly isn't Dee. I silence the call.

And then, for the first time in literal years—certainly the first time since I started working at this online dating tech conglomerate—I put my phone on Silent mode and place it screen-down on my desk.

I suddenly feel way too hot. My shirtsleeves are already rolled up to my elbows, and I've undone two of the buttons at my collar. Any more, and I'll look like I'm auditioning for that ridiculous "Stripping Mike" movie.

Which, on a side note, appears to be the intended goal for many of the male users on our dating platforms, if the shirtless bathroom selfies and flexing gym mirror photos are anything to go by. One of my teams is running stats about the efficacy of those photos with our female users. It's not looking great.

What happens now?

"Mr. Chase?" a high-pitched squeak comes from the direction of my doorway. "Mr. Niles wants to see you."

3

I look up to see Ariana hightailing it away from my office... silently, because she removed her heels to run back to her desk.

I guess that says everything you need to know about my attempts at being charming.

"'Bout time," I mutter hoarsely, grabbing my suit jacket from the back of my chair.

As I step out of my office, I pretend not to notice the dozens of heads popping out from doorways and alcoves. The employees at SparksFly are *nosy*. Might be a by-product of working at a company with one of the biggest dating app and website portfolios in the world. But it's very unlike my own "live and let live" perspective.

Or, you know, "work and let work".

I make it to Mike's office in a few strides and knock twice on the mahogany door before stepping into the room. It's a bare space, the large cherry wood desk at the center drawing immediate attention. Two stiff, behemoth leather chairs are pulled up in front of the desk. I know from experience that those chairs feel about as comfortable as they look.

"Mike, listen. I know how this must lo—"

"Hey, Chase!" my boss and the CEO of SparksFly says boisterously, leaning back in his desk chair. "How you holding up, sport?"

I blink, thrown. When I speak, my voice is gruff. "Seriously?"

Mike laughs. *Laughs.*

Which is pretty much the opposite reaction I was expecting. But I suppose it's better than the alternative when a company's CEO calls you in for a meeting on the heels of a PR disaster that *you* caused.

"Sit, sit. Seems we have a few matters to discuss."

"I'll say." I don't bother trying to appear jovial. Mike knows me well enough to see right through it anyway.

My boss clicks his mouse, and an article appears on his

4

computer monitor. An article featuring a photo of me, front and center.

It's not a good photo. It's a candid, taken while I was leaving the office. I'm wearing one of my tailored charcoal suits, a hand in one pocket, and my Ray-Bans folded into the crook where the top button of my dress shirt is undone.

Problem is, my shoulders are thrown back in a way that looks deeply arrogant, even to me. All I can think is that I must've been stretching my back or something.

On top of that, though, I'm glaring. Full-on *glaring* at the person taking my photo.

Honestly, I can't remember that day, or the person taking that photo, but I look very much like I have a "charm problem."

It isn't news to me that I have a resting glaring-while-also-somehow-eye-rolling face. But it *is* news to see it like this. In the news.

"So." Mike steeples his hands on his desk, peering at me with his animated brown eyes. "Can't say that SparksFly has ever encountered anything like this before."

"I don't know if *anyone's* encountered something like this before."

Mike nods against his steepled fingers. The guy's nearing sixty, but you wouldn't know it. His dark hair is graying only slightly near his temples, and he somehow knows all the new generation's slang and upcoming trends. It also doesn't hurt that he exclusively dates women who are a few decades younger than him.

"Why don't you take a seat and tell me the full story," he insists, gesturing towards the leather chairs again.

I hate literally everything about this moment. But I sit.

Because when Mike Niles tells you to do something, you do it.

Mike is what you'd expect for a man once named in LA's top 40 under 40. He's complex. Intelligent. Driven. He co-

5

founded the SparksFly Group and has dedicated his life to growing his empire—and he did it all while maintaining a complete "not an a-hole" reputation.

As one of the high-level VPs, I've seen him in action, and he can be cutthroat at times, but it's always in the best interests of our company. Plus, he does it in such a way that the other party sometimes *thanks him* at the end.

The guy is probably freaking amazing at his romantic breakups, too.

I take a deep breath. "First off, I never, ever intended for my personal life to affect my work and this company. I'd never do anything to jeopardize my career... and you know that I don't date all that much."

Mike smirks. He knows this all too well, has tried to set me up multiple times with friends of his twenty-something girlfriends. But I've always declined (even though, at my thirty-one-years-old, they're far closer in age to me than they are to Mike).

Thing is, I'm not husband—not even boyfriend—material.

My work, my career, is *it* for me.

"It was one date." I set my jaw. It's sore from grinding and clenching my teeth all morning. "I'm not even sure why I said yes. I mean, Carly seemed nice enough. We'd run into each other at the gym or the coffee shop, and she asked me out a couple times, but I always said no. Until I didn't."

It didn't help that, at the time of that conversation, I was dealing with some pretty intense work stuff. Was trying to save one of the many independently owned dating apps that SparksFly bought and then tried to trash after taking part of its code.

Needless to say, I was distracted that day. And I agreed to go out with her.

If only I'd known that said date would create a total dumpster fire here at work. I hate blurred lines, try to keep my life

6

compartmentalized. But now—per one of my favorite *Friends* episodes—the line is one big splotch.

"The date didn't go well. There was just so much silence. I think I shared some inane fact about croutons. And then, you know me... the whole charm problem thing." I grimace. "I probably could've tried harder to be more charming, but I knew within minutes that I'd made a mistake agreeing to go out with her. And I don't have a ton of skill letting people down easy."

Mike snorts but waits for me to continue.

"Well, you've seen the tabloid articles." I wave a hand towards his computer screen. "Probably heard the ridiculous tell-all podcast episode that broke the story in the first place. I was a 'terrible, terrible date,' which isn't a good look for a VP at a company that runs dating apps and websites."

Look. I could give two flying fridges what people think of me—as a date or otherwise. The problem is that my "reputation" has now, apparently, become linked with how well I can do my job.

"So, everything they reported was true?"

"*Reported* is a strong word," I mutter. I listened to the episode yesterday evening—it was trashy and sensationalized in the vein of a tabloid, but it was more or less factual. This new media, I swear. "What they said was accurate, but taken *completely* out of context. I would've actually preferred for Carly to be on the podcast and roast me herself."

Mike frowns pensively at the article again. "Well, Carly didn't come off nearly as badly as you did. And she's certainly getting her fifteen minutes of fame now. She's quoted in this article reflecting on the story, and there's even a nice little picture of her at the bottom holding her guitar. Must be doing wonders for her follows."

I try hard not to roll my eyes. About midway through our date—as we sat across from each other eating our mains in a

7

painfully awkward silence—Carly was approached by a fan of her music.

There was no more silence after that.

Carly told me literally *everything* there was to know about her fledgling country-pop music career. Which, to be fair, might have been a nicer alternative to the quiet.

Although, she hijacked my phone, and she must've made me follow her or something because, ever since, my Spotify recommendations have been off the ever-loving wall. I'm talking Miranda Lambert. Shania Twain. Mickey Guyton. Maren Morris. Old school Taylor freaking Swift...

Have I *accidentally* listened to a couple of the songs the whole way through? Maybe. And have I enjoyed them more than I would've expected?

That's not important right now.

"How did it end?" Mike asks.

"It ended well. Or so I thought."

At the end of the (albeit not great) date, I thanked Carly for her time, shook her hand, and we went our separate ways. I thought that was it. Done and dusted and never to be repeated.

But I clearly don't have Mike's penchant for breakups because here I am, a couple months later, my dating mistake coming back to haunt me *very* publicly.

When I speak again, my voice is a low rumble. "So, what happens now?"

Mike doesn't answer right away. He stares at the stupid article and that terrible photo for another few moments before exiting the screen. "Look, Chase. You know how much we need you here. Your teams count on you—*I* count on you—in so many ways. You are totally invaluable to this company, and we're going to do everything we can to make sure that this media circus blows over and makes you look good. Really good."

"I don't need to look good. I need to be invisible and anonymous again so I can go back to doing what I do best: my job." I

8

lean back in the uncomfortable leather chair. *This*, at least, is something I can do—brainstorm solutions, think of next steps. Strategize. "So, where's the PR team at with this?"

Mike's mouth twitches. "You're not an idiot, Chase. You know that I was in a meeting with the board just now."

"I do."

"And you know that this isn't only affecting *you*. The SparksFly name is being dragged through the mud along with yours. We're an online dating empire, and one of our highest level VPs is currently entrenched in a dating scandal."

"I know." I swallow thickly.

"Well, you can understand that this is a sticky situation." His expression turns soft. Kind. *Pitying*. "Some members of the board are thinking that it's best you lie low for a while. Take time off until this all blows over."

"Hang on." I hold up a hand. "Do you want me to 'lie low,' or 'take time off?' Because those are very different things, Mike."

"*I* don't want you to do anything of the sort." He shakes his head, seeming uncomfortable. In the years that I've known him, I've rarely seen Mike Niles be put on the spot. It's deeply unsettling. "I fought for you to stay on. Give your side of the story to the media. But there was a vote and everyone went the other way. Felt it would cause too much drama, too much of a media frenzy, if we engage with this."

I consider what he's saying. There has to be a way to fix this.

But the way Mike's looking at me... I have the distinct feeling he already has a solution. And I'm not gonna like it.

"What happens now?" When I ask this again, my voice sounds far away, disengaged. I also feel far away, disengaged. Probably because this is a nightmare. My work, my job, my career is *everything* to me.

I have nothing else. And I like it that way.

Mike clicks his mouse again and brings up a new screen.

9

My jaw practically hits the floor. "Not the vacation calendar."

"Why don't you take a break, Chase? You must have *months* of vacation accrued by now. I can't even remember the last time you called in sick." Mike offers me a tiny, encouraging smile. "You can escape this record January rainfall we're having and go somewhere nice. Mexico. The Caribbean. Italy. I had the best time in Rome last year, sampling those fancy ice creams and eating pizza. Plus, the women..." He kisses his fingertips. "Bellissima!"

"I don't eat dairy," I say robotically. As if this is the only thing stopping me from dropping freaking everything and flying to freaking *Italy*.

"It was an example. The world is your oyster right now. With your bonus from last year alone, you could fly business class to Antarctica if you wanted to."

"I don't want to go to Antarctica. I want to stay here. Work."

"Well, I'm afraid that's the one thing you can't do." His voice is resigned but firm.

It was one date! I want to yell.

"I see," I say instead.

"Now, why don't you go back to your office and take notes on where you're at with all your projects, put anything that isn't pressing to the side, and then, take a week off. Two, if you so choose. Leave this to us." His expression softens again. "A break could do you some good, Chase. You might be surprised how much you need it."

Doubt it, I answer in my head again. Out loud, I say, "Sure thing."

Mike gives me one final smile, and I know I'm being dismissed. So, I stand, grab my suit jacket, and head out the heavy mahogany door, letting it slam shut behind me.

This is fine.

People go on vacation all the time. It's not like I've been given three weeks to live, for crying out loud. It's *one week* off of work.

This is the mantra I repeat to myself as I pack my briefcase. Newsflash: the mantra is *not* working, my skin is clammy, and my stomach is rolling.

I feel like I'm heading into exile. Which might be a touch dramatic. I still don't completely understand what my reputation as a good or bad date has to do with my ability to do my work, but if this isn't a glaring confirmation of the fact that I've been right not to date much in my past, I don't know what is.

But I'm choosing to trust Mike. Choosing to believe that the board and the SparksFly PR team will resolve this issue and call me back to work ASAP.

So, I will take this vacation.

I probably shouldn't leave LA, though. I should stay close, in my penthouse apartment that I haven't decorated since I bought the place staged for the open house. I like that it's stark, clean, neat. Uncluttered.

I'm shoving my keys and wallet into my pockets when I remember that I never took my phone off Silent mode.

I grasp for it and check the screen.

Frick. A ton of missed calls from various unknown numbers, a stack of messages from women I've never met asking if they can get their chance to prove the media false (what is wrong with people?), and finally...

Five missed calls from Dee.

I press her number, and the phone starts to ring. It barely completes one round.

11

"Lachlan!" Dee's voice is like music to my ears right now. "Finally! What's going on?! Where are you?"

"I'm at the office, I—"

"WHAT?" she screeches. Which is new for Dee. I don't think I've ever heard her operate at that octave. The woman's unflappable; is about as even-keeled as I am. "You're not in the hospital?!"

"Why would I be in the hospital?" I ask, taken aback.

"I don't know!" she's still screeching. I hold the phone away from my ear. "You left me that weird message, and then I tried calling you but you didn't pick up, and then I played the message for Noah, and he's been worried sick thinking you got into an accident or something."

Ah, that explains it.

Diandra Griffiths-Jackson—better known as Dee—heads up a few different projects under my supervision and doesn't usually give time to dramatics or big emotions. The same can't be said for her husband, Noah. The guy comes across as jokey and easygoing, but he wears his heart on his sleeve.

"I'm not in the hospital, I'm at the office," I say calmly. "Everything, physically, is fine. But we do have a problem here."

I sense Dee change tack. There's a shuffle, the sound of her computer keyboard, and then, "What's up?"

So I tell her.

I tell her about the date I went on with Carly a couple months ago, and the gossipy LA "news" podcast that, for some reason, featured said date on last night's episode. I tell her that this feature created a snowball effect in the media, and now, major gossip sites are pouncing on the story—and calling both myself, and the SparksFly conglomerate, huge frauds.

"Wow," Dee says when I've finished telling her that Mike wants me to step away for a week. "Lucky you."

"Excuse me?"

12

"You have a week off work. *Paid*. They're practically forcing you on vacation."

"Doesn't feel like luck to me."

"I get it. I would've felt the same a couple years ago." She's clearly smiling, and I keep from rolling my eyes. Dee and her husband, Noah, are so blissfully in love, it's annoying. It would be *deeply* annoying if I wanted that for myself. But I don't. "Any idea what you're going to do?"

I grind my teeth again. I need to stop, so I clench my fist instead. "Probably stay in LA. Although, honestly..." I trail off, thinking aloud. "That sounds *miserable*."

"Warm and sunny California sounds miserable? No way."

"Well, it's not sunny now." I look out at the literal sheets of water running down my windows, blurring my view of the city. "If I stay, all I'll be able to think about is work." Clench my fist. Unclench my fist. "I'll go insane. I won't be able to stay away from the office."

"They'll probably miss you and want you back in a day or two anyway."

I give a small grin, vindicated that Dee had the same thought I did. *This* is why she's my right-hand man. Woman.

"Yeah. Mike and the board want to wait for the media circus to die down."

Dee gives a short laugh. "Shouldn't be long then. The next big tabloid news story will break soon enough."

I give my head a shake. "I just can't for the life of me fathom why these people *care*. The reality TV stars must be hibernating due to the rain or something."

"Well. All that being said, you should probably at least *try* to look like you're taking a vacation." Dee pauses. "And maybe you'll surprise yourself and enjoy the time off. You probably need it—you've never taken a vacation in the couple years we've worked together."

I couldn't disagree more.

13

But logically, she might have a point. Which is also why she's the best right-hand woman.

Some productivity gurus speak about the benefits of restorative rest. So, I suppose it's worth a try. With the goal of increased efficiency and creativity, of course.

"I guess so," I say darkly.

"Maybe you could get away, but stay close. Let's say, within three hours' flying distance from LA. You know you're always welcome in Mirror Valley."

I hear the smirk in her voice. Dee happens to live and work remotely in the small Colorado town where I spent most of my childhood, and the last time I visited her (for business reasons, of course), I was accosted daily by people wanting to nosy into my life, my career, my dating history. Any little thing they could get their greedy, gossip-hungry hands on.

They'd have a field day with today's news.

"No. But thanks. I promised Noah I'd be back to catch some of the MLB spring training with you guys, and that is the next visit that I am mentally prepared to take."

"Fair enough." She pauses. "What about visiting your brother?"

"My brother..."

"Doesn't he live in Washington State?"

"Oh, yeah. You mean Beau." His name feels foreign on my lips. I haven't thought of either of my half-brothers in what feels like months. "He lives on the coast near Seattle. A small town called Cascade Point."

"Seattle's not far. I'm sure it'd be easy enough to book a place out that way for a week, and then cancel it and fly home whenever this mess dies down and Mike wants you back."

"Right." My mouth feels full of cotton balls. I basically grew up in Colorado, but Cascade Point is where I was born. I wouldn't consider either of them home. "Who knows if Beau—or my grandparents—would want to see me."

"I certainly wouldn't know," Dee quips dryly. "You'll need to call him to find out."

Call Beau. Call my grandparents. Well, step-grandparents.

Yeah. Beau is the lesser of two evils.

But do I really want to go back to that tiny, rundown seaside town known for its overgrown seagulls? Not even a little bit.

Although, Beau *has* made an effort in recent years to reach out, has invited me to come back for a visit. He's the only one of my immediate family who moved there, close to Anna-May and Graham, after leaving Colorado.

Maybe I could drop by for a visit. A visit that will likely be cut short anyway.

It would cover me on familial obligations for the next couple years, at least.

"Hello? Lachlan?" Dee says.

"I'm here. And I think you're right, I'm gonna get in touch with Beau. In the meantime, with all our projects, just—"

"Don't worry, I've got them 'til you're back."

"Which will be in a couple days."

"A couple days," Dee repeats cheerily.

We hang up, and I scroll through my contacts to find my younger brother's number.

"Beau Brighton" is all it says. No photo. No address. No note. Just his name and number.

I write up a quick text asking how he'd feel if I came to Cascade Point for a couple days.

The response is immediate. I know the guy's a firefighter in a small town on the rainy Washington coast—and therefore probably has loads of downtime—but this is extreme.

Beau Brighton: You should come. Would love to see you.

Before I pack away my laptop, I look up rentals in Cascade Point for the next week. I could probably ask Beau to stay with him—could maybe even ask Graham and Anna-May—but that

15

seems like a huge favor to ask of family members that I haven't seen in years.

Plus, I like my own space. Private, quiet space.

In the end, I find a quaint seaside cottage that looks perfectly private and quiet, and it has a flexible cancellation policy. I book it using our company name instead of my own for an extra dash of anonymity in what I know to be a ridiculously gossipy little town. I haven't lived in Cascade Point in literal decades, but I don't want to take the risk of drawing attention.

Then, I decide that, instead of flying, I'm going to drive the twenty hours to Cascade Point. Not in my own sporty little hybrid Lexus, of course. I'll rent a luxury SUV and cruise it up the coast, because the best way I know to deal with something *this* big is to drive.

All I can hope is that, by the time I arrive, Mike will already want me back here.

2

LUCY

I might not have been on many third dates in my lifetime, but I'm *pretty* sure they aren't supposed to end like this.

Because here I am, on a rainy Friday evening, covered in muck and mud and walking on the side of a road in Seattle with only a broken mountain bike to accompany me. I'm grumpy and gloomy, and trust me, Lucy Mary-Ann Summers is *never* grumpy and gloomy.

Though she does apparently think of herself in the third person at times.

Sigh.

I had so many hopes for Brady.

I know most dating experts say not to put all your eggs in one basket, but how could I not? Brady's a witty attorney with a chiseled jawline and soulful brown eyes, who also has dinner with his grandma once a week.

The first time he messaged me on one of the dating apps I've got downloaded, he opened with a casual: "Hey Lucy, what's juicy?"

Which was so stupid, I had to message him back. Because lame jokes are inversely proportional to a guy's future dad potential, right? That's my roommate Jordy's theory, anyway.

As Brady and I got to talking, we just... clicked. He showed himself to be cheerful, kind, and good-natured. He communicated his feelings openly and honestly. And he seemed the type who might like moving from a big city like Seattle to small-town Cascade Point.

He was waving green flags like he was a freaking NASCAR flagman at the start of a race, and my heart was definitely a *go*.

Now, of course, I wish that I'd looked for that one, glaring red flag.

Maybe then, I wouldn't be stranded with a bike with a flat tire, my favorite leggings sporting new holes and tears, and an intensely firm resolution that I will never bike, or go to the mountains, or spend any time outside ever again for as long as I live. Never, ever.

I hear the way this sounds in my head—exactly like the childish whine I know so well.

I can't help but grin as I wonder what my five-year-olds would think of this situation.

Ping!

The noise comes from the sopping wet pocket of my raincoat. I shudder to think that I almost didn't bring it today. I figured that if it rained hard enough, we would stop biking (wrong). And that, seeing as I don't have a car and took a long bus ride out here with my rental bike, Brady would drive me back to Cascade Point after the date (also wrong).

Could this be him apologizing? Offering to give me a ride given the torrential downpour?

Not saying I'd get over what happened today, but I sure wouldn't mind a drive home in my current state.

I find cover under a tree next to the road and take out my phone. I tap at the screen, and it lights up, but my fingers are so wet, it keeps sliding into camera mode. The camera clicks a couple times, capturing my sneakers that were once a baby pink suede and are now ruined to the point of being unrecognizable.

18

I let out a strangled grunt. There is truly no need to commemorate this moment.

Finally, I manage to check the text preview, fully expecting it to be Brady at this point.

Nope. It's Jordy.

Jo-Mo: Hey babe, how's the date going?? Sorry to bother, but that blue bowl above the fridge wasn't anything special, was it?

That *wasn't* says it all. There's a small pang in my stomach as I type a quick reply.

Lucyloo: Nor blather, bow was moooooos

Dang it. I tap at the screen, trying to correct the text, but the water on my fingers only makes it worse. *Why* do smartphones sometimes make you sound so, so dumb?

I send the text as is and hope that Jordy can translate. She responds immediately.

Jo-Mo: Oooh! Is this Lucy's pocket? What a treat.

I exhale loudly and tap the button to call her as I get to walking again. The rain's letting up a bit—more of a consistent drizzle than a monsoon.

"Hey Lucy's Butt, it's been awhile!" Jordy shouts into the phone in her *I'm your fire woman, and I'm saving you* voice.

"Ow, Jordy!"

"Oh, so Entire Human Lucy," she responds at a normal volume. "Sorry for yelling, I thought you were butt dialing me while whizzing around corners and kicking up dirt on the trails." She crunches what sounds like a carrot. "How's Dream Man? Say hey for me, will ya?"

"I will not. Dream Man has turned into Nightmare Man."

"Oh, no. Tell me more."

She's kind to say that. Or maybe just wants the gossip, as many people in our chatty (but loveable) town often do.

19

And Jordy has witnessed enough of my crooning and swooning over Brady at this point.

For our first date, he drove the two hours from Seattle, and we went down the coast in his classic blue Camaro. Unlike Shania Twain, I couldn't blame the guy for making me take off my shoes before he let me get in. We parked by the beach, I bundled up in my cutest knit jacket and matching beanie, and we had a picnic as the wintry sun began to set.

It was perfect, even with the screeching seagulls. And the strong winds that whipped my hair into an unfortunately too-literal beehive (who could've guessed we'd park close to an apiary?).

Our second date was even better: Brady drove to Cascade again so we could catch a movie, and he brought all of my favorite snacks from Trader Joe's. It was *magical*.

Today was our third date. And it was anything but magical.

"I'll tell you the full story when I'm home, but let's just say that the whole mountain biking thing *should* have been the first sign of our downfall."

Jordy snorts. "Yeah. Can't say I ever saw you as the sporty, outdoor adventurer type."

"I thought I'd give it go. Thought I might be a secret biking prodigy. A Simone Biles on two wheels."

"But you don't like biking. Or the mountains. Or being outside."

"Can confirm that is still the case." I sigh, adjusting my grip on the handlebars. "Brady and I just got along so well, you know? So, when he asked me to go downhill mountain biking with him and his friends for date number three, I couldn't say no. I mean, the next step after meeting his friends is meeting his *family*. This felt like a logical progression for us."

"It felt logical to take yourself on a perilous outdoor activity you've never done before for the sake of meeting some guy's friends?" There's another crunch of carrot. "Lucyloo, you know

20

I love you. But your optimism sometimes makes you act like a bit of a dumb-dumb."

I roll my eyes with a laugh. "Thanks for the honesty, Jo. I'll tell you what actually happened on the date—and with said *friends*—when I'm home. Which should be soon."

"Brady's driving you back?"

"Nope. I'm walking to the bus station in Seattle."

The crunching stops. "Wait, *what*?"

"Well, Brady and I are very much over and done with, so I'm getting myself home." I don't really want to get into this now; I'm not liking this whole self-pity-party thing. "But, anyway. I was calling to find out what happened to the blue bowl. The ceiling's not still leaking, is it?"

The kitchen in the adorable little rowhouse that Jordy and I share has recently sprung a leak in the ceiling above our fridge. The blue bowl, made of a delicate Italian blown-glass that my mom found in a consignment shop, was the only container we had that was large enough to catch the steady droplets while Jordy and I were at work.

The bowl is—was?—a treasure of mine. Mom only left me a few things when she passed away a few years ago, and that bowl was one of them.

At that moment, a car speeds past me and kicks up an actual tsunami of water and mud directly onto my torso.

"What was that?! It sounds wet."

"It was raining a little bit earlier." I squeeze out the bottom of my raincoat. I'm soaked right through, and there's nothing to be done but to just accept it. "Seriously, though, is—"

"Let me get this straight," Jordy cuts me off. "You're walking on the side of the road at this hour, alone, in the rain, to catch a bus out of Seattle." I hear the clink of keys in the background. "I'm coming to get you."

A ride would be amazing, but Cascade's a couple hours away by car. "It's a far drive, J. I don't want to put you out."

21

"Not at all. This is ridiculous. And unsafe. I can't believe Brady let you go like this."

"I didn't give him a choice. I kinda just left."

Jordy's silent for a moment. "I'm on my way."

"Are you sure?"

"I'll call Chief from the car. I'm sure Beau can cover for me."

"Ohmygosh." I clench my eyes shut. "You're working tonight. No. No way, you need to go into work."

"Don't be silly, I'm coming to get you."

"No, really," I insist. "It's just a little rain, and you could literally save a life tonight." I'm nodding, knowing that I can't take Jordy away from her job at the fire station. "There's no point in you driving all the way out here. I'm almost at the bus station, and goodness knows I can't get any more wet than I am now." I choke out another laugh. "Really, I'm fine. I'll just have a heck of a story to tell you tomorrow morning."

Jordy makes a noise in the back of her throat. "Are you sure? Because Chief will let me go if he knows you need me."

"I'm sure." I put on a smile. "I'll let you know as soon as I'm home."

"Okay... but I'll have my phone on me, so if you need me, I'll come get you."

I'm about to insist that she shouldn't worry, but I know Jordy. So, I just say, "Thanks, J."

And as soon as I hang up, I feel my luck improving. Because in the distance, I see the lights of the bus station. On top of that, the rain has stopped.

Maybe today's going to turn around after all.

3

LACHLAN

I'm crossing from Oregon into Washington on Friday evening when my phone blares loudly through the car's sound system, cutting through my thoughts. And through a horrifically twangy guitar solo.

It's only just occurring to me that I've been listening to a country playlist since I set off from my hotel in Healdsburg early this morning.

Who would've thought that listening to *country music* would be my response in a crisis?

It's always reminded me of my roots. Which I don't particularly *want* to be reminded of. Very few people know about my past—where I come from, where I grew up. In fact, most people don't even know my full name.

Lachlan Chase is what I go by in the city, but my full name is Lachlan Chase Brighton. I dropped the last name when I started business school. My first and middle ones are succinct, to the point—they look good on a business card. "Brighton" bogs it down.

Plus, it sounds so... *cheery*.

The name doesn't mean much to me, anyway. It's not that I

hate my family or don't want to be associated with them or anything so dramatic. I just prefer to keep things simple. Black and white. And our family dynamics are anything but.

Take my step-grandparents, Graham and Anna-May. They are two of the most eccentric, uppity, *colorful* people I've ever met in my life. All of my memories with them feature take-out dinners (ladled out onto fancy dinner plates), excessive amounts of wine-drinking (on their parts, not on mine), and summer nights spent in their dilapidated (read: haunted) Victorian mansion on the outskirts of Cascade Point.

I shake myself out of my thoughts and answer my phone handsfree without checking the caller ID. It has to be Mike.

"Lachlan Chase," I say, turning on my signal to get into the fast lane.

"Wow. Official."

I blink in surprise. "Hey, Beau."

"Hey, bro," he responds cheerfully. "What're you up to? On your way to Cascade?"

I clear my throat, feeling all of a sudden like the wind's been knocked out me. I left LA yesterday afternoon. Drove for literal hours. Slept overnight in a hotel in Healdsburg and continued on my way this morning. But somehow, hearing Beau's voice makes it all feel very real.

I've left the city. I'm on vacation. No work.

What on earth am I doing?

"Passed Portland an hour ago." My voice is uneven, but I'm not sure Beau would notice. "Should be there in a couple hours."

"Cool," he responds brightly. Like I just told him some of the best news he's heard in a while. "I'm about to start my shift at the station but wanted to see if I could do anything for you. Need a place to stay?"

"No need. Rented a cottage for the week."

24

"Well, just let me know if you need directions or anything. The roads are tricky in some places, and I bet I'd know how to get you to the right address." He sounds so... happy. Is he happy like this all the time? Must be exhausting.

"I have my Maps."

"I figured."

There's a beat of silence, and I flounder. I'm a confident guy; a VP at a big company with no shortage of accomplishments to be proud of. There's no reason for me to feel awkward, and yet, I do. "So, is that all?"

"Pretty much. Was also curious if you'd even pick up. I assumed you'd fly to Seattle and rent a car when you landed."

"I like driving." *With country music, apparently.*

"Right. I forgot how much you love a solo road trip. Sounds like fun."

I glower at the busy freeway. "So fun. I should probably go."

"Drive safe, and I'll see you in the morning. My shift's gonna go late tonight." He pauses for a moment. "Have you told them you're coming?"

I debate acting like I don't know which *them* he's referring to, but I already know that he won't fall for it. "No, I haven't."

"Your call. Anyway, I hope you packed a raincoat, it's meant to be real stormy the next couple days."

Ugh. This west coast weather, I tell you.

Before I can hang up, I hear a scuffle on the other end of the line. Some movement, a grunt.

"Uh, see you tomorrow then," Beau says, clearly distracted.

"Is everything okay?" I ask. Against my better judgment.

I then hear what sounds like a woman muttering. Beau comes back on the line. "Yeah, everything's fine. It's just Jordy. She's leaping on me, wanting to know if you're driving through Seattle."

"She your girlfriend or something?"

"Jordy?! Absolutely not." Beau lets out another of those loud, barking laughs. "We're just buds. But she—okay, Jordy, one sec! I can't speak if you're blocking my mouth."

"Ask him!" the woman hollers.

"Alright, sheesh! Hey, Lockie, she wants to know if you're driving through Seattle because her roommate's stranded in the city."

I narrow my eyes. "I wasn't really planning on stopping—"

"Gimme it!"

The woman's shout interrupts me, and Beau heaves a loud sigh before saying, "Fine! Lockie? Jordy wants to speak with you."

Before I can protest, she's speaking. "Hi. Lockie, is it?"

"Lachlan," I correct her.

"Jordy." I hear the smile in her voice. Is everyone in Cascade Point so *cheerful*? "You're not a serial killer, are you?"

I blink, her question surprising me so much that I almost want to laugh. "No."

"Well, I had to make sure before asking my next question, didn't I?" She actually sounds impatient. With *me*. "Because if you're not a serial killer, will you pretty please stop in Seattle and pick up my dear friend and roommate, Lucy?"

"As I was saying to Beau—"

But Jordy's not listening. "She's stranded at the bus station all wet and covered in mud from the rain, and totally deflated and down on her luck because she had a bad date. You've had a bad date before, haven't you, Lockie?"

If only she knew.

"Lachlan," I correct her again.

"Anyway, she got to the bus station, and it turns out her bus is two hours late because of the storm. I'm sure she'd super duper appreciate a ride to Cascade, and since you're already coming here..."

She trails off, finally silent. I pause, too, mulling it over. Of

26

course, I don't want the woman—whoever she is—to be cold and wet and stranded at a bus stop on a Friday night, but I've been on the road for two straight days at this point. Plus, I don't pick up hitchhikers.

Nonetheless, I type the address into Maps and groan. "It's an hour detour for me."

"Consider it your good deed for the day. And it'll only take one hour to complete!" Jordy replies all too reasonably. "Lucy's one of the sweetest, kindest, most happy-go-lucky people you've ever met, so she'll definitely be good company. And she's had a very bad day. I was about to go get her myself when Beau mentioned you were coming to town."

"You would've left work to drive a couple hours just to pick her up?"

"'Course I would. She'd do the same for me."

I clench my jaw. Remember my resolution to use my fist instead and take it off the steering wheel.

What's another hour on top of this already long drive across three freaking states? With a soaking wet and muddy woman who will probably be complaining about her bad date until we reach town?

Ugh.

"Fine," I say stiffly. "I'll swing by and pick her up."

"Good man. I'll give you back to your brother now. Bye-bye."

And just like that, Beau's back on the line. "She wore you down, huh?"

I signal to change lanes and stay on the I-5. "Call me a softie," I grumble.

"I would never dare do that," Beau says laughingly. "But you've just won over a Cascadian, so that can only ever help you."

How? I want to ask, but I say, "Great."

27

I hang up right as huge drops of rain begin to pelt the windshield again.

Guess I'll be making a couple stops in Seattle: one for a forlorn but apparently friendly woman covered in mud, and one for a tarp for her to sit on so she doesn't completely mess up my rental car.

4

LUCY

What are three perks from today?

I hold out my fingers. This is an exercise I give my class sometimes when they're particularly grouchy or low energy. And yes, I do it myself when I'm having a bad day. I always try to go for five, though. Just because, if I can get to three, surely I can think of two bonus perks, right?

But as I stare at my mud-caked, rain-prunified hand with the nail polish I applied last night already starting to chip off, five feels like a *lot*.

"C'mon, Lucy, you just need three," I mutter under my breath, squeezing my hand into a fist.

"You alright, ma'am?"

I startle and look over at the man who's sitting on the other end of my bench. He looks to be a few years younger than me, and has a nose ring and wide brown eyes.

Brown eyes that are currently *full* of wariness as he angles his body away from me.

"I'm fine, sorry!" I giggle in a weird, high-pitched kinda way. "Look at me, just talking to myself."

The young man's expression doesn't change. Instead, he sits up, like he's preparing to flee.

29

"I'm not crazy, I swear," I add. Which, of course, makes me look the exact opposite.

He smiles thinly. "Okay, ma'am."

I kinda get it. Here I am, sitting alone at a bus stop with a broken bike. I'm covered in mud and my clothes are stiff and half-dry even as it starts to rain again. I'm sure I'm a sight for sore eyes.

Add on to that the fact that the sun has set, and the sky is darkening by the minute. I'm also hungry, but it's not so bad yet that it's worth dragging my bike all the way to the small convenience store down the road. With the way my luck's going today, if I walk away for a minute, my very late bus home will come and go without me on it.

And now, on top of all that wonderfulness, I'm scaring off a local.

But if I can't think of my perks, maybe I can distract myself by talking to Judgy-Pants. "Where you headed?" I ask conversationally in my best, normal, not-crazy voice.

He doesn't look at me. "Aberdeen."

There's a beat of silence. And then, the guy very quietly (and somewhat reluctantly) says, "And you?"

"Cascade Point."

More silence. But for some reason I can't justify, I continue talking.

"Just had a heck of a day. I came to Seattle this afternoon to meet the friends of a guy I was dating who are all big into mountain biking. As you might be able to tell, I am not." I choke out a laugh. "I figured I'd give it a go, and lo and behold, not only did I absolutely *not* impress my date, but said date ended up enthusiastically proclaiming to me that he's in love with his best female friend."

I believe his exact words were *Lucy, dating* you *made me realize I'm in love with her!!* Which felt pretty terrific, let me

30

tell you. Especially as the sky chose that exact moment to be all dramatic and start raining.

But he did thank me for it.

So, you know... that was nice.

"I can't even blame him," I continue with a shake of my head. "The girl's awesome. Super pretty, great biker, really funny. So, after that, I knew it was time for me to bow out. And, here I am."

The guy doesn't respond to my stupid word-vomit. And now, I feel even more stupid and low than I did before. I heave a sigh and look down at my hands again.

Then, he speaks: "Maybe you should've asked him if he was in love with someone else."

Hmm. Is that *how third dates are supposed to end?*

"And," the guy continues. "Maybe you talked too much for him."

I press my lips together, stung. Okay, I do have a reputation for talking a lot. And, fine, maybe I shouldn't have been looking for sympathy from a stranger at a bus stop. I'm all out of sorts.

I'm about to break down and call Jordy when two huge, familiar, wonderful headlights shine in the distance, coming our way.

Finally!!

I leap to my feet and grab my bike, hauling it awkwardly towards the stopping zone. I smile, counting one perk off my list: at long last, the bus is here.

It pulls up, the brakes shift, and the bus beeps as it lowers to collect me and my bike. Normally, I'd be polite and would let Judgy-Pants on first, but I'm too hungry, exhausted, and generally eager at this point to do anything but stand here, smiling at the bus driver through the door-window like a loon.

I'm about to step inside when the driver addresses me. "Where you going, lady?"

31

"Cascade Point," I say brightly. "Man, am I happy to see you."

"Sorry to break it to you, but this bus is only going to Aberdeen."

I literally feel my face fall, and I take a step back in shock. "Aberdeen?! That's still, like, forty minutes away from Cascade."

Judgy-Pants takes this opportunity to hop lithely onto the bus. What a guy.

"Dunno what to tell you." The driver shrugs. "It's raining like crazy out that way. You should probably talk to someone at the ticket counter and see if there are any more buses going out to Cascade tonight." He must notice that I'm currently spiralling into despair because his face softens. "Hey, it's alright. Worse comes to worst, you sleep in the station and catch the first bus tomorrow morning, right?"

Well. That *would* be a fitting end to today.

Before I can respond—or decide to get on the bus anyway— the doors shut, and the engine starts up again, and I watch from the sidewalk, alone, as the taillights disappear into the twilight.

About those perks of mine?

I've got nothing. I am currently living a perk-free existence with zero perks in sight.

I collapse onto the bench again and finally allow myself the pity party I've been holding at bay all evening. I remove my favorite orange bandana from where it's tied oh-so-cutely around my neck and use it to tie back my soaking wet, stringy brown hair. The bright color, with its white polka dots, makes me think of sunshine, and that's exactly what Brady said when I wore it in my hair, just like this, for our first date.

Last night, I painted my fingernails the exact same orange. I scratch at the color on my index fingernail now. It chips off unevenly.

I let out a final grunt of frustration before picking myself up

32

again. Sitting here, wallowing in the darkness by myself isn't going to help anything. I need a plan of attack:

Step one: Talk to the ticket counter person.

Step two: Food.

Step three: Call Jordy for help (AKA take her away from her job where she could literally change lives tonight. No big deal. Feeling great about that.)

At that moment, a pair of way-too-bright LED headlights wash across my body, and a big SUV comes to a stop a few feet away from me. I take my handlebars again, staring warily at the tinted windows where a muddy, wet, drowned-rat-looking *ma'am* is staring back at me.

Oh, dear. Guess I can't blame Judgy-Pants for almost fleeing.

As I'm staring at my miserable reflection, the passenger side window rolls down.

And there, staring back at me, are two icy blue eyes that practically glow from the dark interior.

Scratch that. They're *glaring* back at me.

"You Lucy?"

The voice is deep and rough and gravely, somehow sounding like cement being poured. Beneath the voice, there's a twangy banjo noise that feels very much at odds with this moment, which should probably feature intense piano playing and synths a la *Halloween* or *Jaws*.

I look around, as if the man could be speaking to anyone else. But I'm alone here.

All alone.

"Hello? Are you Lucy?"

My survival instinct kicks in. Stranger danger is still a thing when you're almost thirty, right?!

"Nope!" I shout as I grasp my handlebars and tug my bike away. Of course, the bike doesn't roll but instead lags sideways,

33

ricocheting me abruptly so that I almost topple back into the mud.

"You sure?" the man asks, and his door slams.

"Stay away! I can karate!"

Holy... People don't actually say that, do they?? Especially people who actually *know* karate.

Because I don't. Clearly.

The man is standing behind his SUV, looking at me, but not approaching. I see that he's wearing black pants and a white shirt. And loafers. Really nice, clean loafers.

I take note of these details, committing them to memory in case, ya know, I need them in a police investigation later.

Then, my eyes land on the man's face. And I'm actually stunned for a moment.

This guy looks exactly like Superman, with his jet-black hair and light blue eyes. Which *would* be incredibly attractive if Superman was your type (which is not the case for me). He has a strong, square jaw covered with a layer of groomed stubble. Full lips that are such an innocent rose-pink, they don't seem to work with his tough features and expression. There's not a single laugh line in sight.

In fact, he's glaring at me with so much intensity, my breath locks in my throat.

As I stare back at him with a mix of abject fear and wonder, one corner of his lips twitches up. I get the sudden sense I'm amusing him. Somehow.

"If you wanted to scare me, you probably should've said you had mace. I think that's a little more believable." He says this evenly. Like he's happily volunteering this simple fact about the best way to keep him away from me.

"Mace," I mutter, kicking myself.

Superman's mouth twitches again, and I'm immediately put off. Is he trying not to *laugh* right now?! Getting his jollies scaring the living daylights out of a woman standing alone at a

34

bus stop after sunset? That's incredibly anti-Supermanly of him. What kind of sicko...

At that moment, his glowing eyes drop to my hands, which are locked tight around the handlebars of my rented bike. He frowns, and it's an astonishing sight. This frown alone could move mountains.

"You have a bike," he thunders. It's the only way to describe it, though he's speaking at a perfectly normal volume.

"Uh," I trail off, still wondering who in blue blazes he could be, and why he's here, and why he hasn't started attacking me yet. "Do you... do you want it?"

The blue eyes are on mine again. Is this guy even human? He's got this strange energy to him, seems almost robotic or alien.

Superman was an alien, wasn't he? I'll have to ask River about that on Monday.

Focus, Lucy!

Point is, the man looks totally out of place in real life. *My* real life. Shouldn't he be swanning about on a movie set somewhere? Or else hanging around on his maybe-alien planet?

In any case, it's *quite* shocking when his lips stretch into a very real smirk. "No. I'm good. But why on earth did you bring that mess of a bike on a date?"

A shiver travels the length of my spine.

"How did you know I was on a date? And hang on, how do you know my name? Who in the living heck are you?"

The man's eyebrows pop up, and I realize I've surprised him. "I'm Lachlan Chase. I assumed your friend Jordy told you I was coming."

"No." I try to read his micro-expressions in the fading light.

He doesn't *look* like a kidnapping/murderer type—I mean, the shoes *alone* would surely make chasing his victims difficult—but a girl can never be too safe.

So, I set my jaw, straighten my spine, and meet his gaze with

35

resolve. "Listen, I don't know who you are or why you're here or how you happen to know my best friend's name, but if you're not here for my bike, I should probably tell you that I'd make a very annoying kidnap victim."

"You don't say."

"Yup." I hold up a hand to count my most annoying tendencies on my fingers. "For one thing, I talk a lot. For two things, I've been told I laugh too much and have quite a loud screech. And for a final thing, my bladder is tiny, so I will have to stop for pee breaks on the way to wherever you're holding me hostage."

The man's lips twitch again on point one, but this time, they twitch downwards. He regains a neutral expression and just says, "I'm taking you to Cascade Point, you absolute nutcase. I'm driving from California, and I'm headed to Cascade to visit Beau Brighton. Your friend Jordy practically forced me to detour through Seattle to pick you up."

"Oh." The air leaves my lungs. "You know Beau?"

"Yup." The Superman lookalike better known as Lachlan Chase offers no more information.

"And you're not here to steal my bike. Or kidnap and murder me."

His lips twitch again. "No, that rusty pile of junk is of no interest to me. And Jordy already asked if I was a serial killer. I confirmed that I'm not."

That *does* sound like something Jordy would ask a complete stranger.

"I see... Well, okay." I gesture towards said pile of junk. "Want to give me a hand?"

Lachlan's strong nose, which I can now appreciate is a perfectly straight line that hints at the fact that he's never broken it (not an athlete then?), wrinkles up. "Not particularly."

"That's fine. Probably don't want to get your shoes dirty."

This is meant to be a joke. Lachlan's face—appropriately statue-esque—doesn't move.

36

So I grab the bike by the center rail and hoist it up against my body. The frame is heavy, muddy and covered in bits of grass.

I'm waddling awkwardly towards the SUV when my grumpy Superman friend checks a very shiny watch, exhales in a forceful whoosh, rolls his eyes, and takes a total of four strides towards me. He takes the bike right out of my hands and lifts it onto his shoulder like it weighs nothing.

It's only once he's in front of me that I realize how *big* he is. He's a good half-foot taller than me, which would put him around 6'5", and just... bulky. I suddenly wonder if he hung back to talk to me because he's aware of how threatening he might've seemed up close like this.

Lachlan walks over to what I can now see is a new BMW, leans the bike against the back bumper, and opens the trunk.

That's when I spot the roll of plastic wrap, and I idly wonder again if I really *am* about to be murdered. But in a matter of seconds, he's laid out a sheet of plastic on which he places the bike, and then he closes the trunk. He wipes down his shirt and pants—which appear to be of the expensively-designed-to-look-cozy variety. He managed to get not a single speck of mud on his person.

Those bright blue eyes meet mine again, and he raises a singular, skeptical brow. "What was it you were saying about my shoes?"

His tone makes me bristle. Without giving a response, I head to the passenger side of the SUV.

"Wait. Hang on a minute, Lucy."

I pause.

"You're a mess. You can't sit in the car like that." He strides towards me with more plastic wrap in hand, which he lays down on the passenger seat like I might pee myself or something. He goes on to put more plastic on the floor and along the door. "Think you can keep things clean?"

37

My cheeks flare red, and I'm glad it's too dark for him to see. "I think I can just about manage it."

I wiggle onto the plastic sheet. It squeaks embarrassingly beneath my soggy leggings.

Lachlan smirks as he leans in to say, "I'm not taking any risks."

Then, he slams the door in my face.

5

LACHLAN

We've just passed a town called Aberdeen when the announcement comes over the radio.

"Due to heavy rains and flooding, some roads to the coast are closed."

The mud-drenched woman otherwise known as Lucy grabs her phone. Within moments, she lets out a groan and knocks her head back against the headrest. I wince—I didn't put any plastic there, and I'm really not lying when I say she's mud-drenched.

"The road's closed," she says in a voice full of what can only be described as despair. "Can this day get any *worse?*"

I stay silent. It's rare that anyone complains in my vicinity, let alone expects my sympathy.

Don't get me wrong, I do what I can to help people—I donate to charities, support important events and causes, that kind of thing—but rarely are they sitting in my freaking passenger seat.

"The road to Cascade Point?" I ask gruffly.

She simply nods.

"Surely there's another option."

"Nope." She stares at the darkness ahead of us. In the headlights, the road blurs, clears, blurs again before the windshield wipers can swipe the water away. I've driven in heavy rain before; it doesn't scare me. But I am surprised that this Lucy person isn't afraid, or even nervous. She apparently trusts me—a complete stranger she not long ago thought was a kidnapper—to get her home safe.

I frown. "So, what should we do..."

It's not a question so much as me thinking aloud, but Lucy answers anyway. "Stop somewhere, I guess. I could eat."

I'll say.

I heard her stomach grumbling over the patter of rain before we even got to Aberdeen. Given her apparently tiny bladder, I suggested we stop for a bathroom break, thinking we could get food at the same time, but she declined. Said she just wanted to get home.

So far, the woman hasn't lived up to her kidnapping promises: she has neither needed to use the bathroom, nor been overly chatty since I picked her up in Seattle.

When I first pulled over, I could hardly believe that the soaking wet woman standing alone could possibly be the "happy-go-lucky" Lucy that Jordy spoke about. She seemed so down on her luck, even as she shouted at me that she "can karate." Which she clearly can't.

Another gush of rain hits the hood of the car, and Lucy shifts in her seat.

Hmm. Maybe she's more nervous than she's letting on. And honestly, it's not exactly fun driving in this torrential downpour. I check my watch and notice that it's getting late.

All of a sudden, I spot a light up ahead that isn't a reflection of my headlights on raindrops.

I see the sign next: a roadside motel aptly named The Last Stance Motel.

And it says there's vacancy.

"Oh!" Lucy exclaims. "Perfect!"

The woman has a loose definition of the word "perfect."

40

I pull into the parking lot and stare at the front of the building for a moment—chipped maroon paint, dirty windows, a wooden sign above what is apparently the restaurant with a letter "e" missing so it spells out "Last Stanc Saloon."

This looks *nothing* like that Healdsburg hotel I stayed at last night.

I have half a mind to head back to Seattle and find a proper hotel, but Lucy bounds out of the car before I can say anything. With a frustrated grunt, I go in after her.

The lobby is what I'd imagine stepping back to the 1920s would feel like. Must, dust, and every other -ust. Worn couches and armchairs take up the center of the room. Rickety tables are smattered with brochures that clearly haven't been touched in ages. An unnameable but recognizable *old* smell makes my nose crinkle.

"Last Stanc," indeed.

I find Lucy at the reception desk, waiting to be helped, and it's only then that I notice the orange bandanna tying back her hair. It's a pop of color against her otherwise dark and dirty outfit, and it makes me wonder what sort of a person chooses to wear something so impractical while mountain biking.

I'm usually pretty good at reading people, but I'll admit that Lucy is kind of a blank for me. I get the feeling this whole "gloomy" thing isn't the usual for her.

If anything, she has features I'd describe as *sweet*. Like if freaking Belle from *Beauty and the Beast* stepped out of her storybook and landed in Seattle. Cheeks that turn red when she's upset and that I would guess become even more apple-red when she blushes. Bright green eyes that shine out behind thick lashes. Bow-shaped lips that move to express her every emotion.

I decide that she might be quite pretty beneath all the mud.

All of a sudden, she shivers. She's probably one of those women who's always cold. Probably wraps herself in blankets with a cup of hot cocoa and wholesomely reads away a Sunday

41

afternoon. I wonder what she'd choose to read—fiction, non-fiction? Science fiction?

What am I doing?

I snap myself out of it. I don't *want* to know this Lucy person. And it's not like we'll be seeing each other again after this journey comes to an end.

"Any luck?" I ask, approaching her.

She startles a little, like she didn't realize I was there. "What do you think?"

I almost smile. She might look like a princess, but she's got some fire to her. Princess Belle, perhaps.

"Have you tried that?" I nod towards the old-timey bell tucked away next to a gas lamp (seriously, what century are we in?).

She gives a swift roll of her eyes. "Aren't you just full of bright ideas?"

But she taps the bell, avoiding my gaze and keeping her tiny, angular chin tilted up.

The door behind the desk creaks open, and an older man pops his head out. "What?" he asks, sounding almost as agitated as I feel.

"Hey, there!" My muddy passenger is suddenly beaming, her face alight. I barely recognize her. Or her voice, which sounds sweet as pie and laden with sunshine. "I'm Lucy Summers, and I'd love to book into one of your rooms."

The man harrumphs. "Tonight?"

"Next week, actually," I deadpan before I can stop myself.

Lucy and the old man shoot me shockingly identical glares, and Lucy steps a little in front of me. Like I'm a misbehaving child that's just embarrassed her in front of this wizened gentleman.

"I'm from Cascade Point and was hoping to get home tonight, but the road's closed due to the downpour. So, me and my, uh... friend,"—*oh, she means me*—"are looking for a couple

42

rooms to crash in while we wait out the rain." She lets out a light laugh that sounds like she's hiccuping freaking cloud bursts or something. "Not that I'm scared of rain, being from Cascade. But, you know, better safe than sorry."

The man is zeroed in on Lucy, and I see him soften as she speaks. I, myself, am surprised at the calm, even way she's taken control of the situation. The way she sounds genuine and friendly while also being firm. She'd make a good teacher.

"Well, miss, you and every other person on the road have had the exact same thought." He lets out a guttural choke of a laugh that turns into a cough (cobwebs, perhaps). But he seems almost sorry when he says, "The motel's full tonight."

Lucy visibly deflates. "Oh. The sign said there was vacancy."

His mouth slides to something resembling a sympathetic grimace. "Unfortunately the 'No' in the sign went out a few years ago and has never been fixed. Has never needed to be before tonight." He coughs out another laugh, and I'm about to propose that we find another motel when he speaks again. "I've got friends who work at other places in the area. Let me make a couple calls."

Lucy nods. I nod, as well, though the man has apparently forgotten I exist.

We step away from the desk, and I can see Lucy's face again. Her dark brows are drawn together in worry, and she's biting her lower lip. Her arms are crossed, and I spot the goose bumps peppering her skin.

Normally, this type of thing wouldn't affect me, but she looks so hopeless that I have the urge to run my hands down her arms to warm her up. It's so distracting that I'm annoyed.

"I can get you a sweater," I offer, just wanting her goose-bumps to go away so I can think clearly.

"What?" she asks, meeting my eyes.

"I've got some sweaters packed in my car. I'll grab you one."

43

"Oh, no, that's okay. I wouldn't want to get them dirty."

I don't want her to get my wool sweaters dirty either, but my irritation at her discomfort right now outweighs my love for clean clothes. "I'll dry clean them when we get to Cascade Point."

One corner of her mouth quirks up a little. "You think Cascade has a dry cleaner?"

Well. Guess I'm not doing laundry 'til I get back to LA.

"But, really, I'm fine." She smiles fully. "Besides, it's good to be a little uncomfortable at times. Makes you appreciate it when you're comfortable again."

"That sounds like some overly positive, irrational B.S. to me, but okay," I grumble, which Lucy fully ignores.

Nonetheless, I try to convince her to take a sweater, but with every offer, she insists even harder against it. Here I am, trying to help her, trying to keep her warm, and she won't let me.

It's frustrating. *She's* frustrating.

The old man returns to the front desk and looks directly at Lucy with a small grin. "I have good news and bad news for you, miss. Which would you like to hear first?"

"Good news," I say.

"Bad news." Lucy smiles.

Of course, he defers to her. "The bad news is that all of my friends' hotels and motels are full for the night due to the road closures. But the good news is that I might have space for you two, after all."

"You do?" Lucy lunges towards the desk. "Thank you. Thank you, sir."

"Don't thank me yet. It's not exactly luxury accommodation."

"That's fine. We'll take the rooms."

"Okay." The man rifles around behind the desk, presumably looking for keys. "You see, so few newlyweds come through here

44

that the suite is now being used as a storage closet. It's full of brooms and mops and extra tables and sheets, but give me some time to clear it out, and you'll be good to go."

The singular isn't lost on me.

"Excuse me," I interrupt swiftly. "*One* suite? *One* room?"

The man is bent over, scrounging around the keys like a rabid chipmunk. "Yup. The honeymoon suite." He finally pops his head up above the desk, jangling an old brass keyring on his fingers. "Was that not clear?"

It's certainly clear now!

What *isn't* clear is the fact that there are people out there who would consider this ancient, moments-from-being-condemned motel as a potential *honeymoon option* (who in their right minds?).

Lucy looks at me with alarm. I raise my eyebrows back at her. "I'll sleep in my car. You can have the suite, Lucy."

She bites her lip, then turns back to the man. "I know it's the honeymoon suite, but would there happen to be a pull-out couch? A cot?"

"I think there was a couch in there at one point."

Promising.

And then, perceptive as ever, he squints at the two of us. "Aren't you two together?"

I purse my lips. Lucy shakes her head.

The man's eyes widen a touch, but he waves a hand. "Ah. I'm sure we can figure something out for you, miss."

"I hope so. But in any case, we'll take it. Thank you..."

"Gene."

"Thank you, Gene." After a moment, she looks over her shoulder at me and gives me the scariest eyes I've ever seen in my life.

I get the memo. "Oh, right." I clear my throat. "Thank you."

"My pleasure." He smiles at Lucy, clearly warming to the expression. "Why don't you get yourself some food at the restau-

45

rant before it closes? I'm sure you're hungry after your long journey."

"I really am. But I'll help you clean out the suite first. We *both* will."

I stare at her again. It's not that I don't want to help the old man, but I'm usually the one taking control in these types of situations. Instead, this deluded, unreasonably optimistic mud-covered person is running the show, and I feel very weird about it.

Lucy and I follow Gene to a covered walkway out back of the motel. Well, actually, I follow Lucy and Gene, who are chatting away like the best of friends while I trail along behind them, looking for lurking spiders or cracks in the foundation that hint that this building might collapse tonight.

In the end, I decide I'd rather not see either, so I pad along silently, keeping an eye on Lucy. I feel strangely protective of her. Like I don't want anything to happen to her while she's in my care.

Not that she's actually *in my care* as she can clearly take care of herself. Karate or not.

"Here she is!" Gene announces, throwing open a peeling door at the far end of the motel building.

The room is just as musty and dusty as the lobby, and is full of old furniture, blankets, and cleaning supplies. At the end of the room is the bed.

One bed.

Thankfully there is, indeed, a couch. Or *not* thankfully, given the disgusting state of it.

After we've finished cleaning out the room, Gene says a gruff goodbye, hands us two sets of keys, and heads back to the front desk, telling Lucy to enjoy a meal at the restaurant on him.

Only Lucy. Apparently, I'm chopped liver.

And finally, reality hits me: Lucy and I will be sharing this room tonight.

Lucy collapses onto the bed (which emits a literal cloud of dust) and sighs happily. "We're so lucky."

I stare at the brown and green stains on the couch cushions. "I don't know if I'd call it luck," I grumble.

"So. Are you taking the couch, or am I?"

"The real question is, do you or I want to be the one catching some sort of skin disease from those cushions." I gingerly press a hand onto the bed. The mattress is firm, which I can appreciate.

Her mouth pops open. "Surely, you're not suggesting we...?"

I'm not suggesting anything, but for some reason, I find myself leaning into her reaction. I blink at her innocently. "What? You don't want to share a bed with me, Miss Passenger?"

Her eyes flash. "Do you want to share a bed with *me*?"

I grimace. "Not particularly."

"Well, then, we agree. Neither of us wants to share the bed with the other."

I glance at the couch again. I feel slightly nauseous even looking at it, let alone at the thought of having *physical contact* with it. "And neither of us wants to sleep on the couch."

Lucy bites her cheek. "Well, we know what we have to do."

"*You'll* sleep in the car?" I'm kidding, of course.

"*No*. We're going to have to make the best of this situation and be thankful that this is a king bed that will allow us to put *lots* of distance between ourselves." Her green eyes lock on mine with a surprising and slightly terrifying intensity. "And I have to warn you... I might not know karate, but if you even *try* to cuddle me tonight, I will pin you to this nasty carpet."

"I'd love to see you try."

Her eyes widen, and I press my lips together. "That sounded flirty. It wasn't meant to be. I'd like to literally see you, Passenger Princess, try to pin me to the ground."

47

She smirks. "You have no idea of what I'm capable, Mr. Kent."

"Kent?"

"That's right."

I frown. People from Cascade Point normally have a hard time with my first name but this is a new one. "The last name's Chase."

Lucy's busying herself grabbing a couple of very thin, very worn pillows from a side cupboard and arranging them down the middle of the bed as a sort of makeshift barrier. "Pretty sure Superman's last name wasn't 'Chase.'"

I roll my eyes. "Ha, ha. Anyone ever tell you that you're hilarious?"

"Sometimes."

She stands straight, apparently satisfied with her pillow barrier. I don't have the heart to tell her that the pillows are so flattened from age that, even if there *was* a possibility of cuddling tonight (which there absolutely is not—I am not a cuddler), they wouldn't do much.

"What, you've never heard that before?" She grimaces as she waves a hand towards my face. "With all *that* going on?"

I blink at her in abject confusion. We have far more important matters to attend to at the minute than whatever *that* she's talking about. Like the fact that we'll be sharing a bed tonight. In this dilapidated motel. And I *still* haven't heard a peep from Mike.

Lucy's stomach roars yet again.

I clench my jaw—no, my *fist*—and face her squarely. "Okay, look, this is what's going to happen. I'm going to go to the car, grab my things, and take a quick shower in what I hope isn't a totally disgusting bathroom. And you are going to go to the restaurant and get yourself some food. And I am going to bring you a sweater. Because if I see another goosebump on you, or if I hear your stomach make one more sound..." I let my sentence trail off.

Lucy opens her mouth to protest, but I hold up a hand.

"I mean it. Go."

Her nostrils flare with irritation, but she lets out a frustrated breath. "Fine. I think better on a full stomach anyway."

"I'll meet you there after I shower."

She doesn't respond. Just walks out the door and slams it shut behind her. Only, it doesn't close, so she has to come back in to try and shut it again.

"Twist the lock the other way."

She doesn't acknowledge my words but does turn the lock. Then, she shoots me a saccharine smile—I have a feeling she wishes she was flipping me the bird instead—and closes the door firmly behind her.

6

LUCY

I'm sitting at the bar in the motel restaurant, literally inhaling a cheeseburger, when Lachlan finally makes his appearance.

He was right, by the way.

After the way-too-clichéd one-bed incident (or it *would* be clichéd if Lachlan and I had even a shred of something in common on which to base a romantic dalliance), I couldn't handle it anymore. Couldn't handle *anything* more on an empty stomach, not even a shower. And now that I'm somewhat satiated, I feel prepared to face the man... and the situation at large.

But as Lachlan steps into the dark, dingy restaurant, plastic bag in hand, I almost start laughing. He looks so out of place here, with his perfectly styled hair, and designer stubble, and pressed gray slacks. The suite's bathroom was clearly acceptable for a shower.

He looks around (presumably for me?), and I can't help but notice the way everyone else's eyes swing towards him.

Which checks out. Not only is Lachlan impossibly tall and well-built, but his overall presence somehow dominates the room. He's like one of those heavy planets or a black hole. He has his own center of gravity, tugging every gaze towards him.

And I guess it doesn't hurt that he's fairly nice looking with that dark hair and brooding blue gaze framed by thick lashes. His black sweatshirt hugs his upper body, making it abundantly clear that the man works out.

Okay, fine. He's handsome.

But that doesn't mean there's any chemistry here. At all.

I have more chemistry with my greasy cheeseburger than I do with Lachlan Chase.

So, when his eyes meet mine, and my stomach does a weird turning-over sensation, I know that it's due to the delicious five-hundred calories I've just ingested.

And besides, it's nothing compared to the full-fledged butterflies I had with Brady.

In just a few strides, he's towering above me.

"Good shower, Mr. Kent?" I ask brightly.

Before he answers, he pulls out the barstool next to mine and takes a seat, placing the plastic bag on the bar next to him. Now that I've eaten, I'm noticing his careful, precise movements. It's almost like he's aware of his height and how intimidating he might seem. And yet, on first meeting, he came across so cold and arrogant. It's contradicting and confusing.

But I guess first impressions aren't everything. They certainly weren't with Brady.

"Fine," he says in what I now know is his normal clipped tone. "Water was hot, pressure was okay."

"Good to hear. I'll clearly be needing one tonight."

He doesn't respond. Just grabs a menu and scans it quickly. "Burger good?"

I'm beginning to realize that Superman isn't big on complete sentences. "Yup. One of the best I've had, actually."

He nods to the drink in front of me. "And the beer?"

"Also good." I run my fingers along the glass. It's still cold, though it's only half full. "I don't drink except on special occasions. And today is *definitely* a special occasion."

I'm enjoying the warm buzz through my extremities. As a

51

once-in-a-blue-moon drinker, I had no idea what to order, and so I very coolly (if I do say so myself) asked for the most popular beer on tap.

It occurs to me now that I probably should have eaten the burger *and then* ordered the beer, but as soon as the calories hit my bloodstream, I should be fine.

I take another sip as Lachlan waves down the bartender. I can't help but watch him. Notice the small freckle where his angular jaw meets his neck, the carefully trimmed stubble with not a hair out of place.

The man is so *groomed*. Too groomed and perfect and "city" for a motel like this. Or a town like Cascade Point.

Not for the first time, I find myself wondering why he's going to my hometown. What sort of business could he possibly have there? And how does he know Beau?

I get the feeling that, with Lachlan, I'm only ever going to have more questions than answers.

On a whim, I lean in slightly and inhale. He's wearing a woodsy aftershave that isn't too strong. Here I was, expecting him to be doused in Hugo Armani No. 7 or something.

"Are you sniffing me?"

Those bright blue eyes are suddenly on mine, and I jerk back so quickly, I almost topple off my stool. "What? NO!" I say too quickly. "You're delusional."

That skeptical eyebrow of his crawls all the way up near his hairline. "Am I?"

"You know, if you're asking a question, your intonation is meant to rise at the end," I say innocently. "Otherwise, people might think you're a sarcastic a-hole."

His lips twitch again. An indication of amusement, perhaps? "Thanks for the tip."

The bartender returns with waters for us both (Superman must've ordered them), and I tune out as he orders something

52

else, swirling the remnants of my beer around my glass (how am I almost finished already?).

As soon as the bartender walks away, Lachlan grabs the plastic bag and holds it towards me. "Here."

"A bag? For me? Shucks, you shouldn't have."

His nostrils flare. "It's what's *in* the bag, Princess Belle."

I pop a brow at him and his choice of nickname (which isn't the worst I've heard—Belle likes books), but I take the bag, only now seeing the logo splashed across the front.

"Hang on. This is from the motel?"

Lachlan nods. "Who'd have thought this dump would have a gift shop?"

"Hey now, don't speak ill of my new favorite hotel ever."

"I'd say I'm sorry..." He trails off into silence.

I reach into the bag and take out a bundle of maroon fabric. "What is this?"

"It's a change of clothes. I can't stand you looking like that anymore."

I gesture down at my mud-ified self. "Clark Kent doesn't want to be seen with the likes of me?"

He stares at me, and his expression so confused, I almost laugh. "That's not it at all."

I grasp the fabric, intending to take it out of the bag, but Lachlan catches my hand. His grip is firm but surprisingly gentle. For a moment, I'm distracted by how big and warm his palm feels against my skin and the way his index and thumb form a perfect circle around my wrist. "There's a bathroom back there."

"And there's a door over *there* if you want to leave."

Lachlan purses his lips. "Have you always been so stubborn?"

"Have you always had a fetish for maroon clothing?"

"Not *maroon* clothing."

Wow, was that a joke?

53

I pause for a moment, but then, he says, "Go now, or I'll tell you about my other clothing fetishes."

Well. That's that.

I stride off towards the back of the restaurant and do, indeed, find two doors side by side—one with a photo of a cowboy, and the other with a photo of what looks like the damsel in distress on the cover of old romance novels.

I press my lips together, relating unfortunately a little too much to that damsel at the moment.

The bathroom is dimly lit, just like the restaurant, and smells of cigarette smoke and cheap air freshener. Nonetheless, I shake out the fabric and discover that there's not one piece but two.

"Ohmygosh."

It's a sweatsuit.

Grumpy Superman got me matching maroon sweatpants and a hoodie.

In bright yellow writing, the front of the hoodie reads, "I <3 One Night at Last Stance" with the "at Last" being so small and faded that it instead seems to proclaim that *I Love One Night Stance.*

Lovely.

I stand in the tiny bathroom, debating. What I should *probably* do is go back to the suite, take a shower, and make myself somewhat presentable. But I have a sneaking suspicion that if I get anywhere close to a mattress, I might fall over into a deep slumber.

I really *would* love to get out of these dirty, mud-caked clothes, though. And aside from the unfortunate text across the front of the hoodie, the sweatsuit feels warm and comfortable, the fabric soft beneath my fingers.

Before I can think too much about it, I go into a stall and change into the sweatsuit. It fits perfectly, and it baffles me that Lachlan was exactly right with his sizing—small up top, medium on bottom. No hourglass figure or slim straight lines here, I have a God-given shape like a teardrop diamond (I used to say "pear-shaped" until one of my kids pointed out what it means when "things go pear-shaped," and I couldn't bear to think of myself, or any other person, that way).

Oh, man. These warm, dry clothes feel incredible. A luxury.

I meant what I said earlier—sometimes it pays to be uncomfortable for *this* level of happiness.

I come out of the stall grinning, and not even the fact that I look like an over-enthusiastic One Night Stance fangirl can stop me. I give my face a wash in the sink, and with my full belly and clean clothes, I feel like an entirely different person. Like the girl who was on a terrible date today doesn't even exist.

When I hop onto my stool again, I wave the bartender over. "Another beer, please, and this time, it's a happy beer."

I plop the plastic bag, now full of my dirty clothes, on the empty stool next to mine. On my other side, Lachlan swings his head to look at me. His blue eyes do a quick scan of my body, pausing to read the writing across my chest.

Then, his gaze meets mine, and I hold it, pushing my shoulders out a little.

"Yes?" I ask, challenging him.

He shrugs. "That's a good look."

I open my mouth to reply, but I deflate, frowning. I can't tell if that was meant to be a joke, or if this comment was sarcastic, or if he's simply stating a fact. I still can't get a read on the guy. And before I can settle on a response, he's turned away to face the TV above the bar where a hockey game is underway.

The bartender places my second beer in front of me, along with a glass of amber liquor and a burger for Lachlan. He eats quickly, taking huge bites that make me wonder if he was just as ravenous as I was. My curiosity about the man is growing more intense by the minute.

I take a sip of beer. It's really doing wonders for my mood.

55

"I should thank you," I say.

"Sounds genuine."

"It is. *Thank you*, Lachlan Chase, for picking me up in Seattle, and for driving me all the way here, and for getting the suite, and for buying me clean clothes." I pat down the front of my hoodie. It's very cozy. I'll probably keep it after this nightmare trip.

"I wouldn't say I'm happy about it."

He says this so matter-of-factly that I have to snort. "At least you're honest."

"Most of the time."

"I assumed Brady was honest." I swirl the beer around my glass. "And it turned out his honesty was nothing more than a lie he was telling himself."

"Who's Brady?"

"Long story." As if I want to get into all *that* right now. The guy at the bus stop made it very clear that people don't want to hear my sob story. But that doesn't mean I'm not curious about *his* story. "So. Care to tell me why you're visiting Beau in Cascade Point?"

He pauses mid-dip of a fry in ketchup. "No comment."

"Hmm. That sounds like something very important people say when they're being interviewed on TV." I chuckle. "Are you a very important person?"

"No comment." He's still looking away, but I swear his lips quirk up at one corner. He then glances at my bag of muddy clothes. "Is Brady the reason you were stranded at the bus station?"

"Also no comment." I smile humorlessly. "But seeing as I'm going to be sharing half of a bed with you tonight, can you tell me a little more about yourself past being 'Lachlan Chase from California?'"

"Sure." He pauses. "I'm not a murderer or kidnapper, and I

56

have no intention of coming anywhere near your little pillow barrier tonight."

Not exactly what I was going for, but it's something, I guess.

I push away my empty glass. At some point, the bartender placed another beer in front of me, and I grasp the new glass, the condensation cold on my fingers. I sigh deeply into the silence. "What a riveting conversation this is turning out to be."

"Isn't it."

"Well, it *could* be riveting if you'd just answer my questions properly."

"I could say the same."

He's too captivated by what appears to be a mattress ad on TV to see the look I give him. "We can't just sit here in silence, can we?"

"Doesn't bother me."

I decide I didn't hear that. "If I don't want to talk about Brady, and you don't want to talk about yourself, I'll tell you about myself, if you'd like."

"Please don't."

I stare at him, appalled, and he actually looks at me this time. Shakes his head. "It's not about you. I just won't be in town for very long, so there's no point in us getting to know each other."

I suppose that does make sense. "Can you perhaps tell me how many days you'll be in Cascade?" He narrows his eyes, and I hold up my hands. "I'd like to bake you something or get you a gift when we're back. To thank you."

He shrugs a hulking shoulder before pushing his empty plate to the side. "Unclear. And I don't need your thanks."

"Well. If nothing else, I know that you're good at keeping things to yourself."

Now, those icy blue eyes meet mine, and they cut through me like liquid fire. "Maybe you shouldn't want to know anything about me."

57

He turns back to the hockey game—which has apparently just ended—and takes a swig of amber liquor.

And all I can think is that, whether I *want* him to or not, this man intrigues me. This mysterious man with eyes cold as ice and an attitude that falls somewhere between brutish and aloof, and yet, who also opts to pick up stranded strangers and buy them sweatsuits.

It's funny. I thought I knew exactly who Brady was, thought I understood him based on a few words from a dating app profile and two in-person meetings. I believed he was everything I was looking for. And it turns out that I'd fabricated something in my mind. Made up a story about who he was, and who we could be.

Now, here I am, running the risk of doing it all over again. Creating an entirely false narrative about this total stranger.

How much easier would it be to *know*, for a fact, when something isn't true?

I place my chin in my palm. "Well, if you don't want me to know anything about you, why don't you make something up?"

This catches Lachlan's attention, and he looks at me curiously. "You want me to lie to you?"

"Kinda." I shrug, warming to the idea. I value honesty as much as the next person, but it's been a long day—a long few *weeks*—of living by someone else's lie without being aware of it. And who knows, maybe this could be fun. Which is clearly something my grouchy friend is in need of. "We could make it a game."

"A game where we tell each other only lies." Once again, he says this as a statement and not a question.

"Yes. A lying game."

"Whoever heard of a lying game?" Lachlan is staring at me like I've gone insane. Maybe I have. Maybe I *am*. It's abundantly clear that he has no intention of seeing me again once we get to Cascade Point, so who cares if he thinks I'm a bit loopy?

58

"I just made it up." This beer is making me feel buzzy and daring. I'm excited about this now. "But think about it. It'll give us something to talk about while we're stuck with each other this evening, *and* it'll allow us to still part ways as strangers who don't know anything about each other. See? Win, win, win."

"What if I don't want to talk? What if I prefer to sit in silence?"

I nod at the TV, where a series of post-game interviews appear to be taking place. Of course, the volume is all the way down so we can't hear anything anyway. "In that case, don't mind me as I entertain myself with some lipreading."

On the screen, a very bald man with a very official jacket is shaking his head. I drop my voice all the way down low. "Well, Steve, as I said to my wife, the raccoons in the attic are a-flutter—"

"Stop." Lachlan heaves out a sigh. "Alright. Hockey game's over anyway, so I'll indulge your ridiculous whim. You go first."

"Okay." I tap my fingers against my glass, thinking. "First off, I'm not Lucy Summers. My name is Ava Kinava."

"Like Evel Knievel?"

"Nope. No relation."

He makes a noise that sounds suspiciously close to a chuckle. "Nice to meet you, Ava."

"Nice to be met, not-Lachlan." I wrack my brain for other non-truths. "I am an eighty-two year old woman who hates cats and lives with her boyfriend of five years." I wince. "Ooh, that hits too close to home. Maybe I'm single and that part is just true." I glance his way. "But no comment on that, of course."

"No comment," Lachlan agrees, his lips twitching upwards again. Yes, he seems amused this time. It's strangely gratifying. "So you *didn't* go on a date today then."

It takes me a minute—my head's feeling light and foggy—but I realize he's playing along. "No. I *didn't* have a date. I *didn't* go to Seattle to go mountain biking with a guy named not-

Brady, only to completely fail at biking and then have said date proclaim that I helped him realize he's in love with his best friend." A sour taste fills my mouth at the memory.

"Wow. That sucks. Honestly."

"No comment." I nod. "But hey. You win some, you lose some. So, what about you?"

"What about me?" Lachlan's voice is heavy with wariness.

"Do you have a special someone back in California? A girl-friend? A wife?" My eyes drop to his large hands. "I don't see a ring. Though maybe it wouldn't fit on your finger."

He gives me a look. I smile back cheekily. I kind of feel like little red riding hood taunting the wolf. Poking the bear. I like teasing him like this.

"Next question," he grumbles, turning back to his drink.

"Duh, you're meant to make something up," I say sassily. Liquid courage, apparently.

He's silent for a moment. "Okay. I am a married man who is deeply, deeply in love with his wife."

Oh! Those words do something to me. Something in the timbre of his voice, the way his breath skates over the word "love." The word "*wife.*"

I suddenly have to know if he has one.

"Really?" I ask, a little breathless.

He smirks. "Maybe."

I swallow thickly. No, this man couldn't have a wife. The poor woman would surely be skewered to death by his glare.

Anyway, time to move on. And maybe it's time I call it quits on my beer drinking for the evening. I push away my half-empty glass and lean my full weight on the counter, frankly staring at him. "Okay. Now you know about my situation. So, tit for tat."

"I would've been very happy not knowing your *tat.*"

I snort with laughter. "Remember. Just make something up."

Lachlan peers at me. And maybe it's the buzzy optimism

60

I'm feeling right now, but I'm fairly certain he definitely seems amused. "To which question, exactly?"

"You said you're going to Cascade Point to visit Beau. Why?"

"Because I am *happily* taking a *voluntary* vacation to the coast."

I screw up my face. "Not what I meant. But if you're from California, I can't imagine why you'd come all the way up here for a coastal vacation." I shake my head. "No. I meant *how* do you know Beau?"

He purses his lips. Really very nice lips. "I... *haven't* known Beau for a really long time."

"So, you're friends? Family?"

His jaw clenches over the last word.

I'm slightly taken aback. "Oh. Beau's your family?"

Lachlan looks at the TV, where Bald Jacket Man is still speaking. "No comment."

I frown, processing what this means. Beau Brighton's lived in Cascade Point for years, is such a staple of our community that I almost can't remember a time when he wasn't living there. Back when I was in high school—when I would spend the summer months in Oregon with my dad—Beau used to spend *his* summers in Cascade Point with Graham and Anna-May, his grandparents and our town's founding family.

It was Beau and his two brothers. One younger, and an older half-brother. Not that I've seen either of *them* in years. What were their names?

My eyebrows shoot up.

"You're Lockie."

He swallows, and I watch his Adam's apple bob. "No comment. But it's Lachlan now."

"Right." I think of Graham and Anna-May Brighton and the drama with their wild-card daughter Darla when she (to every-

61

one's shock) got married and subsequently adopted her new husband's young son... Lachlan.

Darla and Alan had two more sons (Beau included) before they suddenly moved their family to Colorado, leaving the grandparents behind.

That was all before my time, of course, but my mom used to say that it was a whole can of worms. According to the Cascade rumor mill, something went down between the parents and grandparents that forced the former to leave, but no one knows what happened.

And I have the distinct sense that the grumpy man next to me wants nothing less than to talk about it.

"That explains that," I say, and then correct myself, "*Doesn't* explain that."

Lachlan doesn't move. There's certainly more to his story, but he's clearly not eager to share it, and I don't want to push him.

Anyway, this was meant to be a game. Something fun. So, I change tack completely. "What else can I tell you... Oh, I'm a circus performer!"

He takes a long swig of his drink, downing the glass. "A clown, perhaps?"

"Rude. I'm an acrobat, actually. Extremely flexible and coordinated."

"You don't say."

"And I hate knitting. Knitting is the worst thing that has ever happened. Yuck." *Says the girl who has literally an entire section of her closet dedicated to clothes she's knit for herself.*

"Yuck," he repeats.

"Oh, I love driving. I drive all the time. I love narrow streets and terrible weather and parallel parking. Yup. I'm just constantly driving places."

Lachlan smirks. "I hate driving."

I'm nodding aggressively now. I'm past the point of being

buzzy and happy, and now, I feel sleepy and happy. "I despise reading also. Reading is the absolute worst. I don't have an overflowing bookshelf at home."

"What's your least favorite genre?"

"Well, fantasy is horrible. And romance is my guilty displeasure."

"I also hate fantasy."

"Wow. Look at us having *nothing* in common. Real 'opposites distract' sort of situation." Is that the expression? I'm not sure. Also, this stool's feeling a little tippy. And I'm so tired. This day is catching up to me, and now that I'm full of burger and beer and wearing cozy clothes, all I can think about is bed.

Actually, I feel a little drunk. Should I be this drunk after two and a half beers?

I place my arm on the bar and lie across it.

Lachlan's facing me now, and his brow's crinkled. "Hey, you okay?"

"Fine!" I giggle happily. Or drunkenly. Or tiredly? Can't tell. "Sorry. Not fine."

He looks me up and down. "I'll get you more water."

"Had enough water through osmosis today."

I lift my shoulder in what should be a casual shrug, but it instead makes my head slide off my arm and hit the bar. I grunt, though it didn't really hurt. Suddenly, there's a warmth on my shoulder, and I realize that Lachlan's big hand is steadying me.

I gaze at it in surprise. "Wow! You have nice hands!"

Lachlan holds a glass of water out to me. His icy blue eyes appear in my line of sight, and this time, I know I can read him. He's... worried.

I take a couple long gulps and then place my head down again. Just gonna take a tiny, little catnap.

"Don't you have rules for overserving?" Lachlan's talking to someone else now. His voice is rumbly and deep and threatening, like those mushroomy storm clouds forming over the ocean.

63

"She only had a couple beers." The person pops his gum, sounding way too chilled out to be facing stormy Lachlan.

"Which beer?"

"The stout."

I open one eye to see Lachlan holding a sticky laminated menu. "You mean the only beer in here with 15% alcohol content?"

He's doing that thing again where he asks a question without *asking* a question.

But 15% alcohol content? Well, that explains it. Who on earth drinks beer that strong?

Me, apparently.

I giggle at the concept. "Ya know, I'm pretty tired. Maybe I should go to bed."

"Not a bad idea." Lachlan's talking to me again, and his voice is no longer thundery but solid and warm. Like thick, slow-moving honey. He should narrate sleepytime audiobooks. "Can you walk?"

"Yup. No problem."

And yet, it's with my full weight leaning on him that we make our way across the bar.

At the other end, he stops. Faces me. Through the blurry haze that is my current beer-goggled state, I can see the concern in his eyes.

"Do you trust me?" he asks. And for some reason, as I stare into the glacier blue of his irises, and I consider what happened today, and despite the fact that we agreed to only lie to each other... I realize that I do.

For absolutely no logical or understandable reason, I trust this complete stranger who picked me up from a bus station only hours ago. Because even though he's a bit intimidating, I've also noticed the ways he's checked in on me. Asked if I wanted to stop when my stomach was grumbling loud as a freight train

64

outside of Aberdeen. Bought me clean, dry clothes as soon as we got here. Made sure I had water. Made himself smaller.

So, it's not a lie when I say, "Yes."

The warm pressure of his hand moves from my elbow to my back. Another hand lands near my knees. And I'm airborne.

No, not airborne; I'm being *cradled*. Literally cradled in strong arms, my body held against a firm chest and a heart that's beating steadily against my cheek. For the first time since I left Brady, my entire body relaxes.

And as I close my heavy eyelids, all I can think is that Lachlan Chase doesn't feel so much like a robot or alien anymore, but like a mahogany tree. Solid, reliable, alive.

7

———

LUCY

When I wake up, the first thing I'm aware of is that I'm too hot.

Like *way* hot. To an unbearable degree.

"AGH!" I grunt, kicking my legs and arms out, only to discover that there's a blanket over me. A very warm blanket. On top of very warm clothes. *What the?!*

My eyes shoot open, and I blink against a painful, blinding light. Where am I? Why is it so hot in here? Why is my head *aching?*

I raise one hand to shield my eyes and pat the mattress beneath me with my other. It's firm, and slanting down towards the middle, and certainly not *my* mattress.

Oh no.

The storm. The motel. The bar. The beer.

Oh, no!

I sit up as it all comes rushing back, too panicked to pay all that much attention to the pain pulsing behind my eyes. I look down at my maroon-clad self. Yup, still wearing the sweatsuit. One of my legs is on top of a blanket I don't remember putting on myself, and my other leg is sprawled off the side of the bed.

The one bed.

But Lachlan couldn't have slept here, because clearly, I was

66

spreadeagled. And judging by the trail of dried saliva on my cheek, I was drooling. Mouth open and probably snoring.

I spot the couch beneath the window. There's a mess of sheets pulled across the dirty cushions and tucked in on all sides. A nicely folded blanket sits on top. One of the pillows from the bed sits half-on, half-off the arm of the couch.

Guess *that's* where he slept. In a prime position to witness my snoring and drooling.

But at least we didn't share the bed.

And now, where is he?

The suite's bathroom is dark, and it's only then that I see the sheet of paper on the night stand, right next to a plastic water bottle and a container of Advil. I edge myself carefully to the side of the bed and pick up the paper.

Morning, Sleeping Beauty. Assuming you wake up. Here's some Advil and water. Take two of these before you even think about leaving this room

—L

I blink a couple times, still totally confused and bewildered and trying to remember last night's finer points. Lachlan and I talked, didn't we? For awhile, I think. I told him I was in the circus? And he told me something about his connection to Cascade Point. He's coming to our town because he... doesn't know Beau?

And yet, the faded memories don't fill me with anything particularly negative (aside from utter embarrassment, of course). I have a feeling that Lachlan was actually kind to me in my drunken, exhausted state. Is that possible?

Ugh. My thoughts are hurting my brain.

I down two Advil and finish the bottle of water.

I'm wondering if I can trust myself to stand when there's a heavy knock at the door. The sound is unfortunately similar to the pounding in my head. This must be some sort of punishment for making it to almost thirty without being a big drinker.

"Yes?" I squeak after the knocking finishes. Lachlan has his own key to the suite, so this can't be him. Which is good, as I'm way too discombobulated right now to face what we talked about last night—or to face *him*.

"Housekeeping!" a woman's voice calls.

Phew. "One minute, please."

I edge myself off the bed. Those Advil can kick in *anytime*.

All of a sudden, there's the sound of keys and the door handle jiggling. Before I can do anything, the door's launched wide open, blinding me with light from outside.

"ARGH!" I shout, covering my eyeballs and shrinking away in a distinct *I'm a woodland troll who never sees daylight* kind of way.

I'm trying to see past the spots in my vision when the woman speaks again. This time, to someone else. "See? She's alive. We've had very, very few deaths here."

She sounds absurdly proud of that statement.

"'Few' isn't *none*," a familiar voice rumbles in response, echoing my thoughts exactly.

I blink blearily a few more times, starting to adjust to the light. A gray but bright light. Which is promising. Lachlan's massive shadowy outline stands in the doorway, facing a stout woman who mutters indignantly as she stalks off.

"Has it stopped raining?" I ask, rubbing my eyes.

"For now."

Shadow Lachlan steps into the room and walks towards me. But he stops before getting too close, placing a takeout cup onto a side table near me. "Coffee. Didn't know if you liked cream or sugar, but you seem like the type, so I got you both."

I'm surprised at the gesture. I do, actually, take my coffee with both cream and sugar. "You got me a coffee?" My voice is croaky. "I thought you were more the type to leave me for dead."

"Hmm. I was tempted. But I figured your friend Jordy

68

might make things hard for me when I get to Cascade Point all by myself, and I just don't have time for that."

"True. Jordy might've confirmed *you* weren't a serial killer, but she's never made such a promise herself." I take a sip of my drink. It's the perfect temperature—I like my hot drinks more lukewarm.

"Sorry if it's cold," he says gruffly. "The motel's coffee smelled like fresh tar so I walked to a cafe down the way. And came back to discover that the second key doesn't work. Lucky for me—or unlucky, perhaps—that woman was at the front desk. She was rather rude about the fact that she had to put down her book in order to assist me."

"Well. Sure seems like you charmed her."

He ignores me. Takes a long pull of his own takeout cup.

I tilt my head. "Let me guess, Americano with an extra shot of espresso?"

Lachlan meets my gaze. "Do you want the truth or a lie?"

Ohmygosh. Our lying game!

I clear my throat. "Surprise me?"

"Cinnamon mocha with extra whip." He doesn't give any indication, one way or another. I decide it's the truth, and it makes me smile.

Lachlan then checks his watch before grabbing his bag—which is packed by the door. "How long do you need to get ready? I'd love to hit the road soon."

"What time is it?"

"Past 11am. Gene gave us—gave *you*—a late check-out, and I figured you could do with a sleep-in. It's not like this room's gonna be occupied tonight unless some unfortunate newlyweds get turned around on their way to their *actual* honeymoon destination."

I hold back a snort. "That's kind of you to let me sleep."

"Not kind. Practical. I don't want a sleep-deprived passenger princess. Plus, the road only just opened." He nods

69

towards me. "Get yourself ready and meet me at the car. I found a place we can get breakfast close to here."

I open my mouth and close it again. I'm usually the one making the decisions. Choosing the best course of action. But for today, in my delicate state, I'm happy to defer to this bossy, grumpy man, who might actually be a little sweeter than he looks.

The thought unleashes a sudden memory. One of Lachlan, just last night, asking if I trust him. And equally strong is the firm, totally inexplicable knowledge that I do.

"Okay." I glance around the room, and my eyes land on the pitiful couch. "Your back feeling okay after a night on that thing, Clark?"

He follows my gaze. "It's been better. But it's not like I could get much sleep in the bed after you broke through the pillow barrier. You practically rolled on top of me while trying to cuddle me. Had to move to the couch just to get a minute of shut-eye."

Oh. My. Goodness!!

The blood drains from my face so fast that I feel faint. Lachlan, meanwhile, gives me that tiny smirk of his before turning on his heel and leaving the suite.

Please. Please let that have been a lie.

8

LACHLAN

It seems that Jordy was, in fact, correct.

Lucy is so... *kind.* Happy go lucky. Cheerful. Friendly.

Well, to everyone but me.

Since opening the door of the honeymoon suite on her this morning—her brown hair piled into a messy knot on her head with tendrils hanging out and her lips pouted in a way that was almost cute—Lucy has gone out of her ever-loving way to be sweet as pie to literally every person she's come across.

I waited for her by my rented SUV for ages and was about to drag her out of the motel by her unfortunately sloganed hoodie when she exited the lobby accompanied not only by my friend Gene, but also by the grouchy woman at the front desk who unlocked the suite's door for me.

Lucy then hugged them goodbye. *Hugged them.*

Seems she has a habit of wrapping herself around total strangers.

I could only stare at her with a mixture of curiosity and wariness as she removed all the plastic wrapping I'd put on the passenger seat yesterday (streaked with dried mud and grass, I'll have you know) and then sat down without a word. Her dark hair—the exact color of chestnuts, I noticed—was freshly

71

washed and tied back with her orange bandanna. Her skin smelled of cheap motel soap mixed with a sweet, clean scent reminiscent of the sea breeze.

Now, we're seated at a diner twenty minutes away from the motel, and Lucy is making conversation with our waiter. Making him laugh. And she said a bright hello to everyone we passed as we walked in. Which you would just never do in LA. People there keep to themselves, hustle through their days without paying much attention to anyone else.

You know, like you'd expect *normal people* to do.

It makes me wonder how Lucy gets anything done. Unless her job involves this much smiling and cheerful chatter and laughing. According to her little lying game last night, she's *not* an acrobat or circus performer.

So, I can scratch those off the list.

But I stand by what I said: there's no point in my wondering, or in us getting to know each other. I certainly don't want to know Lucy. And she doesn't want to know me. So that's that.

I take out my phone and place it screen-up on the table. It's been almost forty-eight hours since that conversation in Mike's office, and I still haven't heard from him. A part of me was hoping he'd get through Friday and realize what a huge mistake it was for me to step away. No dice.

How the frick did the podcast even know about the bad date in the first place? It's not like they just *happened* upon the story.

Carly. She must've fed the story to them.

She—and her music career—are the only ones benefiting from this nightmare.

"Waiting on a call?" Lucy asks sweetly. "Maybe your *wife* checking up on you?"

She blinks her aquatic green eyes at me before taking a loud sip of her double-cream, double-sugar "coffee" from a comically large mug that covers almost her entire face as she drinks.

72

"Memory coming back to you, then?" I ask dryly, making sure my intonation stays down at the end.

Her nostrils flare with indignation. "My memories are intact, thank you very much."

"Oh, yeah?" I don't break eye contact as I take a sip of my water. I know, I *know* I shouldn't be engaging with her like this, especially given that we'll never see each other again after today, but I can't help myself. It's just too easy. "Which part of last night do you remember most: when you cuddled up close to me? When you tried to spoon me?"

I was right. Lucy is an apple-red blusher.

And it's not just her cheeks. Her neck and the tiny slice of her chest visible above her One Night Stance hoodie turns the exact same red.

"You. Are. A. Jerk." She punctuates her words, her tone even. "And you're lying, I've decided. No way would I spoon with the likes of you, even in my deepest REM cycle."

My lips lift into a smirk. It's an expression I've been using a lot since meeting Lucy. "No comment."

What I don't say is that Lucy wasn't a bad co-sleeper at all. *I'm* the problem. A full night's sleep for me is usually five hours, and it's a miracle if I make it through the night without waking up at least once.

After tucking Lucy into her side of the bed and making sure the pillow barrier was intact, I stuck to my side, teetering on the edge of the mattress and facing away from her with my arms crossed.

I actually managed to sleep fairly well... Until I woke up with her entwined around me.

At some point in the night, I rolled onto my back, and she'd migrated over the pillows and onto my side of the bed. She wasn't spooning me, but she *was* tucked up against me so that my arm was around her, and she had one of her arms and a leg draped over me.

73

I peeled myself away from her and made up the disgusting couch to try and get more sleep. Mission unsuccessful.

Lucy waits until our food arrives, and I'm mid-bite into my breakfast sandwich, egg and ham falling everywhere, before innocently saying, "You're going to Cascade Point to see your brother Beau."

Frick. She *does* remember. And while I debate for a moment calling up our lying game again, I decide to opt for the truth. "Half-brother. And yes."

Lucy smiles and nods at my phone. "Are you waiting for a call from him, then?"

"Haven't talked to him."

She tilts her head, looking at me with confusion. "Didn't you tell him we stopped at a motel last night so he wouldn't worry about you?"

The proposition is so insane that I can't stop the derisive laugh that erupts from my mouth. "Beau?! Worried about me? Absolutely not."

"You're his family." Lucy's eyes search mine. For answers, maybe? But I don't know to what question.

Because my family? We're simply not close. I'm a few years older than both of my half-brothers, so the age gap was a definite factor when we were growing up. My parents—my dad Alan and step-mom Darla—are nice enough, though we keep our distance. My biological mom isn't in the picture, and Darla adopted me when I was four years old, so for all intents and purposes, she *is* my mother.

As for my step-grandparents, I haven't spoken with them in literal years. Which might be why visiting them isn't at top of my list when I get to Cascade Point. Who knows if they'd even want to see or hear from me.

I just shrug, not liking being put on the spot. "Doesn't mean much."

"It means something." She presses her lips against her ginor-

74

mous mug, apparently lost in thought. Her dark brows are drawn together, and she looks... upset.

Am I the only person who makes this woman feel anything but cheerful?

"You should message him," Lucy eventually says decisively. "And *anyone else* who might be worried about you."

I quirk my head at her. Miss Passenger Princess here seems very intent on finding out my relationship status.

I don't think she'd like to hear the truth, though. Which is that there isn't anyone in my life who could possibly be concerned about where I am right now, and I like it that way. Love, relationships, family... they've always been on the back burner for me. Low priority.

I'd guess she's the exact opposite. Lucy looks like the type to happily marry and pop out babies yesterday.

She insists on paying for breakfast seeing as I got the suite last night, and she forks over wrinkled dollar bills to our waiter with a smile.

But just as we're about to leave the diner, she stops. Standing on tiptoe, she grabs a knitted duck stuffed animal from an assortment of knit birdlife on one of the shelves by the door and then runs back to the till to pay for it.

When we're back in the SUV, she holds up the duck proudly and offers me an explanation I didn't ask for. "It's for my kids."

This surprises me. "You have kids?"

She's got the duck in her lap, is petting its little wings. "Yup, a whole ton of them."

Oh. So, she *has* already popped out babies. *A whole ton* of them, apparently. "But you're not married, or have a partner."

She gives me a look, like I'm deranged for asking such a question. "What does that have to do with anything?"

I blink, placing Lucy into an entirely new category in my

75

mind. And I have to say, I'm impressed. "Nothing," I say firmly. "Nothing at all. Good for you."

"Maybe I should've gotten a couple. My five-year-olds go crazy for birds."

My eyebrows rise again. "Twins?"

She screws up her face. "No."

What in the world does that *mean?*

Lucy's staring down at the duck, running her fingers over the knit pattern. And she once again looks so forlorn and thoughtful that I'm annoyed.

What is up with this woman and her emotions getting under my skin?

I also get the feeling that she's going to be regretfully petting that little duck all the way to freaking Cascade Point, and I'd rather not have her crying in my passenger seat.

So, without a word, I march back into the diner. When I emerge a few minutes later with a canvas bag full of stuffed birdlife, Lucy's green eyes go wide, and she presses her palms to the passenger window in excitement (ugh). And then, she smiles.

I open her door, throw the bag at her feet and return to the driver's side, starting the engine so we can get on the road and I can get away from this woman for good.

It's a slow, painful slog to Cascade Point through dense evergreens with branches that dip dangerously close to the road. Parts of the highway were damaged in yesterday's deluge, so we're down to one lane in some areas.

Sometime after we pass a sign reading *Cascade Point – 5 miles*, Lucy turns down the volume on the car's sound system.

I startle a little, so absorbed in my thoughts about SparksFly

76

and Carly and the media circus that I almost forgot Lucy was here. She hasn't been particularly chatty today either, but we *have* had to make more than a few emergency pee stops. The last of which involved me throwing on the hazards while she ducked off into the brush, and keeping my gaze averted from any squatting women in the forest.

It's yet another thing on the long list of items I never imagined I'd be doing just a couple days ago.

"Not into country?" I say into the silence.

"I am. Just not after two hours straight."

The road worker ahead of us holds up a very useless "Stop" sign. Pretty sure only one car squeaked through when he had it turned to "Slow". I turn the BMW off again so I'm not idling, and Lucy bounces her head back on the headrest with a loud groan.

I get it. Sitting here in traffic like this is a colossal waste of time.

All of a sudden, I think of Lucy's little lying game last night. The suggestion was entirely unhinged, don't get me wrong. But I can't say that it wasn't a way to pass the hours.

"Country music is all I ever listen to," I say. "Because I'm actually a cowboy, back in California."

Lucy rolls her head my way, and her expressive lips quirk up at the corners. "A cowboy, huh? Is that where you learned your whole 'no comment' business? Ranch life?"

"Sure thing. We ranchers and cowboys are all very important people who *love* to get featured in the media. We're all just craving the limelight and want to be in the midst of all the hustle and bustle." I look at her with a well-worn expression of skepticism. "Did you not know that?"

"Makes total sense. Cowboys definitely *don't* have a reputation for being stoic, silent lone wolves." She pauses. "So, I assume you rodeo and horseback ride and wrangle bulls and the like."

77

"Absolutely. Wrangling bulls is my favorite pastime."

"From the moment I saw you, I knew you'd make a good rodeo clown."

I look at her innocently. "Pretty sure there's only one clown here."

She narrows her eyes at me. "So, you *do* like country music."

"I'm on a female country singer kick these days. Lauren Alaina. Carrie Underwood. Shania Twain."

"You're lying."

I smirk. "No comment."

She grins. "Well, I absolutely *hate* metal music."

I'm surprised. *This woman* listens to metal? "Do you hate metal as much as you hate knitting?"

Lucy goes still, and I have a feeling I just unlocked another memory from last night. "Knitting is the worst," she responds passionately, petting the stuffed duck again. "I never make little knit toys and stuffed animals."

She mentioned this last night as well. Of all the hobbies a woman aged twenty-five to thirty (can't get an exact read on her age) might have, knitting is *not* what I would've expected.

The road worker turns his sign back to "Slow." I have half a mind to roll down the window and oh-so-helpfully yell that his sign is *completely* useless given the gridlocked traffic.

Lucy utters another sigh.

"You can go, if you want," I tell her. "We're less than five miles from town and the rain's holding off. Why don't you walk past the traffic and call a ride, and I'll drop off your bike when I get to town."

She looks at me with abject horror. "You want me to *walk* a couple miles along a flooded highway? Are you insane?!"

I shrug a shoulder. "Would probably be faster than waiting for the traffic to clear. It takes me about an hour to run ten miles so it shouldn't take you *that* long."

"You're also basically Superman incarnate with freakishly long legs."

"That has to be the nicest thing anyone's ever said to me." I purse my lips. "No, it was just a suggestion. It sounds like you know people who would pick you up on the other side of the gridlock, and this is a *much* shorter drive for them than going all the way to Seattle."

Lucy's silent for a long moment, debating. "That's okay," she finally says. "We've made it this far, haven't we? Not gonna abandon you at this final hurdle. And besides, the chances of you seeing me again after this trip are exponentially higher if you have to drop off my bike."

"You make a good point."

Lucy lets out that light, airy laugh I've only heard her use around other people. Honestly, I can't tell what's more unsettling—having her expect my sympathy, or having her find me funny.

A mere forty-three minutes later, taillights begin to light up and cars start to move.

"Finally!" Lucy cheers, clapping her hands like a child. Which makes me wonder what her "whole ton of" kids are thinking about her being gone unexpectedly for the night. She must have a friend or family member watching them.

It's at a crawl that Lucy and I eventually get to the T-intersection, and I take a left towards Cascade Point while the majority of the traffic goes right. As soon as the road is clear, I press on the gas and relish the feeling of going faster than a snail's pace.

The paved road begins to crack and bump with potholes as we enter the town limits.

I recognize Main Street immediately by the old-timey brick and wood buildings, some with white, blue, or pink cracked paint. It's like driving right into a memory, into an image I haven't seen in decades. And nothing looks different. Not the

79

old bakery at this end of town, not the dilapidated city hall, and certainly not the rundown fire station tucked in behind everything.

Shivers crawl down my spine as I take it all in. From the overweight seagulls perched like tiny gargoyles on every building, to the mingling smells of algae and sea bream blowing in through my open window, to the cool breeze coating my skin with fine salt.

Only then do I realize what a terrible, terrible mistake this was.

"You okay?"

Lucy's voice startles me, and I come roaring out of my memories and back onto Main Street. Where we've rolled to a stop. Luckily, no one is driving behind me, though some passersby are staring.

"Fine," I choke out gruffly. "Just been awhile."

Lucy nods with understanding, and I want to ask if she grew up here, and why she never left. But before I can say anything, she belts out one of those loud squeals she warned me about.

"EEE, it's Jordy!!"

The passenger door is suddenly wide open as Lucy throws herself out of the BMW, waving frantically—entire body waving, really—at a speck of a woman across the street. The woman is seriously tiny, with a blonde bob and a constellation of freckles. Her face splits into two with a wide smile.

That's Jordy?!

The trunk opens and Lucy's clearly struggling to grab her bike, so I get out to help her. But by the time I get there, she's already half dragging, half rolling the bike towards the freckled woman, the bags of stuffed birdlife and dirty clothes hanging off her arms.

But then, she stops in the middle of the road and turns back towards me. Her green eyes are shimmering, her lips pulled into a smile. The kind of smile she hasn't given me in all the time we've known each other.

"Thank you, Lachlan," she says sincerely. "All lying aside, I'm glad that it was you I was stuck in a motel with last night."

Behind Lucy, Jordy's eyes are erupting with a thousand question marks. I can only imagine the actual inquisition that Lucy will soon have to deal with. But my focus is on the passenger princess—no, the *woman*—who accompanied me here and wasn't terrible company after all.

I give her a nod. "Could have been worse."

Lucy laughs again, rolling her eyes at me like we just shared an inside joke. She continues on towards Jordy, who I find is staring right at me. As soon as my gaze meets hers, she winks.

I look at Lucy once more, taking note of her suggestive motel hoodie, the orange bandanna tied in her hair, her cheeks that turn pink as she laughs at something Jordy said.

And then, I turn on my heel, get in my car, and drive away. Alone.

Just the way I like it.

9

LUCY

"You have some 'splaining to do, Lucille Summers."

I crinkle my nose. My first name isn't short for anything, and Jordy knows it. Still, I put on my best and most innocent tone of voice. "Whatever do you mean, Jordana Murphy?"

"You got stuck," she speaks slowly, like she's spelling something out for the very old and very senile. "In a motel room. With that... *specimen*. Can he even be called human?!"

Jordy—who, to this point, has been holding the majority of the mountain bike's weight while I cradle my bags of dirty clothes and stuffed birdlife—suddenly releases the handlebars to fan her face, thereby tilting the full weight of the bike onto me.

The fact that I almost topple right over speaks volumes about my arm strength (which is directly opposite to Lachlan's arm strength, if those tight sweatshirts and the feel of his biceps when he carried me last night are any indication).

"Superman, perhaps?" I suggest.

Jordy takes the handlebars back, and I can stand upright again. "I was gonna say marble statue. Hopefully he's not cold as marble."

"No, he's got very respectable body heat," I say without

thinking, and my cheeks immediately turn red. "Okay, before your mind goes straight into the gutter, let me clarify. We hardly touched and certainly had no good reason to touch. But he did kind of maybe carry me back to our room after I had a couple beers."

Sigh.

The way Jordy's eyes are bugging out of her head, that explanation only made things *worse.*

"Lemme get this straight," she shrieks, startling the older man walking on the sidewalk ahead of us. He spins to give us an annoyed glare.

"Sorry, Mr. Sidhu!" I call out with a feeble wave.

But Jordy's off, paying no mind to the poor soul she just lightly terrorized. "YOU, Lucy Summers, had a *couple* of beers, and you had to be *carried* back to your *room* by a man who may or may not have just stepped out of GQ?!"

Jordy appears to be mere moments away from a full conniption, complete with hyperventilation.

"No!" I say quickly. "Well... yes. But not like *that.* The road was closed because of the storm, so we had to stay somewhere overnight, and there was only one room available at this motel. So, we had to share it. Platonically, non-romantically, and every other acronym for the fact that we are non-acquaintances who had to bunk up together for one night. It was as sexy as sharing a camp dorm room with ten stinky strangers."

I leave out the fact that the room sharing also involved bed sharing.

And that said room was the honeymoon suite.

And that there is a very slight (and I do mean *slight*) possibility that I unintentionally spooned that man...

Jordy might have a heart attack on this sidewalk if she knew those details. And I need her heart to be intact at least until we get to the rental shop to return this bike.

83

"Ten strangers, huh?" Jordy waggles her eyebrows. "Ten of *him* wouldn't be such a bad thing."

"You really think he's that hot?"

"You don't?! He looks like Henry Cavill and Daniel Craig's brooding, sexy baby. With very appropriately sized hands."

"Need I remind you that said sexy baby shares a large portion of his DNA with your best friend, Beau."

"Ew." Jordy's lips press together, and she lapses into silence. "Anyway, hottie with a body or not, it was kind of him to pick you up in Seattle and save you from a night sleeping in a bus station."

"I don't know if *kind* is the term I'd use for the guy." I say this with a smirk as I look down the street, where Lachlan's taillights turned left a few moments ago. Not a lot of people drive in Cascade Point, so the huge, new BMW *definitely* stands out.

Honestly, I get a kick out of his overall grouchiness.

Got a kick out of it.

It occurs to me that I might have enjoyed our bizarre little road trip more than I realized. Lachlan was a comforting presence beneath all the grumpy. He's steady and solid and reliable. Totally unflappable to my easily flapped.

It's strange to consider that I might not see him again. I mean, it's a small town so chances are I will, depending on how long he stays here. But we certainly *will not* be spending time together like we have been—AKA with the proximity and intensity of a pressure cooker.

I brush off the almost wistful emotion. This is really just a touch of Stockholm syndrome from being trapped in a car and motel room with the guy for the past twelve hours.

"I'll also never be drinking again," I say to Jordy, holding my head. "I thought I'd treat myself to a couple of the beers last night given the chaotically hot mess that was yesterday. Seriously, the moon must've been in retrograde or something."

84

"Pretty sure that's not how the moon works. And pretty sure that, as a teacher of young children, you should know that."

"Well. Turns out the beers I treated myself to were a light 15%."

Jordy's jaw drops. "Are you serious?" Her expression turns to one of despair. "I missed drunk Lucy?!"

I stare at her flatly. "Yup, and I don't think she'll be making any more appearances anytime soon. Drunk Lucy went straight to bed and woke up with a nasty hangover."

Not to mention an increasingly un-patchy recollection of feeling cold in the night and then gravitating like a freaking wrecking ball through the pillow barrier and towards the other warm body on the bed.

Mortifying.

I snap myself out of that line of thought. "I thought my head was gonna fall off this morning. It's so embarrassing—I only had two. And a half." I squeeze my eyes shut. "Don't tell Mabel about this. I'll never hear the end of it."

Mabel is our lovable resident wine connoisseur, complete with a posh British accent. She loves all things grapey, often going on about her preference for New World wines. She usually brings a bottle or two to our town's book club meetings on Wednesday nights.

"And speaking of..." Jordy turns to me, brown eyes sparkling. "What on earth happened on the date with Brady?!"

So, I tell her the full story. My first attempt at biking down a small pitch that instead pitched *me* headfirst into a bush. The hill I finally succeeded at going down, only to realize that my rear tire kicked up a slew of mud that coated my entire backside so that it looked like I had some sort of colossal bathroom emergency. Joking around with Brady's friends and feeling like I was being accepted. And then, Brady's confession.

By the time I'm done, we've dropped off the bike and are

85

almost home. Jordy and I share a tiny one bedroom plus den rowhouse, but I have no complaints. The location is excellent, mere steps from our historic (read: old and rickety, but still very cute) port and a short walk from the fire station and the elementary school.

"Holy bananas. I'm so sorry, Luce." Jordy's shaking her head, looking as flabbergasted as I felt yesterday. Today, though, the date almost feels like old news.

"It's okay. At least he was honest in the end. Saves me wasting my time. And now, onto the next."

"Back onto the apps, then?"

"Ah. I might take a break from the apps." I choke out a laugh that sounds hollow.

Truth is, it's slim pickings for dates here in Cascade Point. This is a small, coastal town, and given that most of the guys here have, at one point or another, accused me of having cooties, tugged on my ponytail, and/or is the brother or cousin or ex-boyfriend of a close friend, well... there's not a ton to work with.

Seattle is the biggest metropolis close by, so I often joke that I'm going to try and lure a city boy out this way. Which kind of maybe makes me sound like one of those sneaky sirens in Greek mythology.

My dating history is much more mythology than Greek, though.

"Besides," I continue. "Apps or no apps, my person's out there somewhere. It's just a matter of time."

Jordy laughs. "Luce, your optimism really is something else."

"I just choose to live my life the Hallmark way. I mean, there's got to be *some* truth to those movies where the big city businessman, or the hot lumberjack, or the exiled prince find love and move to a small town, right?"

Because that last part is *key*. It beats out everything else.

86

Cascade Point may come up short in terms of jobs and those easy amenities and services you get in cities. But this is my home. It's where I'll choose to stay.

My mom used to say that living in a town like ours either suits you or it doesn't. It didn't suit my father, which is why he left us and started over somewhere new with a new family. Broke my mom's heart when he left. But it taught her—taught us *both*—a valuable lesson:

You can't force someone to be something they aren't.

We're climbing the steps to our house, arms linked, when I suddenly remember. "Is the ceiling in the kitchen still leaking?"

"It was when I left for work last night. We should probably call the plumber on Monday."

"Hmm. Maybe it stopped. Leaks can do that, right? Just suddenly stop... leaking?"

She laughs. "Maybe in a fantasy book."

I suddenly remember yet another snippet of my conversation with Lachlan last night. The guy reads fantasy novels, of all things. I would've guessed he sticks to non-fiction of the inspiring-self-help or biography-of-a-titan type. Or books about horses and cowboys. Who knows.

The man's like a funny little onion. Has so many unexpected layers.

"Oh! You never told me what happened to my mom's bowl."

Jordy stops so abruptly that I almost topple back down the front steps (because yes, she may be tiny, but she's built like a freaking tank).

"Luce, I didn't know it belonged to your mom." She takes my hands earnestly. "I wanted to empty the water out of the bowl before I left for work, and so I pulled up a chair, and I... well, I dropped it and it shattered. I'm so sorry."

I shake my head. There's no need for her to apologize. "It's not your fault, J. I should've probably mentioned it."

87

"Do you know where she got the bowl? I'll try and find one exactly like it."

"It's not necessary. Really."

"No, I'm on a mission." She sets her jaw. "You *know* how I get when I'm on a mission."

I do know. I've never met anyone with such a one-track mind in my entire life.

"Well then, your mission is taking you to Italy."

She frowns pensively and then looks at me with twinkling eyes. "That's that. Next time I'm in Italy, I'm buying you a bowl."

I have to laugh, glad that we're moving on. My mom was my best friend, but her death wasn't exactly sudden. She'd been sick for awhile, so I had time to grieve and feel the emotions and be sad. These days, I try to only think of her with a happy heart. And I've mostly succeeded.

"Oh, yeah? When's that trip scheduled for?"

"Any day now." She affects a posh accent. "Just as soon as Jake gets his act together and flies me business class to Europe."

Jake is Jordy's new man—they met on the same dating app I met Brady, and she's been seeing him for a few months. As happy as I am that she's found a guy who seems to like Cascade, I'm also internally more than a little leery of Jake. Who, in my opinion, was grossly misnamed given that he is the epitome of a Chad.

I'm trying to be excited for my friend's relation-situation-ship, though (a point that Jake refuses to clarify, by the way), and I throw an arm around her shoulders, laughing along with her as we open the front door.

As soon as we step into our house, it's clear that something is wrong. There's a damp, mildewy smell that I don't remember being here when I left yesterday.

Jordy takes off down the hall towards our kitchen, and I'm hot her on heels.

There, we find that the ceiling leak has evolved into an ugly brown splotch hanging out right above our fridge.

"Uh, Luce... I don't think the leak has stopped leaking. I also don't think we have a big enough container to catch all that water."

I look at her with wide eyes. "I'll call Benny."

10

LACHLAN

What kind of an absolute waste-of-space town doesn't have a single container of oat milk anywhere on its premises?

I've got the answer for you: Cascade Point.

This town has remained in the 1800s when it was first established (per the Brighton family records) and doesn't have any lactose-free substitutes in its biggest (and only) grocery store. Regrettably, the Cascade Market is not quite Erewhon.

"Louis, it's an allergy," I say to the store's owner and manager, not wanting to have to use my work voice. Which is a few octaves lower and significantly more threatening. "I cannot have anything with lactose."

"Psh. Lactose allergy. Never heard of such a thing," Louis Gramercy responds with a wave of his hand.

I pinch the bridge of my nose. My original goal was to keep to myself in Cascade Point. In my mind, ideally, only Beau would know that I was visiting.

But the minute I dropped Lucy off, I realized that there wasn't a snowball's chance that this tiny town had any sort of food delivery service. So, before going to my rental, I came to the grocery store with the hope that I wouldn't run into anyone I recognized.

No such luck. Louis certainly knows who I am, just as I remember him from my past summertime visits. He's in his sixties now, and his round cheeks, too-long facial hair, and wide eyes are all familiar. Though he's quite a bit more portly.

"You city people," he continues. "You always need your organic, grain-free, dairy-free, sugar-free, *everything*-free meals. Might as well eat air, is what I say." He laughs boisterously, patting his sizeable belly. "Here in Cascade, we eat everything. And we enjoy it, just as it is."

The man must be at least partly losing his marbles. Or his hearing.

I pinch the bridge of my nose, try not to bark my next words. "Louis. For the last time. If I have dairy, I will be in severe pain. I just can't understand how you don't carry a single dairy alternative. This isn't an unreasonable request."

"Toughen up, son. A little discomfort might do you some good."

Funny. That's essentially what Lucy said yesterday.

The entire population of this town are clearly gluttons for punishment. They do live *here*, after all.

Louis beams at me through his scraggly beard, pats my shoulder, and then trots off down the aisle, whistling a cheerful tune.

"Guess I'm having my coffee black," I grumble while grabbing a bag of ground beans. The market doesn't carry any of my preferred brands, of course, so I pick up some locally roasted coffee that actually smells decent.

I take a quick scan of my basket. I've got rice, chicken, eggs, a no-name wholegrain bread, and some fruits and vegetables to get me through the rest of the afternoon and evening. Because surely, Mike will call by tonight.

I just have to hope that my rental has a good enough kitchen to cook. And cell service.

After a stop by the liquor aisle, I head to the checkout

counter. Because on top of a lack of food substitutions, Cascade Market also doesn't have self check-out.

I look at the time while the cashier rings up my groceries and notice that my wristwatch—a Tissot I bought with my first ever bonus from SparksFly—appears to be off. Yes, the second hand is ticking weirdly.

Great. Of course my watch breaks the minute I leave the city.

Frustrated, I look around the small store, jiggling my foot. Louis is nowhere to be seen, but I can hear him somewhere, terrorizing another poor soul with a monologue about... eggplants?

"Yup. He's talking about vegetables."

I startle, turning towards the cashier who somehow read my mind. He can't be older than sixteen, and he has thick dark hair and coal-black eyes. He's not even looking at me, just scans through my bag of broccoli with a bored expression.

"How did you know—?"

"You looked confused." The boy shrugs, and when he glances at me, it's clear that this whole bored thing is an act. I have a feeling he's been watching me. "Louis loves his veggies. They're his pride and joy. If you give him an ear, he'll talk it right off."

"*His* veggies," I repeat.

"Grows them himself. Fruits, too, but he's less proud of those."

"I see."

"A lot of the food here is local." The boy's words pick up speed (and his scanning slows) as he looks at me full on. "Louis grows a lot of the produce. Agnes brings over eggs and milk from her farm. Wyatt and Cheyenne make breads, and they have rolls and buns and stuff at their bakery."

I tilt my head at the boy. "Why are you telling me this?"

He lifts his chin slightly. Back to playing it cool. "You're

92

new here. Thought you should know what you're dealing with, coming from the city." He glances at me again, and there's no hiding the eagerness in his eyes. "LA, right? What's it like there? I heard the girls are *hot*."

"LA's busy." I frown in the direction of the dairy aisle. "Has everything you could ever need, right at your fingertips."

"Me and my friend Ainsley—he goes by Ace, like Ace *Bam*tura, wrestling detective—want to go there someday. Join the Pro Wrestling Guerilla on our way to the WWE. Become *huge* stars..." The boy trails off, starry eyed.

"I get it. I'd want to leave this place, too."

"Oh, no." He gives me a funny look. "I'd go back and forth with my awesome private jet."

This amuses me. "Private jet, huh?"

"Well, *yeah*." He snorts, like he's spelling something out for me that is embarrassingly obvious. "I could never move away. My sister and my mom and all my friends live here. And the fishing and surfing are so good. And the cinnamon rolls at the bakery? Hands down the best *I've ever had*."

I continue to stare at him, frankly baffled. Even the sixteen-year-olds are in love with this rundown truck stop in the middle of nowhere. They've clearly all been brainwashed by the fresh, unpolluted, ocean-tinged air.

Then, the boy puffs out a sigh that deflates his chest. "We'll see if this wrestling thing works out. I've been watching this guy's YouTube videos about the WWE. It sounds almost impossible to break into. Ace doesn't seem worried, but I kinda feel like it's a pipe dream."

He's fiddling with the straps of my grocery bags, lost in thought. I don't think he's looking for sympathy or advice, but for some reason, I feel for the boy and his big dreams. "Hey, don't let anyone tell you that you shouldn't try and go for what you want. Especially not some nobody YouTuber online."

93

He looks up at me, surprised. I'm surprised too, if I'm being honest.

"Thanks," he says. I grab my bags, give him a nod, and am about to turn away and leave this place for good when he follows up with, "And don't worry about the people here. They'll get over it soon enough."

I pause. "What?"

"You." He waves a finger towards me. As if this is any help.

I open my mouth to ask him exactly what he means when Louis appears out of nowhere like a red-cheeked, messy-bearded poltergeist. Was he hiding behind the gum and chocolate display?

"Jensen, what did I say about scanning through alcohol?" Louis is peering at the boy with his lips pursed and his chin tilted down. From this angle, he looks alarmingly like a stern owl. "Not until—"

"Not until I turn twenty-one. I know, I know." Jensen rolls his eyes with a sigh as he grasps one side of my case of beer and pushes it towards Louis.

Holy. In that little exchange, I almost forgot about the life-saving beer I need to get me through tonight.

Louis steps around Jensen, scans through the case, and hands it to me. He gives me a too-wide, too-bright smile as I pay for the groceries. "Pleasure doing business, Lockie. Now, Jens, care to help me stack the tomato cans? I'm envisioning a pyramid today."

"Again?" Jensen whines. "Look, I saw something the other night on Reddit. Someone stacked their cans to look like Mario! It was so cool!"

"We're not in this business to be cool, my boy—"

"Clearly," Jensen mutters.

"—This is serious. What did I tell you the other day about patience, hard work, and professionalism?"

The two bicker like father and son as they disappear down

94

one of the aisles. I take this as my cue to leave and practically burst out of the market.

But as I'm placing my bags in the back of my SUV, Jensen-the-aspiring-wrestler's bizarre warning about the people here rings in my ears.

11

_____

LACHLAN

It wasn't just Louis at the Cascade Market.

There was also Gina at the hair salon, and Mr. Sidhu at the laundromat.

I went into three different businesses this afternoon and was greeted each time by very cold shoulders. Not that I would've wanted Louis or Gina or Mr. Sidhu to be friendly or, heaven forbid, *chatty*. But their overall unhelpfulness towards me—a potentially paying customer—was not what I expected.

In LA, the customer is king, and I guess I had the (apparently wrong) impression that small town folk were generally a friendly bunch.

I expected them all to be like Lucy. Instead, it felt like I was meeting a bunch of...

Well, *me*'s.

And while it would've been a more pleasant experience to be helped as a customer—instead of having my allergies thrown in my face, getting laughed at when I asked Gina if her salon carried my preferred men's shampoo as I forgot mine, or having to chase an impressively avoidant Mr. Sidhu around the laundromat to ask about dry cleaning (which they don't do, it turns out)—I have to appreciate that these people aren't running their town on frivolous pleasantries.

By the time I'm driving down the road towards my rental, I'm looking forward to cracking open a beer and plotting out how I'm going to successfully avoid speaking to another living soul in Cascade Point for the rest of the night (or, worst case, a few nights).

This street isn't one I remember. The house should be a five-minute drive from town, but it's much longer given the twisty-turny roads and potholes. There are only a couple houses down this way—quaint, cottage-style homes separated by overgrown thickets of trees.

My rental is at the end of the street. Or it should be.

All I can see right now is very thick brush. Which, admittedly, does bode well for my privacy and seclusion requirements on this mandatory vacation.

The British woman on my Maps calls out twenty feet, ten feet, five feet...

I roll to a stop. And I can't tell what I'm looking at, but it *certainly* isn't the "charming, historic two-story cottage by the seaside" from the vacation rental website.

The photos showed a white and pastel-blue cottage with a red front door and huge bay windows. The screened-in porch looked to be intact, complete with a porch swing, and a somewhat manicured garden.

I've been catfished. Because let me tell you right now, a manicurist hasn't been anywhere *near* this garden in at least a decade.

As for the house? Well, I'm not sure I'd go so far as to use that word for this pile of wood with peeling paint, and cracked windows, and a dirty front deck.

I shudder to think what the inside looks like.

I swear under my breath as I assess the decrepit building. After a moment, I reluctantly decide I should check it out. Get a

97

full scope of the situation before sending the owner a strongly-worded message.

So, with a grunt, I head up the front steps. They creak beneath my weight but don't break and send me plummeting. Which is good.

Per the automated welcome message, I find two keys beneath the empty plant pot next to the front door. When I open it, the door doesn't fall into a pile of dust, as I expected. Instead, it opens into a foyer with hardwood floors covered by an old navy rug.

The house smells slightly stale, but clean. The living room is dark seeing as a huge, custom-made blind is pulled over the bay window. As soon as I open it, the room floods with light, and I can see what I'm dealing with—white walls sporting scuff marks and holes where artwork or shelves must've once hung, a series of old family photos, a navy couch and armchair that are faded white on the seats, a cast-iron wood stove that looks like it hasn't been touched in years.

I head to the kitchen next, where I find a set of appliances that would fit into that sitcom set in the 70s. A back door opens onto a spacious, screened-in porch that looks to be in fair shape and must have provided the photos of what I mistakenly thought was the deck out front.

My tour then takes me to the master bedroom, which has another huge window looking onto the back of the property.

The cottage might be old and rickety in parts, but it's been cleaned recently, if the lingering smell of antiseptic products is anything to go by. It occurs to me that this place might've been quite nice at one point, when it was decorated and filled with life.

It certainly *isn't* that way now.

I head upstairs to another dark bedroom that must connect to the balcony out front. I turn on the lights.

"WHAT the—"

My voice cuts off as a thousand eyes stare back at me.

The room is full to bursting with animals. Stuffed animals, that is, of all shapes and sizes. Most of which are sporting googly eyes all turned towards me.

Terrifying.

I turn off the lights and head across the hallway, where I find another bathroom. With carpet.

Back downstairs, I stand in the foyer for a moment, weighing my options. This is an old, very quiet, very isolated house. Trees and bushes separate it from the next houses over, and I doubt anyone from town is going to just *wander* up this street.

I wanted a calm and quiet place for myself, and this place does fit the bill. Even if it would need some *serious* work to get back to what it looked like in the photos.

The irony is not lost on me that catfishing is fairly common on my company's dating apps.

And now here I am, being catfished by a short-term rental.

House-fished.

As soon as I've brought my things inside and stashed my grocery bags in the fridge, I crack open a beer and head out back to the screened-in porch.

One entire panel of the screen is torn right down the middle. I idly wonder if this was done by a human or animal.

I stare out at the dense shrubbery in the yard. The sky cleared up earlier in the day, and the light is a soft gold as sunset approaches. It sounds like the ocean waves aren't far away, and I wonder whether there's a beach within walking distance.

The loud and insistent squawks are promising. The over-grown seagulls are a sort of mascot for this town. Seems someone very smart and wise a few years back made the decision to feed the gulls in an attempt to placate them. Needless to say, it didn't work.

There's a rustling in the bushes to my right. After a moment, it stops.

When I look away, the noise starts up again.

"Hello?" I call. This time, I swear the bushes are moving. Whatever's in there is pretty big. Bigger than a seagull or a cat or a dog. "Anyone there?"

Hang on. That looks like—

"Who you talking to?"

The voice comes from directly behind me, and I whip around, sloshing beer all over the place. I swear, brushing off my clothes, as I face my half-brother. "Where'd you come from, Beau?!"

He smirks at me from behind an impressive beard as he leans against the doorframe. "Little skittish, are we? Don't worry, Cascadians don't bite. For the most part."

I raise a skeptical brow at him. "I'm not skittish. Just thought I saw someone in the bushes."

"Could be a raccoon. Or a bear. Or a cougar." Beau flops down in one of the Adirondack chairs like he owns the place. "The animal kind."

I roll my eyes at him. "What're you doing here?"

"Came to find you. When you said you rented a cottage, I figured it was on this street. I saw a fancy new BMW at the end of the block, and..." He twirls his fingers my way, then glances at the door through which he came. "Haven't been so far down this street before. I don't even know whose house this is."

"Probably because it's been lost in the trees back here since the Prehistoric Era."

Beau laughs freely, crossing his arms over his sizeable chest as he continues assessing the house. And I take a moment to assess *him*.

He looks... the same. But taller. And hairier. He's filled out, looks more like a man than the boy I last saw him to be. He's got to be twenty-five now, and even in adulthood, Beau and I look

100

nothing alike. Where I have black hair and ice-blue eyes—courtesy of my mom's Irish side—his hair is dark brown and his eyes are green-hazel, just like Darla's. Clearly, our dad's light blond hair and deep blue eyes canceled out in both of us.

"Aren't you gonna offer me one?" Beau suddenly asks.

"One what?"

"A beer." He beams at me. "And I will take one, thank you."

After grabbing him a beer from the kitchen, I sit back down in my own Adirondack chair. Beau takes a big gulp of the drink and smacks his lips together.

"Decent setup here, Lockie."

"Lachlan. And it's okay. Looks *nothing* like what I paid for, but I'll make do. It's only for a couple days." I shift in my seat. The beer is helping, is making me feel a little more relaxed around the brother I haven't seen in years.

Beau smirks. "A couple days, then back to the city."

"Yeah. The city." I clench my jaw. "Everyone seems pretty hung up on that."

"What do you mean?"

"I got some attitude today when I was running errands. People kept calling me out for being a 'city boy,' telling me to 'toughen up.'" I do the quotes with my fingers, repeating Mr. Sidhu and Louis's words respectively. "These people don't even know me."

"Oh. They know you," Beau mumbles.

"And look, what's wrong with liking the city, anyway? This town has no dry cleaning, no lactose-free alternatives, no watch repair. The road is essentially one big pothole—"

"Almond milk," he interrupts me.

"What?"

"Almond milk is dairy-free."

I frown at him with full irritation. "I know that. But there is no almond milk here. According to Louis, lactose allergies don't exist."

Beau's beard twitches, for some reason. "Have you unpacked your groceries yet?"

"No. What does that have to do with anything?"

Without a word, Beau walks into the cottage and comes back out holding something...

Almond milk.

My eyes widen. "I didn't buy that."

"Louis probably snuck it into your bag when you weren't looking. We have a couple lactose-free people here that he orders in for specially. Gluten-free, too." He shrugs. "I bet that if you'd asked nicely and weren't being a jerk, he probably would've showed you where to find it."

"How do you know I was being a jerk?"

Beau just stares at me with an eyebrow raised.

"Fine," I acquiesce. Clearly, my reputation precedes me here in Cascade. "That was... kind of him." The wind's slightly knocked out of my sails now, and I shake my head, resigned. "I still don't know how you guys get anything done. It's all so much easier in the city."

I take another sip of beer. Like everything else I purchased today, this was brewed locally. And honestly, it's not half as bad as I expected.

"Can I give you some advice?" Beau finally says. "Don't burn your bridges 'round here. It might be a small place, but people do what they can—do the *best* they can—for their community."

I hear the edge in his tone, the admonishment, and I start to feel bad. Start to feel like maybe I *was* a jerk.

"I get it. I'm sorry. I didn't mean to go off like that," I say quietly, more of a mumble. I rub my palms into my eyes. "It's been a long couple days, and I'm stressed about work. It's not really much of an excuse. But, yeah. Sorry."

"Thanks. I'm sure it's not all on you, though. I told them to

102

go easy on you, but hey, we're a tight-knit group here. We look out for each other. And people hold grudges."

I frown, wondering what he means by all that, but decide that maybe, right now, I don't care. I have enough crap going on to wonder about who else might dislike me and for what reason(s).

Beau suddenly lets out a chuckle. "Who'd have thought you'd be back here in Cascade Point, staying in this random house by the beach."

"So, there *is* a beach close by."

"Yeah, bro. You're literally steps away. If you, you know, catapult yourself through that hedge, the beach is *right there*."

That explains the ocean and seagull noises. "I did think it would be ages before I came back here." I grimace. "Thought I might never have to come back."

"I thought so, too." Beau goes quiet again, and I wonder if he means that comment about me or about himself. He downs the rest of his beer and then stands and gives me a hard pat on the shoulder. "Guess I'll see you around, big bro. For however long you're going to be in town."

"A couple days."

"A couple days," Beau repeats. "But seriously, take my advice. Things will go a *lot* more smoothly if you play nice with the locals."

"Playing nice isn't really my specialty."

"Just pretend, then. Little white lies."

Well, I am rather well-acquainted with lying after last night. *I wonder if Lucy got home okay?*

The thought comes out of nowhere, but I find that I actually am curious. In fact, I've thought of her a few times today, completely without my permission.

This loony town is messing with me. I swear, Cascade Point is a freaking black hole of useless emotions. And misplaced almond milk.

103

After Beau leaves, the porch is silent once again, save for the squawking seagulls and the crashing ocean waves that are apparently *right there*. Beau might've said that I should be nice to the locals, and I will be.

But first, I have a local to confront because this cottage—as structurally sound as it appears to be—looks nothing like the listing. Which means that this *Tammy* who rented it out has pulled quite the bait and switch. I've sent no less than three sternly-worded emails since I got to the cottage, with no response. The audacity.

Tammy doesn't have a photo to identify her, but her profile on the vacation rental website says that she works at Cascade Point's elementary school.

Guess that's where I'll be, bright and early, on Monday morning.

12

LUCY

By Monday morning, the reverse puddle has evolved into a brown stain roughly the shape of Australia.

It's also constantly leaking. Which is alarming. Though Jordy and I came up with an extremely clever solution in case the leak intensifies before Benny can get here.

I'm leaning against the kitchen counter, sipping my coffee and staring warily at the stain when Jordy appears at the other side of the kitchen.

"Good morning!" she says brightly, already clad in her dark blue uniform top and her favorite reindeer-print fleece leggings that she wears beneath her coveralls. "How's Australia holding up?"

She takes a ginormous step over the inflatable kiddie pool in the middle of our kitchen and then pours herself a coffee, filling the mug to the brim. Where I'm a lukewarm, half-full, two sugars, two milks coffee drinker, Jordy likes her coffee strong, hot, and maxing out the surface tension.

"It's holding up. Barely. Benny should be by this morning to look at it."

Jordy tuts, shaking her head. "Still wish he'd been able to

come yesterday. What're the chances he'd have a wedding on a random Sunday in January?"

"Don't forget, he did offer to drive all the way back here before the ceremony to take a look."

"Ah, couldn't do that to the bride. Having the officiant disappear right before your wedding sounds a *tad* stressful." She takes a slurp of her coffee, then smacks her lips together. "Anyway, we took his advice, and I'm proud of our little fix, if I do say so myself."

Benny's advice yesterday was to shut off the water to the bathroom directly above the kitchen, and also to pierce the ceiling in the middle of the Australia stain to let the water drain out. Which is why we required the inflatable in the first place.

I'm not sure it's *still* meant to be leaking, but hey, that's for Benny to look at now that he's not off officiating.

"So, anything exciting happening today?" Jordy cuts a glance my way. "Some Superman sightings, perhaps?"

I shake my head. "He's probably already left the state."

I hold back from mentioning that I was, in fact, keeping an eye out for Lachlan yesterday while Jordy and I were in town running errands. We *did* hear that Louis, Gina and Ajay Sidhu all had encounters with him the day before. There was clearly no love lost there.

"Well, fret not, I'm sure Beau knows if he's still around." Jordy smirks. "I can ask him, if you want."

I have to roll my eyes. "What are we, in third grade? Ask Beau, don't ask Beau. It makes no difference to me if I see Lachlan again."

"If you say so." Jordy finishes her coffee with one loud gulp. "I'm outta here. Talk later?"

With that, she hops back over the kiddie pool with surprising grace and trots out.

It's another moody morning in Cascade, with heavy clouds gathered in gray clumps over the ocean. It'll likely rain, so I opt to wear thick tights beneath one of my favorite wool dresses—a mustard-yellow one with long, bell-shaped sleeves.

I found the knitting pattern online a couple months ago and got to work creating the dress, adding a couple of my own personal touches along the way. It's cute, if I do say so myself. And the bright color practically begs you to smile.

Which is exactly what I'm hoping my kids feel when they see me on this wintry Monday.

I slide into the dress and instantly feel warm. I add a white seashell necklace, my glittery rainboots, and then tie my orange bandana into my hair.

It's funny. The bandana used to make me think of Brady, but now, it reminds me of Lachlan and our misadventurous road trip.

Which all feels like a fever dream, honestly. If Jordy hadn't mentioned him this morning, I might have believed that I'd imagined the whole thing.

After grabbing the last of my things, I head out, leaving a key under the plant pot next to the front door for Benny.

The air is chilly and damp, smelling of algae and salt, and I wrap my raincoat tight around me. As I hurriedly walk to school, head down against the wind, I'm half-wishing I'd worn my inappropriate motel hoodie for an extra layer of warmth.

This makes me think of Lachlan again, and I have to smile.

I hope grumpy Superman is living his grumpy best life, wherever he is.

13

LACHLAN

First thing on Monday, as scheduled, I'm marching towards the front door of the Cascade Point elementary school. Though, not scheduled according to my wristwatch, which is officially broken and is now living in my suitcase until I can get back to LA.

I stop just short of the door. Rub my palms into my eyes.

I didn't sleep last night. Or the night before.

Normally, I use a sound machine, ear plugs, an eye mask, and have a lavender spray for my pillow, and even still, I struggle to sleep well. But these last couple nights have been something else entirely.

It could be that part of me is mildly concerned the cottage might collapse in on me at 2am. Or it could be the seagulls yelling outside my window all night. But every time I close my eyes, I remember what Beau said about the people here in Cascade.

That they're a community. Tight-knit. Looking out for each other.

Which kind of sounds like my nightmare.

But then, I think of Lucy. The passenger princess.

Last night, as I tossed and turned in the master bedroom's squeaky wrought-iron bed, I couldn't keep my mind off her. Whether she knew the people I'd met in town. What she thought about our ridiculous road trip, and whether she thought of it at all. Whether I'd see her again.

It's not that I necessarily want to, but in a town this small, it's hard to imagine that I might not run into her at least once before I head back to LA.

At around 5am, I checked my phone to see a message from Mike. *Finally.*

I was not appreciating the opportunity to empathize with the ghosted users on our dating apps and sites. The message wasn't particularly good news—Mike simply asked me to hold tight and said he'd call later today.

I'm mentally preparing for the worst.

See? Even *this* makes me think of Lucy and how she'd asked my buddy Gene the other night for the bad news before the good news. My philosophy is always to get the good news first so you can deal with the bad without any distractions.

Of course, Lucy would have the opposite approach.

After reading Mike's message, I gave up on sleeping and went out for a run. I considered going the scenic coastal route, but a part of me was curious who—if anyone—I might see in town.

The only people on Main Street this morning, though, were an older couple opening the bakery, a few fellow early birds out for walks, and a woman wearing a hooded raincoat and unreasonably shiny boots who was practically keeping pace with me as she crossed town.

And now here I am, loitering in front of a children's school and debating how to confront this Tammy person.

I should probably take Beau's advice and go easy on her, despite the house-fishing.

"Excuse me, sir."

I turn to see a woman with bright red hair standing directly behind me. She's carrying a teetering stack of books with a glass tank perched on top. The tank looks like some sort of terrarium with a log and some bark inside.

I step towards her automatically. "Let me help you with that."

"Awfully kind of you." She beams. "And they say chivalry's dead."

She then goes on to practically *throw* the things at me. I act quickly, stepping back to catch the books and trying to shift them into a balanced stack.

It's only then that I notice something inside the glass cage— a bizarre, green *thing* that quickly disappears under the log.

"What's that?!"

"You mean Fergie?"

I frown at her. "*Fergie?*"

"My gecko." She stares at me with a *duh* expression. Like *I'm* the one who's crazy for not immediately recognizing her pet lizard. "I bring her in for my ten-year-olds every year. It's a great way to teach kids how to care for other living beings, and to show them how much work goes into it." She brushes her nails against her vest. "Fergie gets results."

The strange little thing pops its head out again and blinks at me. I blink back, totally lost for words.

Meanwhile, the woman places her hands on her hips, popping a quizzical brow at me. "I don't know you. Are you from around here?"

"Nope." I carefully re-balance the books. The tank is looking precarious, and I don't want Fergie to go flying. Again. "Well, kind of. I spent some time here growing up. I'm Lachlan Chase."

"*You're* Lockie?!" The woman's face lights up. "I've heard so much about you! I'm also new here, moved from Texas a few years ago."

"Good for you."

"It has been good. For the most part. Cascade's an acquired taste." She laughs heartily. "What brings you to our school?"

"I'm looking for Tammy. Any idea where I might find her?" I look the woman up and down, registering her flannel, down-filled vest and faded jeans. She looks to be about my age, and she could very well have bought a house already. Crumbling or otherwise. "Are you Tammy?"

"Nope. Gabby." She screws up her face. "I don't know a Tammy, but let's head inside. See if we can't find you some help."

I follow Gabby all the way to her classroom while she chatters on about everything and anything under the sun. By the time I drop Fergie off—placing the gecko gently on a shelf next to the woman's desk and feeling relieved to see a proper tank in the corner of the room—I know Gabby's entire life story. And I sure didn't ask.

"Anyway, my tens are in a morning assembly and should be here soon, so I'm afraid this is where we have to leave off." Gabby begins to usher me towards the door with no small amount of force. "Why don't you head to the classroom across the way? The teacher there knows *everyone* in this school, from the admin staff to the cleaners to the subs. She can probably help you. Good luck finding Tammy!"

And then, I'm alone, standing outside of Gabby's classroom. But I take her advice and cross the hallway to a room whose door is wide open and where I can hear lots of high-pitched chatter and giggling.

Until I arrive in the doorway. Then, everything goes quiet.

A classroom full of eyes turn to me. Eyes belonging to teeny, tiny kids, some of whom are sitting at teeny, tiny desks, and some of whom are gathered on colorful floor mats at the back of the room.

"Hello." I frown at the children. *Where is the adult here? Shouldn't there be an adult here?!*

They're all just... looking at me. These kids can't be older than six or seven, and I am most comfortable dealing with fully-grown individuals. You know, people who don't require you to know the ins and outs of that peppy pig show, or the shark song, or the exploring backpack girl.

"Who are *you*?" A small girl with black hair glares up at me with her arms crossed.

I clear my throat, floundering for a moment. "My name's Lachlan, and I'm looking for your teacher?"

My intonation goes up at the end. Which, once again, makes me think of Lucy.

"She's gone to the potty," the girl responds sternly.

"Okay. I suppose I'll wait." They all continue to stare, like I'm... well, like I'm Fergie. "Nice to meet you, children."

Frick. I know next to nothing about kids, but you're not supposed to baby talk with them, are you?

"Nice to meet you, *humans*." I correct myself. "Tiny humans."

And then, as if I couldn't be any more out of my element, I perch on the edge of a tiny desk close to the door. But the kids don't go back to what they were doing—they're all still staring at me.

Except for the small black-haired girl, who is glaring at me with a rather alarming amount of intensity.

"Uh." I wrack my brain for something to say. *Anything.* "Anyone here like Taylor Swift?"

Silence. Dead silence.

Holy. I don't think I've ever had less to say in my entire life.

I sit there in entirely uncomfortable silence for entirely too long until the glaring girl, of all people, pipes up. "My mommy is a Swiftie. She especially loves 'Mine.'"

A relieved smile tugs at my lips. "I like that song, too. Might be one of my favorites."

Is it?

For heaven's sake. I actually think it is.

The girl frowns pensively. "Or, maybe it was 'Mean.' I can't remember. You kind of look mean at first. But I think you might be nice, mister."

She gives me a shy, gap-toothed smile and skips to the back of the classroom.

"Wow. Who'd have thought Lachlan Chase would be a Swiftie?"

I'd recognize that melodic, tinkling voice anywhere.

I swivel towards the door to see none other than Lucy Summers smirking at me. "Lucy! What're you doing here?"

Her green eyes sparkle. "I could ask the same of you."

I suddenly remember that I'm still perched on a poor child's desk, and I spring to a stand. "I'm, uh..." I lower my voice. "I'm looking for someone."

Lucy laughs that airy laugh of hers as she walks towards a sinfully messy teacher's desk. I almost find myself smiling after her. Something about her laugh, that bright dress... It fits her perfectly, almost like it was made for her. And with the orange tie in her dark hair, she reminds me of a starlet in an old movie brought to life and color.

"I don't know who you think you'll find in a classroom of five-year-olds. And speaking of which..." She suddenly raises her voice. "Kids, say hello to my friend, Lachlan Chase. He's the biggest Taylor Swift fan I know!"

I glare at her, even as a loud, high-pitched chorus starts up, "Hi, Lachlan!"

Everything suddenly clicks into place. "You're a teacher," I say dumbly. "I'm an idiot."

113

"I won't argue with you, but why this time?" she twinkles.

"I thought you were a single mom. To a 'whole ton of' kids, an indeterminate amount of which were five years old."

Lucy snorts. A loud, unladylike snort that weirdly makes me warm to her even more. "Nope. Definitely not."

By now, the kids have lost interest in us and have gone back to talking amongst themselves, and Lucy busies herself moving random items around her desk.

"So, who are you looking for? A distressed Lois Lane, perhaps?"

I can't help but smirk. "Pretty sure the only person in distress I've seen lately is *you*, Passenger Princess."

"Yes. And it's about time we forget all about that evening of blunders, isn't it?" She glances up at me. "I assumed you were halfway to LA by now. Or have you hunted me down this morning solely because of some Clark Kent hijinks?"

"Lest we forget that I'm not here for you, Miss Passenger." I wait a beat. "I don't know if you'd know her, but I'm looking for Tammy."

At this, Lucy visibly startles, her teasing grin gone. "Tammy?"

"Yeah." I assess her face, her cheeks now pale. "You know her?"

Lucy blinks at me, countering my question with her own. "What do you need with Tammy?"

I'm confused by the sudden serious turn this conversation has taken. "I rented her cottage by the seaside, and well, it's nothing like the photos. So, I wanted to talk to her about proper business practices..." I trail off, now feeling like my whole mission is a bit stupid and pointless. I tack on, "I don't need money back or anything, but it's not what I expected, and I think she should update her photos and listing ASAP."

Lucy's eyes widen, but she quickly turns away. "Noted. I'll pass on the message."

114

I tilt my head at her. Once again, I'm upsetting this woman, and I don't know why. I also absolutely, for no logical reason, *loathe* the feeling. "So, you'll be seeing her soon? I don't want you to get in the middle of it."

Lucy bites the inside of her cheek, silent for a moment. And then, she looks at me. "Lachlan, the house is mine."

14

LUCY

Lachlan's blinking at me erratically.

Seriously, his bright blue eyes are flashing at me like he's trying to communicate in Morse code.

"*You're* Tammy?"

"No. I mean, my name is Lucy, but Tammy left the cottage to me, and I never updated the rental listing," I explain. "Cascade Point doesn't get a ton of visitors, and you're the first person who's booked the property since I inherited it. I actually pretty much forgot about it until I got the booking notification." My lips tug up in one corner. "By the way, who on earth books a rental under the name 'SparksFly Group?' There was a moment where I wondered if gigantic bugs were coming to stay."

Lachlan's staring at me. And how is the man still so beautiful even when looking so scandalized? He's wearing a suit today, which is so out of place it's almost laughable in a town like Cascade Point, but I'm willing to forgive it given how dang sexy he looks. The charcoal color brings out the glacial blue of his irises, and the suit fits him perfectly. Wide at the shoulders, tapered at the waist.

My type is more along the lines of Carhartts and Birkenstocks, but you'd have to be blind not to think that Lachlan's attractive in that suit.

It doesn't hurt that I walked in on him and our sweet-but-sassy Olivia speaking about their shared appreciation for Taylor Swift.

"I see," he responds gravely. Which is classic Lachlan, I've decided. "You're lying."

My eyes go wide. "Am not."

"This is part of your lying game. I get it now."

"I'm not lying. Ask me anything. Go on, quiz me."

Lachlan narrows his eyes at me. "I'm not going to quiz you. How do I know you haven't simply spent a lot of time there with this Tammy person?"

"I *did* spend a lot of time there with a Tammy person. Because she was my mom. Tammy was my mom." I take a breath. "I grew up in that cottage, and my mom would try and rent it out when we went out of town to make some extra cash."

Lachlan seems to clue in on the past tense in my sentence, and he hesitates. He still looks skeptical as all heck, but he asks, "Color of the carpet in the foyer?"

"Navy. Or, it used to be."

"Photo in the living room behind the sofa?"

"There are three. One of my mom and me, one of my grand-parents, and one of our pet guinea pig when I was younger."

He seems startled—and by that, I mean that his eyes widen a fraction of an inch as he processes this. Then, they narrow again. "What about the broken back porch?"

"Trick question. The only part of that porch that's broken is the screen. And that happened when a seagull mistakenly thought a pair of shoes I left out to dry were edible." I shiver. "The seagull was fine, by the way. Though he did take off with my sandals. Punishment, I guess, for not leaving actual food out."

117

Lachlan stares at me for three long seconds and then exhales. "Fine. I believe you."

"Good." I smile sheepishly. "Look. I'm really sorry the photos in the listing are misleading. I should've turned the thing off altogether, but like I said, I kind of forgot about it. Nobody's stayed there since my mom passed away, and I had someone clean and dust the place before you arrived. I haven't actually been inside the house myself in ages. I can give you your money back, if you'd like?"

Lachlan shakes his head. "Like I said, I'm not here to get a refund. I just don't think it's right that the house doesn't look as advertised is all..."

He trails off into silence, lips pursed.

"You're right," I concede. "I'll turn the listing off so this doesn't happen again." I then glance towards my kids, who are slowly but surely getting louder. "Can I get back to my class now?"

His strong jaw ticks a couple times, and his brow is furrowed, like he's thinking. "I—"

"Lucy!"

All of a sudden, Benny is in my classroom. And my kids shout: "Hi, Benny!"

He gives them a beaming smile, finishing with a little spin to make them laugh.

Lachlan's blue eyes are flashing yet again as he stares in confusion at the short, stout man twirling in front of the children.

"What're you doing here?" I ask Benny. "Did you take a look at our Australia stain?"

Behind Benny's head, Lachlan's expression is priceless.

"I was dropping off silkworms for Gabby's gecko, and I figured, why not get two birds with one stone?" Benny then turns uncharacteristically serious, his eyes meeting mine. "But yeah, I looked at the stain. It's bad."

118

My smile drops off my face. "Wait. Really?"

"Yes. You've got a major leak." Benny adjusts his work belt. "It's gonna take some time to check the pipes, fix any that are broken, repair the ceiling etc."

"Oh, no! I have to tell Jordy."

"Already did. I had a delivery at the fire station on the way here, and I gave her the news."

"Sorry," Lachlan cuts in. "You're the plumber *and* a delivery man?"

Benny seems to clue into Lachlan's looming presence in the corner, and he quickly pulls out a business card. "Sure am. Plumber, delivery and Uber driver, wedding officiant, horse trainer... I'm the Benny of all trades." He finishes this off with finger guns.

I've never seen anyone look quite so flabbergasted as Lachlan looks right now. But I have to admire the way he quickly recovers and takes Benny's card.

The shorter man turns back to me. "Jordy said she'll stay with Celeste and offered that you stay with them as well."

I'm still trying to process this turn of events. "I... I didn't realize it would be so serious."

"It is. But it's nothin' I can't fix with a couple days and a couple more Youtube videos."

"Okay. I think Celeste's place is small enough for one person, let alone *three*. But someone in town must have a spare room or a couch or something."

Benny pats my shoulder. "Whatever you gotta do."

With that, he salutes the kids and marches out of my classroom.

"You should stay at your cottage."

I blink at Lachlan blearily. "What?"

"It's *your* cottage." He says this so begrudgingly, I almost want to laugh. "There's a whole other bedroom and bathroom upstairs. You might as well stay there."

"You're a guest, I wouldn't want to intrude."

And maybe more importantly, I'm not sure I'm ready to go back there yet...

Lachlan actually smirks at that. "Trust me, no part of this visit has gone according to any sort of plan. I shouldn't be here for much longer anyway, and then I'll be out of your hair. It makes logical sense that you stay in *your* house."

I bite the inside of my cheek, considering. "As much as I appreciate it, I'll look elsewhere. Someone has to be able to host me for a few days until Benny fixes the ceiling."

I don't think I'm imagining the relief flashing across Lachlan's expression. "Suit yourself. I'll leave you to it, then." He goes on to nod sternly at my kids. "Goodbye, tiny humans."

And then, he's gone as swiftly and unexpectedly as he appeared.

15

LACHLAN

By the time I get back to the cottage, it's raining. And of course, I didn't bring an umbrella, which is pretty much on par with how these past few days have been going.

I change out of my wet clothes and into track pants and a gray henley. If I have to stay in this town much longer, I might have to go chase Mr. Sidhu around the laundromat again.

Here's hoping that Mike has some good news when he calls later.

I pad into the kitchen and pour myself another mug of coffee. I'm still reeling from the fact that this is Lucy's house. That Tammy is—*was*—her mother. We might have started out playing a lying game, but I believe what she's told me.

And the thing is, even though I know I shouldn't—even though there's no logical, rational explanation for it—a part of me wants to know these things. Wants to learn more about her.

I've spent years being totally dedicated to my work and my ambitions. Living my life along a clean, straight line, pointed directly towards where I want to go—up the proverbial tech career ladder.

But since meeting Lucy, well... things are becoming blurred

and messy. And it's not simply because I'm on this involuntary vacation.

No. There's something about her that's... different. That makes *me* different.

Exhibit A: sharing a bed with her in the motel and accidentally liking it.

Exhibit B: my offering to have her *move in here with me*?!

I regretted the words as soon as they left my mouth. And I can't tell you the relief I felt when she said no. Because as much as I don't want *anyone* in my personal space, the last person who should be is the one woman I've not been able to stop thinking about.

I just can't understand it. This wholesome, sweet, small-town kindergarten teacher intrigues me with her kaleidoscope of emotions. The expressions that flit easily across her face. Her ridiculous lying game.

Which is exactly why I should not have been offering her the *spare bedroom upstairs*.

I really am an idiot.

Clocking into the rhythmic tapping of the rain on the windows, I take another drink of coffee.

And all of a sudden, I feel totally aimless. I have nothing to do right now—I caught up on everything in my personal life yesterday while I holed up in this cottage and avoided town at all costs.

I'm literally a sitting duck, stuck with my out-of-bounds and totally pointless thoughts of a woman I'll never see again after I go back to my regular life.

I need to be busy. Do something with my hands.

I decide to head to the dining room, which is currently unusable due to the boxes piled on every flat surface. I get to work moving the boxes to a storage space beneath the stairs, being careful not to peek into them, though they're clearly filled with picture frames, old scrapbooks, school projects, and an alarming amount of knitting needles.

Nope. Don't snoop, Lachlan. You don't want to know this girl.

And that's what I'm telling myself even as I do, in fact, snoop.

Now that I know that these childhood photos are of Lucy, I can't *not* see it. She's tiny in these pictures, a speck of the woman she'd grow into. In some, she's missing a tooth or two. In others, she's standing with a beautiful woman with the same chestnut-brown hair, or else she's holding a guinea pig, her smile wide.

There are scrapbooks from countless birthday parties. Fluorescent pink and orange crafts that make it clear Lucy's obsession with bright things started *very* young.

Was she always this happy and cheerful then? Spreading sunshine and rainbows wherever she goes and making everyone smile like it's her freaking job?

If nothing else, seeing this time capsule only solidifies in my mind the fact that Lucy *cannot* be occupying my thoughts like she has been. She *cannot* be occupying my space like she did when she was practically cuddled around me in the bed at the motel.

We're total opposites, down to the fact that Lucy has all these keepsakes from her past, whereas my parents never kept anything from mine and my half-brothers' childhoods. The only real piece of memorabilia I have is an old photo I keep folded in my wallet of me and my brothers one Fourth of July weekend while I was in high school.

As I'm placing the final box into storage, my phone rings. I practically sprint to the kitchen to answer it.

"Lachlan Chase," I say breezily. Which is false as I'm anything but breezy at the moment.

123

"Hey, Chase. Good to hear that voice again." Mike laughs. "How you holding up over there?"

I purse my lips. I was happy to play a lying game with Lucy, but there's no point beating around the bush with my boss. "Honestly, I'm looking forward to getting back there, Mike."

"I can't even imagine. I've never been to Seattle, or Washington State for that matter, but from what I've heard it's rain, rain, rain. You'll be losing your tan soon, Chase."

I assess my forearms, which usually keep a tan year-round. It's the only thing, aside from my height, that I inherited from my father's Norwegian side. "Yeah. Have to get back to California soon so I can keep it up." I scrub a hand through my hair —I wanted to get a cut this week, until everything went to crap. "Not to mention all the other things I'm missing."

Mike snorts. "No electric car ports, I'm assuming?"

"There's barely a gas station. Imagine stepping back in time a few decades, and that's Cascade Point."

"I might like that. Sounds quaint. Charming. Real grassroots."

I hear the derision in Mike's voice and find myself leaning into it, venting my recent frustrations. "It is, until you can't get the things you want or need. Like food substitutions, or a jeweler to repair your watch, or a proper barbershop to cut your hair, or a food delivery service." I'm pacing around the kitchen now. "Oh, wait. There *is* a food delivery man. Who also happens to be the town's wedding officiant and handyman."

Mike gasps. "No."

"I have the guy's business card. Pretty sure he's also the town's premier real estate agent."

"No!" Mike gasps again.

Finally. Someone else agrees that this place is a little loopy. I was starting to think *I* was going crazy.

"I'm sorry you're going through that, Chase. Sounds like absolute torture."

124

A small, unexpected twinge of guilt runs through me at his words. "Well. I might not go *that* far. Although, people here aren't nearly as friendly as I expected. The only person who's been vaguely welcoming was a woman from Texas and her pet gecko."

"Her pet what?"

"Never mind. Needless to say, I'm excited to get back to the city and have all my creature comforts again. Minus any actual creatures."

"Love that spirit, Chase, and we're looking forward to having you back." He pauses. "It's been a crazy few days on this end. The media's still running stories on the whole dating disaster and dragging SparksFly into it. The board's been in meetings all weekend trying to figure out how to play this. But there is one thing that they've agreed on, and I'm afraid you might not like it."

A sour taste fills my mouth. "Let me guess. I have to stay put."

"There's that quick thinking we love so much," Mike says weakly, clearly trying to be positive. "You understand, don't you, Chase? This *has* to be our strategy right now. I'm working closely with our PR team to figure out next steps, and the second you're in the clear to come back to work, you'll be the first to know."

Once again, I should never have agreed to that date with Carly. "Thanks for the update, Mike. And I'm happy to work remote as well, of course."

Mike considers this for a moment. "You know how I feel about my VPs working remotely, Chase. I like being able to call you into my office at any moment." He chuckles. "But no, your second in command in Colorado is handling your projects extremely well. Just take this vacation to yourself, use it to recharge and regroup so you can hit the ground running. How's that sound?"

Boring as can be. But I say, "Great."

After Mike hangs up, I put my phone down on the counter.

"And you said you're honest."

I turn to see Lucy standing in the doorway to the kitchen, a dark eyebrow popped over her inquisitive green eyes.

And the first thing I can think of—before wondering what she's doing here, or how she's managed to surprise me again today, or whether she overheard my conversation with Mike—is that she grew up well. Grew into a beautiful, magnetic woman.

This thought stuns me for a minute, and there's a beat of silence before I speak. "I said I try to be honest. *Most* of the time." I pause. "And surprising me for the second time today, huh? What'd I do to get so lucky?"

Lucy's serious expression cracks, and she laughs, shaking her head. But I could swear her cheeks redden a little at my unintentionally flirty comment. Which makes her even more beautiful.

It also makes me wonder about whether she overheard what I said to Mike. "So, uh... How long you been standing there?"

"Long enough to hear that last lie you told." She stands straight, her brows drawing together, and I suddenly have the distinct feeling that she heard *way* more than just that final line.

"What lie?"

"You said 'great'. But you didn't mean 'great', did you?"

I pause for a moment, reflecting. "No comment."

Lucy nods with understanding. "Because being here isn't 'great' for you."

I set my jaw, meeting her gaze. "It isn't," I say truthfully. "But I'll make do."

She's frowning, her eyes traveling over my face like she's working something out.

And I take the opportunity to change the subject, nodding towards a small bag she placed on the floor. "Brought me something?"

Lucy opens her mouth, but then, she smirks. "I brought *me*. Because, guess what, I'm taking you up on your offer"

"My offer?"

"Yeah. To move in." She picks up her bag. "You said the upstairs bedroom is free?"

My jaw is hinging open. "It is," I croak.

Her pretty eyes dance when they meet mine. "Well, here we go again, roomie. Though this time, luckily, we won't have to share a bed."

With that, she turns on her heel and skips down the narrow hallway. She begins to climb the stairs, but right before she exits my line of sight, she looks back down at me through the wood railing.

"You know... we're always a little wary of outsiders here, but you're technically not an outsider. Just saying that if you remembered your roots, you might have an easier time getting what you want."

And she disappears up the stairs, whistling cheerily as she goes.

Meanwhile, I force myself to shut my mouth as a strange mixture of something I've never felt before gathers in my stomach. It's not entirely unpleasant, but it isn't pleasant either.

Looks like Lucy Summers will be occupying my space after all.

Upstairs, there's a sudden screech. Which is quickly followed by: "My babies!"

Well. There's something that doesn't surprise me in the least.

16

LUCY

When I wake up the next morning, it takes me a full minute to realize where I am.

Because the first thing I see is a pair of eyes watching me.

Well, one eye. One wide, lifeless, googly eye. The left pupil is stuck up in a corner of the white so only the right is looking at me.

"Good morning, Geoffrey," I murmur, patting the blue knit elephant on his bulbous head. I sit up in bed and stretch, gazing around at the multitude of other animals and plants that my mom and I made long ago when she was sick and knitting became one of the only activities she could do.

Back then, I wanted to challenge myself—practice more and more complicated patterns. Which explains why, in addition to his severe case of misaligned eyes, Geoffrey also has short front legs, and his tail is sideways.

He's actually perhaps a bit terrifying if you don't know his story.

I take a moment to look around my old bedroom. The bright green wallpaper with purple flowers is starting to peel away in the corners. The accordion closet door is hanging off its hinges. The carpet has a multitude of stains and imperfections from the times I brewed "potions" using my mom's beauty products; or painted self-portraits in the style, but with none of the talent, of Picasso; or tried to make my guinea pig a wedding dress and, in doing so, cut a hole into the carpet.

It's weird being back here with these memories. With this nostalgia.

Yesterday, after Benny broke the news about our ceiling leak, I asked around at school to see if anyone had a place for me. Gabby, bless her, said that Fergie's room at her house was vacant, but the thought of sleeping in an old gecko chamber wasn't all that tempting. Believe it or not.

At the end of the day though, Lachlan's words were ringing in my ears.

This *is* my cottage now. For so long, I had no reason to set foot back here, so I just... didn't. I thought it would be too difficult to face these memories of my mom and my childhood. But, now that I'm here again, I feel more at peace than I ever could've expected.

I feel closer to her. Feel like I should've come back earlier.

And, don't get me wrong, the thought of being in close proximity to Lachlan again sounds like a pressure-cookery deja vu. But as he's constantly saying—and per that phone conversation I overheard—he'll be going back to California very soon.

So, between the ceiling leak and Lachlan's offer, I had the perfect push to come back here. Maybe I just needed something to force my hand.

I get dressed quickly and sneak downstairs, intending to grab a cup of coffee and run off to school before Lachlan wakes up. But a peek through the open door of the master bedroom confirms that he's not even here.

What's the guy *actually* doing in Cascade Point? It can't be visiting his brother—Jordy confirmed that Beau has barely seen Lachlan at all since he arrived.

I can't help but be curious about the man.

It's at that point that I pass by the dining room, where the normally closed door is now ajar. I push it open fully, and my breath catches.

It's empty.

I mean, the furniture and everything is still there. But when I last saw this room, it was full of boxes. Memorabilia from my childhood that I shoved in here because, back then, I couldn't bring myself to look at any of it.

A lone piece of paper lies on the dining table.

Moved the boxes into the cupboard beneath the stairs. Hope that's cool.

—L

Even in writing, the man doesn't like complete sentences.

Oh, dear. If Lachlan moved my boxes, did he see any of my gawky, puffy-cheeked childhood photos?

Before I can dwell on *that* embarrassment too much, I head to the kitchen and make a beeline for the coffee machine. I pour myself a cup, but a quick look in the fridge confirms my suspicions.

"No milk." A further peek into the pantry makes me squeak. "No sugar!"

Black coffee, it is. Strong, intense, bitter black coffee.

I take a sip. Almost spit it out. How does anybody drink this?!

I rummage through another cupboard, but all I find is some very old salt and very empty pepper. Dang it. Who rents out a place without providing basic kitchen ingredients?

Oh, that's right. It's me. I'm the problem.

I'm shutting the drawer next to the stove—which is filled to the brim with napkins, sauce packets, and other various trinkets —when the thing sticks. I tug open the drawer and try again.

Yup. It's definitely stuck.

And with the drawer stuck like this, I can't open the oven.

Not that *I* intend to do any baking. But maybe my favorite

130

guest Lachlan is a secret baking fiend. The mental image of a six-foot-something grumpy Superman walking around, wearing an apron and carrying a tray of brownies a la Martha Stewart makes me snort with laughter.

"Come on, don't do me like this."

I give the drawer another firm tug outwards. But it must be seeking revenge for the all the rough handling, because the thing comes right out of its hinges, and the contents of the drawer are suddenly airborne.

Pink, purple and yellow napkins go flying around the kitchen. Soy and hot sauce packets smack into the wall behind me. Buttons and thread scatter all around.

And I'm screeching, stumbling backwards with the drawer in hand like I'm the Incredible She-Hulk. Kitchen edition.

I crash back against the wall and slide to the ground, stunned.

Hulk Smash, indeed.

"Wow. What a *mess*."

The deep, rumbling voice comes from just behind my right shoulder, and I yelp in surprise at the looming presence in the doorway.

Of course.

Of course, Lachlan would appear in the kitchen right now. At the very moment that I've made an absolute mess and also look like an absolute mess.

I try to regain some composure, hopping to a stand and brushing down my cute cream sweater-dress—another one I knit. "Hey, Kent! I did that on purpose. Yup. Thought this kitchen could use some... color."

I trail off uselessly. Lachlan glares at the, admittedly messy, floor. "Mission accomplished."

His blue eyes then scour the rest of the room—the open cupboards where I searched for sugar, the coffee splatter on the counter from when I'd missed my mug while pouring, the oven door, which somehow popped half-open during the drawer debacle.

And while his eyes monitor the room, I'm monitoring *him*, my surprised gaze doing a slow exploration up his body. He's not wearing a suit today. He's got on gray athletic shorts over black leggings that hug his calves and legs, and a black long-sleeve shirt that emphasizes the taut muscles of his torso and arms. His cheeks are red from the wind outside, and his tanned skin is gleaming with a sheen of sweat.

Lachlan then lifts one of his arms—giving me a very satisfying view of bicep—and runs a hand through his dark hair. As he drops his arm, I spot a singular drop of sweat at the crook where his angular jawline meets his neck.

I swallow, captivated.

"What am I going to do with you?" he rumbles.

And there's something in his words, in his tone, that sends a sweep of hot shivers across my skin. Though he very clearly isn't talking to me, but instead is growling at the mess I've made.

Then, Lachlan steps towards me, holding out a hand, and I'm fully confused.

He doesn't want me to... take his hand, does he? But he's staring at me, those ice blue eyes of his smoldering into mine. And so, without thinking much of it, I place my hand in his.

An electric thrill shoots up my arm. His warm hand practically engulfs mine, and I have a distinct body memory of these same hands and these long fingers pressed against my back and beneath my thighs as he carried me to the motel room after Beer-gate.

Heat rises to my cheeks, and I suddenly feel a light-headed buzz I've never felt before.

And then, as if *wanting* to destroy me, he smiles. It's a strange, tilted, almost-sweet smile that I've never seen on him.

"Drawer?"

"What?" I ask in a daze.

"Drawer. I'll put it back."

"Oh!" I yank my hand out of his in complete, abject horror. "My drawers!"

Wow. Nothing sexier than the sound of an elderly Victorian woman fretting about her laundry!

Lachlan chuckles. *Chuckles*. Which, beneath my life-ending embarrassment, almost makes me proud. "Yeah. I'll put it back so we can actually attempt to use the oven."

"Yes, that is a great idea!" I'm laughing now. I don't think it's a cute laugh. Nothing this high-pitched and creaky can be characterized as "cute."

He gives me that special smile again as I push the drawer into his hands. My entire face is on fire. What is *wrong* with me this morning? Clearly, staying in this house is having serious effects on my emotional regulation.

His smile turns into more of a smirk as he places the drawer on the counter, opens yet another cupboard to pull out an old tool box I forgot was there, and gets to work.

Meanwhile, I'm trying to come up with a way to salvage even a shred of my dignity. My gut says to blow past it. Start a conversation. *Be normal.*

"So, you're sweaty," I say in a too-casual voice as I jiggle myself awkwardly onto a counter top.

Lachlan doesn't look at me, just grabs a screwdriver. "You're observant."

"Sorry. I mean, *why* are you sweaty?"

"I went for a run."

"In the cold?"

"It doesn't feel cold when you're running." He pauses. "I wanted to find the beach seeing as, apparently, this house is 'right on the water.'"

"Right." My voice sounds sheepish. I *feel* sheepish. I really should have properly checked out the state of the cottage before

133

my first guest arrived. "It is... there's just a little hedge to go through first."

"It's a nice beach. This is a good location. It would be classified as 'great' if we could get to the sand from here, as was promised on that listing I read."

I could swear there's a teasing lilt in his voice. And is it bad that I'm proud I can recognize this? I feel like I'm able to read Lachlan's mannerisms now—his micro-expressions, the small fractures in his tone that give away what he's thinking.

I lean into his teasing and roll my eyes dramatically. "Yeah. This house needs some work to get back to what it was."

"That's putting it lightly." He looks at me with a smirk to match his tone. "Which means you're in luck, because I have nothing better to do at the moment but help fix this place."

"That is lucky." I chuckle. "But don't overexert yourself. Wouldn't want you to get your hands dirty."

He holds up his palms innocently. "Someone did tell me recently that I had nice hands. Quite the compliment. New for me."

"New because you're too busy being a grouch to be complimented?"

"New because people usually compliment *other* assets of mine." My eyes widen, and he casually adds, "You know, my job, my car..."

"Right."

He smirks, nodding towards the yard. "I'll prune back the hedge while I'm here. If you want."

"You really don't have to do that."

He doesn't answer. He seems taken with this whole drawer reassembly task.

I watch him closely, note the quick and precise movements of his large hands handling the tiny screws. He seems skilled at this. "Have you done this before?"

"No comment."

I roll my eyes. "Come on, Kent. If we're going to be living together for the next day or two or however long, we should probably know *some* things about each other, don't you think?"

Lachlan looks at me, blue eyes wide. "Are you saying you want a break from your lying game?"

I have to laugh. He's teasing me. "Yes. I am."

"As you wish." He places one of the screws to the side, and I catch a glimpse of his wry smile. "I *have* done this before. Growing up, whenever something broke in our house, my parents would bring in carpenters, roofers, handymen, whatever, and sometimes I would watch them work. Sometimes they'd ask me to help and would teach me some stuff."

Lachlan's quiet for a moment as he focuses. I wait.

"My step-grandparents, on the other hand, never wanted to get work done in their house unless the problem was urgent. It never made sense to me seeing as they had money, and yet, their cupboards were off their hinges, or the dining table was crooked, or a window had a crack in it. So, when I came to visit in the summers, I would fix what I could around their house." He smirks. "I don't think they noticed. If they did, they didn't say anything. But making those small improvements always made *me* feel better."

I find myself holding my breath. I've never heard Lachlan speak so many words, so consecutively.

He seems to realize this, too, as he grunts, "Dunno why I told you all that."

"I'm glad you did. It's interesting."

Lachlan glances my way. "*Interesting* might be a little much, Passenger Princess."

I smile at his nickname for me. "You can just call me PP for short." I purse my lips. "Actually, no. Please don't call me PP."

"Princess, it is."

I laugh, feeling more relaxed now. And almost strangely shy. What else is going on behind this man's tough exterior?

135

"Have you seen Anna-May and Graham since being back here?"

"I haven't. Don't think I will."

"Why not?"

He shrugs, his eyes on the drawer as he maneuvers it carefully into the slot. The bottom of his shirt rides up as he bends, giving me a nice view of the defined ridges of his lower back. "It's complicated."

I open my mouth to ask what he means, but he reads my mind.

"*We're* complicated. I'm not sure they'd want to see me." He pulls the drawer out. Pushes it back in. It moves seamlessly. "Fixed."

I swallow my curiosity and hop off the counter to come stand next to him. "Well done. I guess maybe you *are* qualified to take care of the hedge as well."

He runs a hand through his hair and looks down at me. When his eyes meet mine, I swear I see something new swirling in those icy blue depths. Something warm and unexpected.

My heart thumps. Hard.

But then, he blinks, and the moment passes, and I force myself to snap out of it. *Get it together, Luce!*

This heart-thumping, head-spinning, lingering-eye-contact thing is completely unacceptable. No matter how weirdly, how unreasonably, my body is reacting to him right now, I have to remember that this is *Lachlan*.

I step slightly away from him and his woodsy scent. "Uh, you haven't come across any milk and sugar in this kitchen, have you? Black coffee is very much not my thing."

"I did have some almond milk, but I finished it." Lachlan glowers towards the coffee machine. "If I'm going to be stuck here for a couple more days, I'm going to need provisions, so I was about to run into town to grab some more. I can drop you at a cafe if you want."

"You're not gonna come in with me to get your cinnamon mocha?" I ask in a teasing tone.

He doesn't respond. Just gives me a playful, totally uncharacteristic wink that makes my stomach tumble in a flurry of somersaults.

As Lachlan heads off to change, I place my hands on the cool kitchen counter.

There's a chance I didn't fully think through what it would be like to move in with Lachlan Chase.

17

LACHLAN

"Now that we're no longer playing the lying game, I have *so* many questions for you." Lucy is back in her position as Passenger Princess, and this time, she can't *stop* talking as I drive through Cascade Point.

"'Course you do," I respond dryly.

"Don't worry, I'll start with something easy—what's your favorite TV show?"

"Pass."

Lucy crosses her arms and shakes her head. "Nope. You *have* to answer, that's the one rule."

A smirk breaks across my lips. *Alright, I'll humor her.* "Shouldn't the rule be that there *are* no rules?"

Lucy looks at me full on, her expression so shocked that I almost laugh. "*Friends*? Seriously?!"

"Can't a guy like a sitcom or two?"

She laughs before taking a long sip of her chocolate, peanut butter, caramel, whatever latte.

I did end up going with Lucy into Cascade's one and only cafe this morning—aptly named Earth's End Coffee & Books— and ordering myself a cinnamon mocha (I made sure she didn't overhear my order. *That*, I'm keeping a secret for the time being).

And for some reason that must be related to the fact that the skies are dumping an entire ocean of rain this morning, I then offered to drive her the rest of the way to school. Though, it probably would've been faster for her to walk given the criss-crossing, devil-may-care-about-the-car-on-the-road pedestrians.

She smacks her lips, apparently not done with me yet. "*A guy* certainly can and should like sitcoms. But you, grumpy Clark Kent? Can't say I was expecting you to suddenly drop a *Friends* reference."

I affect a very serious tone. "How you doin'?"

"Aaaand now you're Joey. Ridiculous."

I give her a look. "I am many things, Princess, but I'm never ridiculous."

Although... maybe she *is* right.

Because I'm now living with this woman, for goodness sakes. I haven't lived with anyone in years, haven't had a room-mate since college. And I've definitely never lived with someone who's in my head like Lucy is.

I can't help it. Anytime her expression flashes with upset, it's like some primitive radar within me goes off—*Stop it. Protect her. Make her smile.*

Keeping a distance between us clearly isn't going to work. So now, I'm trying a new tactic. Trying to be her friend. Despite the fact that she's wearing yet another knit dress that I couldn't help but notice hugs her body perfectly as she perched on the counter next to me earlier.

But what could be more friendly than sharing my intimate knowledge of *Friends*?

The road clears ahead of me, and I'm just about to press on the gas when a couple people step out in front of the car without looking. I recognize the long-ish hair of my favorite cashier Jensen, and another boy his age that must be his friend Ace.

"Traffic's terrible here with all the pedestrians," I mutter,

139

feeling my frustration start to rise. Don't the kids here learn to look both ways before crossing the street? This isn't safe.

Lucy looks at me, and the moment my eyes meet her aquatic green ones, my shoulders relax slightly. I feel a little more calm. "That's because you don't know all the tricks. Turn right here. There's a shortcut."

I follow her directions into a narrow alleyway between two concrete buildings, where a large swath of color pulls my attention to the right, and I'm suddenly staring at a huge colorful mural.

"Whoa." I slow the car to a stop.

"Oh, that's our Banksy."

"Your *what*?"

"Banksy." Lucy stares at me. "Like the artist?"

"I'm aware. But what do you mean, *your* Banksy?"

Lucy shrugs. "It's what it sounds like. Some artist in Cascade Point has been going around in the last few years, painting murals on our buildings. No one knows who's doing it, though. Some people think it's a ghost or poltergeist. Others think it's *actually* Banksy. I personally think it's some kid from out of town honing their skills."

I assess the mural, the careful strokes of paint—practiced, unhurried. "They're talented, whoever they are."

Lucy smiles. "See? There's some beauty to Cascade Point."

"Color me shocked."

She laughs. "It's a cool hobby. I wish I could paint like that."

"Well, I saw the actual zoo of knitted flora and fauna upstairs. I'd say you're pretty talented, too." I shake my head as I drive forward again. "Though I've never known anyone below the age of sixty who knits as much as you appear to. Not to mention the box hoarding. Pretty worrisome."

"What can I say, I'm full of surprises."

"No arguments there."

140

She's silent for a moment, looking down at her hands. "I've actually got a bit of a social media following."

I look at her in surprise. "You do?"

She takes out her phone and opens up her TikTok. I stop the car again to scroll through it. "I mostly just post new designs I've put together or show off my knitting projects."

My eyebrows go all the way up as I read one of the trending hashtags. "You're a *knitfluencer*?"

Lucy's cheeks turn red, and she puts her phone away. I wish I could say that I'm not hyper aware of her clean, sea breeze scent filling the air around me. "I know it sounds stupid, but I love it."

"Not stupid at all," I say, fully meaning it. "You should be proud. It takes real ambition and passion to do something like that."

Her cheeks turn an even more beautiful shade of pink. I love that I made her blush. "Thanks. What about you? Any hobbies?"

"No hobbies. Just work."

"You don't do anything for fun?"

"Work *is* fun." A smirk crosses my lips. "I know that sounds lame. But I'm pretty passionate about my job at SparksFly. You know, with the dating platforms."

"That's right." Lucy blinks. "You booked under 'SparksFly Group.' So, you work for dating apps and websites?"

"Technically, it's a tech company with a portfolio of dating apps and websites."

Lucy shakes her head. "I met Brady on one of those apps."

"Yeah, sorry about that." I lift a shoulder. "And before you ask, I don't personally use our apps—my primary focus is and has always been my job. I help my teams do their best work. They're the geniuses, the ones who know how to code and how to make these apps succeed. I'm just there to support them and

141

offer guidance. And I do like to know that I'm making a difference in the world, helping our users find..."

"Love," Lucy finishes my thought, her smile widening. "Ohmygosh, you're one huge romantic softie, Lachlan Chase."

Heat rises above my collar. I hope that Lucy can't tell I'm blushing. "No way am I in this for the romance. If anything, it feels like my main job these days is to help other people keep their jobs."

She frowns. "What do you mean?"

"We're a big conglomerate." My jaw ticks. "We buy up all these small-time, independently owned apps and websites, and people often get shuffled out. It's the one aspect of our company that I can't get on board with. I hate to see good, smart workers get laid off or moved around when we take over an app. So, I usually do what I can to make sure that the app keeps some autonomy under our umbrella."

"So, you *are* a softie. But not the romantic kind."

I give a grunt.

"Don't worry, I won't tell anyone." She then looks at me from the corner of her eye. "So, you don't have a girlfriend then."

I purse my lips. "I'm not exactly boyfriend material."

"Ah. Eternal bachelor."

"Nah. I just don't date much."

Lucy nods slowly. "That's cool."

I'm happy for her answer. Because this is what *friends* do, right? Talk about dating and relationships. I'll admit I don't have a ton of friends back in LA, and certainly no close friends. I tend to hang out with people in a convenient sense—gym friends, work friends, running friends.

So my contentment has nothing to do with the fact that I get the feeling Lucy's fishing for info. Or the fact that I want to go fishing, too. "What about you? Any big, bad boyfriends in your past?"

"Not really." Her lips tug up at one corner, but it doesn't reach her eyes. "I'm a Cascadian through and through, always will be. My mom used to say that I need to find a man who likes small towns. As you know, this place isn't for everyone." She gives a short laugh. "But he's out there somewhere, I know he is."

"You sound confident."

"You sound skeptical."

I chuckle gruffly, and when I look at Lucy, she's staring at me with a new intensity, her head tilted my way. I've parked the car in the lot outside the school now, but she's making no moves to get out.

"What?" I ask.

"Trying to see if I remember you. I don't think I saw you when we were younger."

I smirk. "Agree. I have a feeling I'd remember those ginormous sunglasses you wore."

Her cheeks turn that beautiful shade of pink again. "You really *did* go through my boxes!"

"No comment."

"It's only fair that you show me a photo of yourself as a kid."

"Maybe I will. If you're lucky." I shake my head. "I doubt we met as kids, though. I only came to Cascade for a couple of summers in high school."

She nods. "I wasn't around in the summers as much. I used to go visit my dad before... well, before I stopped going."

"Your dad doesn't live here?"

"He left when I was three. It was just Mom and me 'til she died five years ago." She shrugs, not seeming upset or angry or anything. She speaks so matter-of-factly about the fact that she doesn't have much—if any—immediate family here. "He lives in Portland, Oregon now. Has a whole new life and family out there."

I monitor her expression, surprised. I never would've

143

guessed she'd have such a complicated family life, just as I do. And yet, she has such a different approach to life, to family, to everything. Where I bury my family problems, she's telling me about hers.

Lucy Summers might be a lot braver than I am.

"It's good that you have this community here, Lucy."

"Everyone needs a community in some capacity. It's just harder and less enjoyable to do life as a lone wolf."

I give her a smirk. "Agree to disagree?"

"Fine." She rolls her eyes with a little laugh.

"Honestly, the way everyone acts here, I can't believe anyone *could* leave. Seems like the type of place a person might get stuck."

I mean this lightly, as a joke given the literal, massive road potholes (and figuratively—given my own situation), but Lucy's face falls.

"Thanks for the ride," she says. "I should get in there."

"Everything okay?"

"Yup, all good."

She's lying.

And as she gets out of the car and walks away, I can't help but wonder what happened. Because at this point, I'm beyond curiosity. Beyond telling myself that I don't or won't care about what this woman is thinking and feeling.

All I know, right now, is that I made Lucy Summers upset. And I can't have that.

18

LUCY

"MORNING, LUCE!!!"

I launch my phone onto my bed from across the room, hoping the blankets muffle Jordy's singsong voice. They don't. So, I dive after it, quickly tapping the button to turn down the volume.

"Hello? Hello, Lucy?" Jordy's saying before emitting a loud sigh. "Oh, gosh. Did hottie-with-a-body finally murder you? I knew it was a bad idea to move in with your kidnapper."

"Shh, Jordy, I'm here," I hiss into the phone. "I had my speakerphone at top volume, so I had to turn your loud-mouthed self down."

"Isn't that a lovely thing to hear from your best friend first thing in the morning." She tuts and then takes a crunchy bite of something. Sounds like an apple. Jordy cannot seem to make it through a single conversation without snacking. "By the way, Celeste is here too, so it's not just me breaking your phone speakers."

"Hey, Luce!" Celeste calls in the background. "And don't listen to a word she's saying. I'm all the way in the kitchen."

"The kitchen of a studio apartment," Jordy tacks on. "Ooh.

145

Mind putting a scoop of ice cream into my pop while you're *all the way* over there, Cel?"

"Ice cream?! It's, like, 7am."

"You say that like an early morning ice cream float is an unreasonable request."

"What's unreasonable is your diet..." Celeste's voice trails off into mutters and grumbles. But I hear the freezer open and close.

I have to laugh at my two friends, snickering beneath my covers like some sort of blanket troll. "Sounds like you guys are getting along."

"Yeah, it's been squishy, but pretty okay. I'm grateful to Cel for letting me stay with her," Jordy says, and there's another crunch as she bites into her apple. "But that's actually why I'm calling. Benny said that he finally got to look at the pipes properly yesterday, and it's going to be a more complicated job than he expected. We might need to hold tight for a couple more days."

I bite the inside of my cheek, thinking of my friends and their "squishy" arrangement. "That's too bad."

"Is it?" Jordy asks mischievously.

"Yes, from what I heard, you've got *quite* the roommate at the moment, Luce." Celeste's voice is suddenly RIGHT THERE on the other end of the line. I can just picture the two of them in Celeste's living room/bedroom, leaning over Jordy's phone like two gossip-hungry sharks ready for a front-page-worthy piece of chum. Which is pretty apt for Celeste seeing as she's a writer for the Cascade Gazette.

But I would never dare talk to the press.

And also, I have nothing worth talking about.

I roll my eyes as I hear a creak from the floorboards downstairs.

"Did—?"

"Sh." I cut Jordy off with a hiss.

146

There's another creak, the sound of a door opening and closing, and the click of a lock turning. Going out for another run, perhaps? "Okay. He's gone."

"Early bird, is he?" Jordy asks. "Man after my own heart."

"Not mine," Celeste grumbles. "Luce, did you know that this insane sugar-cane of a person gets up at 5am every morning, *regardless* if she has a shift? Also regardless if she's sleeping in the same room as someone who enjoys a sleep-in?"

"Hey, if you can stay up watching your shows and reading your books and sketching until 2am, I can wake up at 5am to my birdsong alarm clock," Jordy trills.

I have to snort, emerging from my blanket den. "Well. With all that going on, I'm happy to hear you two are still on speaking terms!"

Celeste laughs as Jordy says, "We are. Though I would just as soon live with a hot businessman with eyes that pierce your soul and a body that seems made to make—"

"Jordy. It's *not* like that."

"Okay, okay. Please at least tell me what it's like to have *him* as a roommate. And how is it living back at the cottage?"

I swallow as I change into my outfit for today—bootcut blue jeans and a long-sleeve top with a penguin print. It's perfect for this week's theme, which is simply "January".

My classroom has a spare whiteboard on which I encourage my students to free draw according to a theme. Last week, it was "winter sports," next week will be "snowflakes," but this week, I want my kids to celebrate everything from National Penguin day (hence my shirt), to New Year's Day, to Epiphany, to the Lunar New Year.

"It's actually really nice being back here. Feels good to create some new memories in this house. Even if those memories involve Lachlan. Who, by the way, has the funkiest glasses he only ever wears in the dead of night."

"NO!" Jordy exclaims. "So, those eyes of his aren't real? Color contacts?"

"Oh, they're definitely real." I nod, remembering the sight of Lachlan standing out front last night with a cup of coffee and staring in a *peak* grumpy-Clark-Kent sort of manner at the messy garden. At one point, he looked straight up at my window, catching me in a very blatant stare. We made eye contact before I could throw myself to the ground.

Subtlety is not exactly my strong suit.

"I heard you two went by the cafe yesterday morning. Tricia could *not* stop talking about the, and I quote, 'tall, dark and handsome drink of water who stopped by.'"

I snort. "Can always count on Tricia to spread the word when someone gorgeous comes to town."

"Yeah. Remember that beautiful man who came by a couple years ago to see Beau? He was with Beau's friend, Sam. His brother or something." Jordy sighs wistfully. "Anyway, better be careful with this one or she might scoop him up."

My stomach does a funny little roll at that. A roll it has no business doing. "She can try. Though the guy's probably gonna be back in LA by the end of the week."

Of course, that's not the real reason my stomach rolled. Because the truth is, I'm attracted to Lachlan. Like, *very* attracted to him.

And it's not just his physical assets. Nope. There's something about the guy that I can't help but feel drawn to. I spend more time than I should thinking about him and his grouchy, prickly exterior. But honestly, I *like* the way he tells you exactly what he thinks, when he thinks it, without sugar-coating it.

Which is the opposite of me, seeing as I sugar-coat sugar.

In a way, it makes it impossible *not* to trust him.

Which might be why I've been avoiding him ever since that conversation in his SUV yesterday. I'm scared of what else I might say, what else I might have to face, if we talk as openly as we did.

I mean, I showed him my knitting TikTok, for goodness sakes!

But more than that, I'm surprised that I spoke about my dad with him. I never talk—barely even think—about my dad these days. Sure, when I was younger, I used to wonder all the time why he would leave my mom and me like he did. Why he would start a new family, somewhere new, while completely forgetting about us. His first family.

I used to wonder what I did wrong. If I wasn't enough.

I've moved past that now. Or I thought I had. Because Lachlan's words hit me funny, prodded at an old wound that I thought I'd successfully buried.

Seems like the type of place a person might get stuck.

I push the thoughts away, burying them deep down where they belong.

Celeste, Jordy, and I catch up for a few more minutes before hanging up.

The moment I step into the kitchen, I remember that I forgot to pick up milk yesterday afternoon. I pour myself a small cup of coffee anyway, intending to down it as you would a shot. I may not be a shots kinda girl—am barely a two-beer kinda girl, clearly—but I've seen movies. I've heard Taylor Swift songs. Just one big gulp, and I'll be caffeinated as all heck.

And then, I see the note on the counter.

Morning, Princess. I know you hate your coffee black, so check the fridge. I left another surprise for you too. Don't show anyone or I might need to revisit Jordy's whole 'are you a serial killer' question.

—L

P.S. Say "morning" to her for me.

P.P.S. You don't have to avoid me.

149

My cheeks heat. So, Lachlan *did* hear Jordy's screech on the phone. That's embarrassing.

I follow his instructions and open the fridge. And next to a full container of almond milk is a gallon of normal milk and a bag of brown sugar.

I'm touched by his thoughtfulness. And forethought. How did he know that I'd forget to pick these up yesterday?

As I take out the goods, a white slip of paper falls to the kitchen floor. I fix up my coffee before picking it up.

"Ba-ah!" I almost choke on my drink.

Because I'm currently staring at a faded, wallet-sized photo of a tall and scrawny, baby-faced Lachlan Chase.

He can't be older than fifteen or sixteen here, sporting a swoopy teen-Justin Bieber haircut. He's wearing blue jeans that are a couple sizes too big and a white t-shirt. His cheeks are full, showing the first signs of the stark definition they'll eventually have. And his bright blue eyes shine out from the old photo, framed with the same thick, dark lashes that he has today.

But something about this photo seems off.

I place my mug to the side and peer closer. And then, I see it.

Lachlan Chase had braces. And the only reason I know that is because, in this photo, he's smiling. Almost like the special one he gave me yesterday.

He has a beautiful smile, with his icy eyes crinkling at the corners.

All of a sudden, I'm taken by an abrupt desire to make him smile again like that before he leaves for good.

I'm not sure why he left this photo for me, why he felt the need to make it clear that he doesn't want me avoiding him. All I can think is that he knew I was upset when I left the car so abruptly yesterday, and it... bothered him.

The thought makes my heart swell for the man staying in the room down the hall. Because the more time I spend with

Lachlan Chase, the more I can see beneath his carefully protected layers. And the more I get the sense that this grumpy big city man is really just a gentle giant underneath it all.

I'm taking another sip of coffee, still staring at the photo, when a shadow falls across the kitchen floor. My head wrenches up, and what I see makes my jaw drop.

Because I was both right and wrong this morning.

Lachlan Chase *did* close and lock a door. But it wasn't the front door.

Nope. It was the bathroom door. And the only reason I know that is because he's currently standing in the doorway to the kitchen, having clearly just showered. His black hair hangs in front of his eyes, and his cheeks are flushed pink from the hot water.

And he's wearing my mom's fluffy pink bathrobe. Which I barely recognize seeing as it hardly covers the strong planes and taut muscles of this man's body. The sleeves go just past his elbows, and the bottom hem barely grazes his mid-thigh. The tie is pulled taut around his tapered waist, and the collar of the robe strains open over his chest.

I avert my gaze immediately.

"Lucy!" Lachlan tries to tug the collar of the robe closed. It doesn't work. "I thought you were... I didn't realize you'd be..."

I smirk at the wall. "Consider this payback for *your* surprise appearance yesterday." I place his old photo on the counter behind me, so that he doesn't (correctly) assume that I've been staring at it for the past year. Then, I venture a nod towards him. "That's a new look for you."

Lachlan glances down at himself, seeming almost agitated. "I put my towel in the laundry, and I assumed this pink thing hanging in the bathroom was another one. Turns out the downstairs bathroom only has this freaking bathrobe, face towels, and nothing else that one could use to cover himself whilst grabbing a new towel."

"Well, you look great," I say, keeping my eyes on his face. They will not wander, will not inch down his skimpy-bathrobe-clad body.

Lachlan meets my eyes and, to my surprise, there's a hint of a playful sparkle there. "You think so?"

"Absolutely," I deadpan. "You should wear that more often. Wear it outside the house, even."

He pops a brow, and I get the sudden, unsettling sense that he *knows* how hard I'm working to keep my eyes above neck level. "Really. You don't think it's too windy 'round here."

"Hey, I'm pretty sure it's windy in the Scottish Highlands, and the kilt-wearing men over there have it figured out."

"You're making some very valid points, Princess." Now, he's stroking his jaw. He shaved, too. I can almost smell his warm, woodsy aftershave. Almost wish I could trail a finger down his smooth cheek...

I lock my hands behind my back.

"Besides," he continues smoothly. "I know you're a hand admirer, but I do often get compliments on my legs."

And that's it for me.

Because of course this makes me look down at his arms and his broad chest. And dang it, he really does have nice legs. Powerful, strong, muscular.

I look away again, but my cheeks are on fire.

And this must be what Lachlan wanted because he laughs, the sound deep and rich and rumbling. "I'm gonna finish what I started and find myself a towel. But for the record, that wallet photo you hid behind you is all yours. Consider it reparations. Or something to remember me by."

With that, he pads away down the hall, and I get the sense that I just showed my hand. Showed it in a way that I really shouldn't have.

I look at Lachlan's childhood photo again, but quickly hide it away in the empty flour jar on the counter. Because despite

152

the fact that I am clearly very attracted to the man living down the hall, and the fact that he seems to actually have a sweet, flirty side to him, I *cannot*, in any way, develop a crush on Lachlan Chase. Not when he's leaving soon to go back to his real life in LA.

That's where he belongs. He's suited to the city.

He could never, and will never, belong here.

19

LACHLAN

I really, really, don't want to do this.

Don't want to be here.

I stare up at the building as an old but familiar wave of emotion rolls through me. I can't seem to take a full breath in.

I told myself I wouldn't go out of my way, and yet, here I am. Very much out of my way. Out of my comfort zone. Out of bounds.

Graham and Anna-May's gaudy Victorian mansion north of town hasn't changed one bit in the last decade and a half. The periwinkle paint is fading in some areas, coming closer to the dirty white of the shutters and railings. The sloping roof is covered with moss and ivy. Those gutters probably haven't been cleaned since I was last here—since *I* last cleaned them. The small attic window is cracked open, and I wonder if they know. If they've wondered why the winters are so cold in this haunted house of theirs.

Will they even want to see me?

I haven't even spoken on the phone with my step-grandparents in years. Every once in awhile, they tried to reach out, but I didn't return their calls. We weren't close, and my family life felt like such a mess that avoiding them all seemed like the best option.

I can't say exactly what's changed, what's brought me to their house this afternoon. Maybe I've gone a little crazy being off work. Maybe that conversation with Lucy in the car yesterday about our same-but-different family lives has been weighing on my mind.

Maybe seeing her this morning holding the childhood photo from my wallet showed me that some things are worth repairing. (It also showed me to always, always be sure I have a post-shower bath towel).

For whatever reason, I'm here. Clenching and unclenching my fists.

"Now *that* is a nice SUV."

I turn to the right to see the older man at the end of the sidewalk, gazing appreciatively at my BMW. A familiar older man.

I don't know how to respond. While he stares at my rental car—which I purposely parked just around the corner of the house in case I changed my mind—I'm staring at Graham Brighton. His groomed hair is entirely white now, and he's losing some on top. He looks shorter and more frail, but not necessarily unhealthy. The lines on his face cut deeper—equal parts smile and frown lines, indicative of a life that's seen and felt a lot.

And just as he used to dress in a way that never seemed to *fit* Cascade Point, he's wearing pressed slacks and a tweed blazer.

I used to think that he dressed for a different time. The time when *his* grandparents founded this town and came into riches from the seafood and clam trade, along with the port they constructed.

His watery gray eyes don't leave the vehicle. "Is it this year's model?"

"Last year's," I manage, taking halting steps closer to him

and the car. I wonder if he can tell that my breath's caught in my windpipe.

He must not, because he smiles in a satisfied type of way. "That's what I thought."

And then, finally... he looks at me.

There's no reaction. None whatsoever.

His eyes skate up my body, cross over my face, and it's like he doesn't recognize me. Doesn't register me. Like I'm a stranger.

"Must be fun to drive," he says with a smirk I know well.

"It is."

"I used to love driving vehicles like that, back when I was a young buck like you." He laughs, and then shuffles past me down the sidewalk and towards the house.

Does he really not recognize me? Should I tell him who I am?

Graham doesn't seem bothered about me in the least. This has to be a sign that I should turn around and get back in my car. After all, I came all this way, saw the house, saw *Graham*. Even if he doesn't know who I am.

I'm about to get back in my SUV when he speaks: "You coming in, Lockie?"

Surprised, I look over to see that Graham's at the front door now, holding the screen door open with an impatient eyebrow quirk.

"You know who I am?" I ask stupidly.

"'Course I do. Just because I haven't seen you in a decade doesn't mean I'd forget the free-loader who crashed here for a couple summers."

His tone is light and almost joking, and I choke out a laugh as I jog up the sidewalk towards him. He pats my back with a surprising amount of force for a seventy-something-year-old.

Stepping into the foyer of the house is like being slapped across the face with memories: the white lace curtains drawn

156

halfway across the windows; the dog-paw printed carpet in the hallway, now more threadbare; and the smell of lavender and dust and Anna-May's fruity perfume.

Graham's making his way towards the kitchen. "Coffee, Lockie?"

I follow him, walking stiffly. "I'm okay. Thanks, Graham." I clear my throat. "And I go by Lachlan now."

He looks at me with a smile. "Not to me, you don't."

I press my lips together and gaze around the old kitchen. So, something *has* changed: they have a new fridge.

I feel Graham watching me as I take in the familiar space. The counter where I used to read books while Beau and Marcus —six and eight years younger than me, respectively—played in the backyard. The window above the sink where I once spent hours fixing the weather stripping.

I spot the markings on the wall next to the door. "You never painted this over?" I kneel down, running my fingers over them.

"Are you kidding? Your grandmother would murder me in my sleep if I even tried."

"Teacup passed away, what, ten years ago?"

Graham tuts. "Twelve this July. You know Teacup will always have a special place here. If we ever wanted to move, Anna would saw out this piece of wall to take with us."

I have to chuckle. Teacup was Anna-May's beloved chihuahua. And yes, she used to bring Teacup—so named because Anna-May used to insist that she could fit into one— absolutely everywhere with her.

Teacup's height markings are the only markings on that wall. Mine and my half-brother's growth spurts weren't wall-mark-worthy, apparently.

"Where is Anna-May, anyway?"

"Ah. She's around." Graham raises a brow at me. "She didn't know we'd be having company."

157

I scrub a hand though my hair. "It's a bit of a surprise to me, too."

He takes a sip of coffee and smacks his lips. Just like Beau does. "So, what brings you to our neck of the woods?"

"I've been in town for a couple days and figured I'd come say hi." I clear my throat roughly. "Been a few years."

"Sure has." There's not a drop of accusation in his tone, and I realize I was expecting it. "We heard that you were here, and I was wondering if you'd stop by. Anna didn't think you'd go out of your way."

My lips quirk up a little. This doesn't surprise me. Anna-May and I have always thought alike. We might not be related by blood, but I could always see some of myself in her.

All of a sudden, there's a noise on the stairs. "Gray? Are you home?"

"In here, my love."

"Oh, good!" The voice becomes shrill. "I can't find my spectacles!"

Graham lets out a sigh. "Which—?"

"Graham? Where are you?" The voice has moved to a far room. "I heard you speak, you silly man. I need my spectacles!"

"We're in the kitchen, Anna," he calls out.

There's a shuffling in the hall, and then, "There you are, dear! I simply *must* find them this instant. I am expected in town at—Oh! Lachlan."

My step-grandmother—the first person to ever call me Lachlan—is staring at me from the kitchen doorway, a manicured hand pressed to her chest. Her fluffy, light blonde hair is permed in the same style that she had it the last time I saw her. Her blue eyes are framed with mascara-thick eyelashes.

"Hi, Anna-May," I say quietly. "It's been awhile."

She pats down her prim floral dress, tilting her chin up and effecting a theatrical smile. "It sure has, my boy. And dear me, how tall you've become." She purses her ruby red lips. "It really

158

is *such* a shame that you've popped by now, as my presence has been requested in town at the cafe. Seems that our lovely Beatrice is hosting an event next week and was hoping for assistance in perfecting the details."

Graham leans my way. "She means Tricia."

"I might also suggest that we workshop the name of the event." Anna-May goes on with a wrinkle of her nose. "She wants to call it simply 'open mic night' or something of the sort. Which sounds so *derivative*. I'd propose we do something with a dash of sophistication." She puts on a grand voice. "A 'soirée of poetic revelry' perhaps!"

"That sounds much better, my love," Graham agrees with a nod.

"Doesn't it? But I can't suggest such a change if I can't see her plan for the soirée because of my misplaced spectacles!" This comes out in Anna-May's signature squawk, her expression one of practiced despair.

Yup. Anna-May and I might think alike... but the similarities end there.

"Don't you worry, love, we'll find them." Graham turns my way. "Lockie, you check the front room while I search upstairs." He quirks a brow at me. "You remember where the front room is, don't you?"

I have to try not to roll my eyes. "'Course I do."

Right as I'm about to head down the hall, Anna-May—who, since her outburst, has taken out her phone and is squinting at the screen—suddenly holds up a hand. "Wait!"

Graham and I stop dutifully.

"It seems that the cafe is experiencing an unexpected afternoon rush at the moment, and so Beatrice has requested that I pay her a visit tomorrow morning." Anna-May tuts. "And thank goodness for that. I have a feeling this event will require *no* small amount of time and effort. Lachlan, have you any idea the amount of work that goes into planning an event like this?"

"Not a clue. Can't say I've ever been to a 'soirée of poetic revelry.'"

"Consider yourself deprived," she croons as Graham pours her a cup of coffee, which she doesn't drink but does wrap her palms around. Her eyes drop to my hands in my pockets. "Gray, have you not offered our guest a beverage?"

"I have, dear. Lockie doesn't want a coffee."

"That won't do. Get him a glass of juice instead. You like juice, don't you, Lachlan?"

I don't. But I also know there's no point in arguing. "Sure."

Graham takes out a glass jug of what appears to be orange juice. My least favorite.

We head to the front room, and Graham and Anna-May take their respective seats—Graham on the brown leather recliner closest to the TV and Anna-May in the wingback chair next to the fireplace, where she crosses her ankles primly.

Meanwhile, I sit on the sofa, and as soon as my butt hits the seat, I have a sense memory of how uncomfortable this couch was.

Is. This cushion feels more like a block of cement.

The three of us sit together in the front room, not speaking. The only sound is the *tick-tick* of the grandfather clock at the far end of the room. Literally counting down the moments of empty silence until I *have* to say something.

"So," I force out. "Have you seen Beau lately?"

Graham gazes towards Anna-May. Neither of them seem particularly bothered by the quiet. "When did we last see him, love? Two weeks ago?"

"Yes. It *was* two weeks ago because we missed last week's book club, remember?"

"That's right." Graham looks at me. "The newest season of the crime show your grandmother likes came out that day, so we spent all evening watching that."

"And let's not forget that there's a reunion episode tomorrow, so we'll have to miss book club once again," Anna-May proclaims.

This book club thing must be new—I don't remember either of my step-grandparents reading. Graham spent most of his time practicing his golf swing in the yard or assisting with town council (not that he was *on* the council), and Anna-May was often flitting back and forth to town for her high teas and seaside strolls.

"I've seen Beau once since being here, and he seems to be doing well," I volunteer gruffly. "He's grown up a lot."

I've taken an accidental sip of orange juice and can't hide a grimace as the sour, acidic stuff hits my tongue.

"That boy." Anna-May smirks. "He's a heartbreaker!"

"'Course he is," Graham agrees. "He's got my genes, doesn't he?"

Anna-May laughs along with her husband, tapping him on the arm playfully. "Oh, Gray." She then assesses me. "Although, something must've gone right on Alan's side as well, because you look like quite the heartbreaker yourself, Lachlan."

I manage a small smile, wondering if I should skate over this mention of my dad. It's no secret that my parents and step-grandparents don't really speak.

Anna-May pinches her lips, almost like she regrets her words, and a tension fills the air. And then, magically, there's a knock at the front door.

"My. I wonder who that could be."

Anna-May goes to answer the door, and in the ensuing quiet, I accidentally take another sip of orange juice.

"Well hello, Lucy!"

Lucy's here?

"I'm surprised you're home, Anna-May!"

My step-grandmother gives that loud, boisterous laugh you can hear from miles away. "It's a rare occasion, but I am home at

161

times in the afternoon. Especially when I've lost sight of my spectacles."

"Funny, that's actually why I'm here. I've got them for —You?!"

Lucy freezes, mid-step into the room, and stares at me... currently in an awkward half-squat seeing as I couldn't decide whether I should be a gentleman and stand for her entrance, or go with the whole "we're friends now" thing and therefore being gentlemanly shouldn't matter.

In the end, I decide I'm an idiot for overthinking it and drop my butt back onto the couch cement-cushion with a wince.

"I wasn't expecting to see you here, Lachlan," she sputters.

"Surprise."

I smile placidly, even as my heart beats a little harder at the sight of her. She's wearing an oversized knit green sweater that I'm certain would look absolutely ridiculous on anyone else. Instead, she looks cute as a button, especially with her orange bandana once again tied around her neck and bringing out the warm tones in her dark hair.

These are things I notice in a very friendly way, of course.

"Sit, dear. Take a load off." Anna-May frets over Lucy, directing her to the other end of the couch. "You just finished your school day, I take it?"

"That's right," Lucy replies as she settles onto the couch, mere inches from me. "I went by the market, and Louis gave me this as he knew I was coming to see you."

Lucy hands Anna-May a red glasses case, which my step-grandmother fawns over for a moment. Graham says something to his wife, but I'll be honest, I'm not paying a ton of attention to them because Lucy's leaning towards me.

"I didn't know you like juice," she whispers.

"I don't."

"So why are you drinking it?"

162

I raise a brow at her, catching her gaze. "It's easier than refusing. Believe me."

She gives me a peculiar look, tilting her head.

"So, Lucy," Graham says. "Aside from the glasses, to what do we owe the pleasure today?"

"Something's come up at the community center, and we can't have the book club there tomorrow evening." She cuts a sheepish glance my way. "So, I proposed that we have it at my house instead."

Anna-May frowns. "You mean your house near the port? The small one you share with Jordana?"

"No. It's, uhm, my mom's old house. A cottage just south of town. It isn't in great shape, but the living room is pretty spacious, and I think it will work in a pinch." She looks directly at me, her expression concerned. "It was a last minute thing. A last resort."

I can tell she's waiting for my reaction to this news, waiting to see if I'm upset. I give her a nod, a sign of permission granted, not that she needs it.

Lucy gives me a smile of appreciation, her eyes lighting up. I hold her gaze until Anna-May and Graham pull her attention away.

This morning, when I ran into Lucy while wearing that unfortunate pink fluffy bathrobe, I'm not sure exactly what came over me. Chalk it up to the heat from the shower or something. But I was flirting with her. And I liked it.

It was unintentional. Very much not purposeful.

After all, I want to be *friends* with the woman.

But when her eyes went down my body, and she blushed like that...

Well. If I'm honest, I can't stop thinking about it.

Now, as she perches on the edge of the couch, speaking with my step-grandparents freely, I'm totally distracted by her. The

163

movements of her hands as she talks, her animated expressions. She laughs often, and it's a beautiful sound.

I'm surprised at how happy I feel to see her. How at ease I feel around her.

Seems I'm not the only one. Anna-May is laughing at her recounting of a student's antics, and Graham lets out a deep-throated chuckle. Any awkwardness or tension in the room is long gone now that Lucy's here, breathing fresh air into this ancient house.

"Lachlan?" Anna-May's voice draws my attention.

"Hmm?"

"Want to come with me to the kitchen to get Lucy a glass of water?"

I stand, orange juice in hand. "Of course. I'd love a water as well."

Lucy shoots me a private little smile, and I'm almost overtaken with an urge to touch her shoulder or something as I walk by.

In the kitchen, Anna-May takes a Brita filter out of the fridge. "Seems my question is of no importance."

"What question?"

"As to whether you're a heartbreaker." She corrects herself: "As to whether you *were* a heartbreaker."

My frown deepens. "I don't understa—"

"I saw that look you gave Lucy."

I stop, heat rising above my collar. "I didn't give Lucy a *look.*"

"Sure you did. I'd recognize it anywhere. It's the same look my Darla gave your father Alan when she introduced him to us." Her voice becomes thick, far away. "I was scared of that look then, of what it meant. You were such a little thing when the two of them met."

I *was* little. Too little to understand what was going on between my parents and step-grandparents back then.

164

Darla Brighton, my step-mom, was a globetrotter, known for taking off for months at a time. But while on a (what was meant to be brief) visit back home in Cascade, Darla and my dad connected, and it quickly became love.

But my step-grandparents didn't approve of their relationship. So, as a way to try and appease the tension, my dad agreed that he and I would take the Brighton name when he married Darla. For some reason, this still wasn't enough. Even after my parents got married and Beau and Marcus came along, things didn't get better.

Which is why, when I was ten years old, we all packed up and moved to Mirror Valley, Colorado. My brothers and I did eventually come back to Cascade for the summers, until we one by one went our separate ways: me to LA, Beau here to Cascade Point, and Marcus to the world (the guy inherited Darla's traveling streak, big time).

I used to wonder what caused the rift between my parents and step-grandparents. But over the years, I've pushed those questions aside. Whatever it was, it doesn't matter anymore.

But as Anna-May turns to me, glasses of water in hand, her blue eyes are heavy with emotion. Regret. It stuns me.

"I've learned a lot over the years, Lachlan. Seeing that same look in your eyes now? It doesn't feel scary anymore." Her lips form a tiny smile. "And if I'm not mistaken, you don't have that look often."

My heart thumps. Can she really tell so easily that I'm starting to feel something for Lucy? Something I can't explain or understand, but that feels strong, all the same?

She must read something in my silence because she sighs. "Look. Far be it for me to give you advice on matters of the heart. I didn't handle your parents' decisions particularly well." She shakes her head sadly. "But please do tread carefully. Lucy is precious around here. Some say she's the heart of this town, so just be careful not to break *her* heart."

165

I swallow thickly as I absorb Anna-May's words.

She's right. Because while I'm realizing that Lucy is in the back of my mind every day when I wake up and until I fall asleep at night, I know that I can't do anything about it.

We're roommates. Friends.

And this whole arrangement is temporary, anyway.

From the living room, there's the beautiful sound of Lucy's cloud burst laugh again. And all at once, I'm hit with a sudden, intense, in-my-bones desire to be sitting next to her again. Hearing that laugh of hers up close. Maybe joining in.

Hmm. This could be a problem.

20

LUCY

"Who did you say did this paint job, Lucy?" Louis asks as he slips his shoes off and prances across the front deck and into my house. He's surprisingly dainty for a guy who, in his own words, "could body-double for Santa Claus."

"You heard me." I smile. "I came home after school this afternoon to a note that Lachlan fixed and painted the deck, and he wrote that there shouldn't be any shoes on it until at least tomorrow morning."

He also called me "Princess" again. Which I probably shouldn't love as much as I do.

I've come out to stare at it more than a few times, and each time, I feel more impressed, more touched that he would do such a thing. Without my asking, without my saying anything.

"I never imagined Lockie Brighton could do this all by himself. Especially not the Lockie Brighton I've seen around lately." Louis peeks further into the house. "Will he be joining us tonight?"

"No. He wrote that he was going for a drive down the coast."

I'm surprised at how disappointed I feel. It's stupid. I

shouldn't be upset that I won't be seeing him. Shouldn't *want* to see him. It's our book club night, for goodness sakes.

Which, if I'm being entirely honest, is not so much about books as it is about catching up on town gossip.

These Wednesday meetings have evolved over time into informal town meetings. Where else would I hear about Benny's latest misadventures with his escape-artist pet cat? Wyatt's ongoing feud with the baker the next town over? Gabby and Ken's on-again-off-again romance?

It all comes out during Wednesday book club. And with the community center out of commission this week, I thought hosting it at the cottage would be a nice alternative. A way to fill these rooms with love and laughter and chatter again.

Louis and I head down the hallway towards the bustling kitchen. There are so many people in here that they've spilled onto the back porch, where Lachlan also somehow found time in the last couple days to fix the tear through the screen.

I'm going to have to write *him* one heck of a thank you note.

Louis leaves my side in the kitchen to join Wyatt, Cheyenne and Agnes. Gina is standing by the dining room with her son Jensen and her daughter, sweet-but-sassy Olivia. Mabel's standing next to the sink, regaling people with stories of her latest wine-and-bike trip (more wine than bike).

My eyes land on Jordy and Celeste, who are staring at something by the fridge. I make my way over to them. "What're you guys looking at?"

Jordy turns to me with a feral look in her eyes as she holds up a familiar wallet-sized photo. "Is this who I think it is?!"

My entire face flushes as I realize that she's holding onto the old photo of Lachlan. The one he specifically told me I was barred from showing anyone. "How'd you find that?!"

"Duh. The flour jar. You always put secret stuff in there." She giggles mischievously. "And this is *gold*. I mean, look at him! He's an absolute child!"

168

Celeste laughs, and I reach for the photo. "Hey. He told me not to show anyone."

"I can see why. How old is he here, like, eight?"

I blink. "No... he'd be, like, sixteen."

Jordy tilts my hand to look at the photo. Her eyebrows shoot up. "Oh! I meant Beau!"

Beau? I frown in confusion and look at the photo again.

Unbelievable. I didn't even notice the two little boys standing right behind Lachlan in the old photo.

"It's too bad he's on a shift right now. What I wouldn't do to see his *face*." Jordy cackles. "He always said he doesn't have any childhood photos. He's gonna be thrilled." She must notice my expression because she turns serious and peers at the photo again. "Ah, yes. The older kid's Lachlan, isn't it? Wow, he was a cute kid, too. Obviously not as drop-dead gorgeous as the man he is now, but you know—"

"You talking about Lockie?" Agnes cuts in from across the room. "He *is* gorgeous, isn't he?"

"What'd I tell y'all?" Tricia adds from outside the kitchen window, where she's standing on the back porch with Ajay Sidhu. "Tall. Drink. *O'water.*"

I roll my eyes in a big way. "Don't you all have anything better to do than talk about Lachlan?"

Louis pffts at me. "What else would we talk about? This is the biggest news to hit Cascade in ages. The prodigal step-grandson returns!"

"Well, he may be easy on the eyes, but he's not so easy to deal with," Ajay grumbles. "The man keeps chasing me around my business with inane questions about laundry machines, and soap, and dryer sheets. It's maddening."

"Have you tried, you know, helping him?" I ask.

Ajay blinks at me. "Well... no. I suppose I haven't."

I purse my lips, feeling some sympathy for the grumpy man whose heart I've come to know is really in the right place. I

169

could hardly believe it when I saw him sitting in Anna-May and Graham's front room yesterday. He told me that he didn't think he'd visit them while he was in town, but seeing him there, clearly trying, warmed my heart.

"Has *anyone* here been particularly helpful towards Lachlan?"

"I've been!" Jensen pipes in. "I helped him at the store. We're tight now."

Ace shoves his friend in the shoulder. "Yeah, right. If you're so 'tight,' why were we creeping in the bushes the first night he was here?"

"We weren't *creeping*. I was just thinking he might want someone to talk to. Man to man." Jensen puffs out his skinny chest. Gina places a hand on his arm with a motherly shake of her head.

"Well, aside from sneaking around the hedges, has anyone else been particularly kind or welcoming towards Lachlan?"

"Why should we be?" Louis asks. "Why would we try and be friendly and accommodating towards someone who left a decade ago and has never come back? Who clearly looks down on our town? Who's ignored invitations to come for a visit?"

Gina shakes her head. "He's never wanted to be a part of this place."

This elicits several murmurs of agreement.

I look around the familiar, normally friendly faces of the people I've grown up with. My family. My community. Fiercely protective of one another. I feel at once a tremendous amount of gratitude, and also a profound sadness that Lachlan doesn't have a family like this.

"Guys, I know he's tough to take. I know he can be grouchy and unfriendly, but I do believe there's more to him. *He's* trying." I nod firmly. "He's fixed up parts of this house, where we're having our book club. He's mending bridges with Anna-May and

Graham. And if he's trying, shouldn't we at least be open to putting a similar effort towards him?" I point around the group. "We've all burned bridges we wished we hadn't at some point in our lives. Isn't there space for a little grace? A little forgiveness?"

Silence follows my impromptu speech, and I wait, strangely invested in whether my town decides to accept Lachlan. Or at the very least, treat him better.

After a few moments, there are murmurs of agreement, and Louis finally says, "Fine, fine. For you, Lucy, we'll try."

"That's all I can ask for. Now, let's head to the living room and get this book club started."

After bringing out the food and drinks, I perch on the far end of the couch. The living room is actually in good shape. Lachlan must've cleaned the scuff marks off the wall at some point, and he removed the tattered carpet, leaving just the hardwood floors. I also added a few personal touches: a couple of plushy pillows and blankets, some artwork I'd found stashed away, and plants I brought over from the rowhouse.

It looks nice in here. Lived in. Cozy.

We're all deep in a bookish-turned-philosophical-turned-gossipy discussion when the front door shuts.

A hush descends over the living room as Lachlan appears in the hallway. His glacial eyes sweep across the room until they find mine, and they stick.

If I'm not imagining it, his face relaxes, and a hint of that special smile of his appears on his lips.

My heart skips.

I wait with bated breath in the ensuing silence, wondering what might happen next. How everyone might react.

And then, Jordy jumps to her feet. Dives towards Lachlan and wraps him in a comical hug, seeing as her head doesn't even reach his shoulder. "Hey, bud!"

This is enough to break the tension, and there's a ripple of movement as people stand to greet him. Louis even calls him "Lachlan" and not "Lockie."

I'm across the room, too far to do anything but wait my turn to say hello. But I'm watching him. Initially, he's stiff and jilted, but he eventually relaxes. He gives a small smile to Gina and Ajay. Jensen looks up at him with starry eyes as he presses his fist to Lachlan's. Benny smacks him on the back and hands him a glass of sparkling apple juice I already know he won't drink.

The guy is by far the tallest person in the room, so it's easy to keep an eye on him. Or so I tell myself.

I also notice that he's wearing casual track pants and a hoodie today. He almost looks like one of us.

Finally, the crowd around him dissipates, and I spot my chance to go over.

Until Mabel catches my elbow. "Can you help me with something in the kitchen, dear?"

Right before I follow her out of the room, I glance once more at Lachlan to find that he's watching *me*. His eyes are like steaming dry ice, and he gives me a slow, deliberate nod. A strange but delicious heat soars through my extremities as I follow Mabel into the kitchen.

21

LACHLAN

I take hold of the black tape with my teeth, tearing off a piece before sitting on the end of the bed. I place the tape along the right side of my knee—I knelt on it funny yesterday while painting the deck.

After tugging on my black running shirt, I throw my clothes into the laundry hamper. I had a chat with Mr. Sidhu at the book club last night, and I have a feeling he might not run away from me at the laundromat anymore.

Actually, I was surprised at how friendly everyone was. Louis Gramercy apologized for making fun of my lactose allergy. The baker—Wyatt—said he used to work with clocks and offered to take a look at my watch, which I did allow him to take home with some trepidation.

I also got compliments on the little fixes I'd made around Lucy's house—the painted front steps and deck, the fixed porch screen, the new coat hangers I installed in the foyer...

Let's just say that I'm keeping The Point Hardware in business.

At the end of the meeting, the town's librarian—a quiet man named Darnell—struck up a conversation about some improvements he'd like to do at the library.

I offered to take a look, and that is where I ended up spending most of today: at the town's tiny, dark library, chatting with Darnell and taking note of fixes that could be made to the space while I'm still here.

Now though, after a day spent cooped up inside, I need to get moving. I'm looking forward to a nice, long run along the coast. The sun's even making a rare appearance today, peeking out from behind hazy gray clouds.

When I walk into the kitchen, I can't help but notice how quiet and empty the house feels after last night. Even more so because Lucy isn't here right now. It feels like I've barely seen her around the house the last couple days, like we're ships in the night. Only crossing paths when other people are around.

I've taken to writing her notes when I leave the house, but I'd rather talk to her in person.

I write a note for her now, saying that I'll be out for an hour or two and will be back this evening. At the last minute, I tack on a "if you're around and want to hang out."

Which I know is stupid. I shouldn't be encouraging this draw I feel towards her, but I can't help it. Lucy is intelligent and driven and passionate while also being tender and kind. Fiery and soft. She intrigues me to no end.

As I jog down Main Street, the breeze a flash of cold humidity against my cheeks, a couple of people raise their hands towards me. I slow, looking around, and am surprised to see that they're waving at *me*. I give a smile, waving back.

I'm rounding the corner onto a gravel road by the coastline, picking up speed, when my foot collides with something protruding from a hedge next to the sidewalk.

"Argh!" the thing cries out.

I swear, catching myself before I can tumble. "Who is that?!"

There's a very defeated, very familiar, "Hi, Lachlan."

I push the branches to the side to see none other than Lucy

174

Summers staring up at me from where she's currently splayed out on the ground next to the hedge. "Hi, Lucy." I frown. "Whatcha doing?"

"Tanning."

I help her to a stand, steadying her by her bare shoulder. My eyes do a quick scan of her body to make sure she hasn't fallen and is bleeding, and I notice that she's wearing workout clothes: orange leggings and a matching orange sports bra that show off her bare midriff.

I force myself to meet her eyes. "Next time, you should go to the beach for tanning."

Lucy picks a leaf off the shoulder of her top. Her cheeks are blazing red in a blush, and it's all I can do not to tell her how beautiful she looks, even covered in twigs. "You got me," she says. "I was trying to exercise."

"*Trying* to exercise?"

She purses her lips. "Serves me right for doing another outdoor activity."

"Yeah. I thought your Seattle mountain biking adventure took care of that."

She laughs that melodic laugh of hers and shakes her head. "This is clearly the final nail in the coffin that is my venturing into the great outdoors. I'll just have to become a gym rat. Get my protein from a smoothie bar and dead-lift my bodyweight."

She raises an arm and flexes her slender bicep, making what I *think* is an imitation of Arnold Schwarzenegger.

She drops her arm almost immediately. "Or, more realistically, give up this whole 'activity' thing altogether and lean into my true destiny as a movie-watching, snack-loving, Snuggie-wearing couch lounger."

I have to laugh at that. "Sounds cozy. But I can't let you give up *that* easily."

"What do you mean?"

175

"Most of my job is to keep my teams motivated. So, how about I try to motivate you?"

Without thinking much of it, I raise a hand to pluck a leaf from her hair. Her green eyes widen at the gesture, her cheeks coloring slightly. "What? You mean now?!"

"Now, Princess." I smirk. "Unless you've got something else on your schedule."

"If you count 'not dying' as on my schedule," she mutters under her breath, almost too quietly for me to hear. She gestures towards the hedge, and her voice returns to a normal volume. "You've seen how successful I am at running, Kent. I think that's pretty much all I have in me."

"We'll walk then. Ease you in. And if it's not for you, then I'll leave you to your destiny."

She scrunches up her face. "Fine. But if I hate the outdoors even more after this, you have only yourself to blame."

"That's a risk I'm willing to take."

She falls into step next to me, and we walk along the gravel road down the coast that I was planning on running today. I think I like this option better.

Lucy and I talk easily as we pass deserted beaches and tall evergreens. She tells me about her day at school, and I tell her about my day at the library. And about my texting Beau to grab lunch together—he, to my surprise, agreed, and we spent a fairly pleasant hour together. She also seems pleased to hear that people have been more friendly towards me.

We've circled back towards town and are passing a long stretch of sand when Lucy stops. The sun is out and shining now, so warm that I've rolled up the sleeves of my shirt. Lucy fiddles with her hair as she stares towards the water.

"Want to go for a swim?" I ask as a joke.

"Oh, sure. I do often dabble in the art of cold water swimming."

I assess her. "You're lying."

176

She laughs. "I am. But the water *does* look welcoming today, doesn't it?"

"Yeah," I say mildly. She then gives me a funny look, and I frown. "What?"

"You do that a lot."

"Secret cold water swims? You got me," I deadpan.

She chuckles again. "No. You say something, but I don't think you mean it."

I turn to face her. "Lucy Summers. Are you calling me a liar?"

She doesn't respond right away, just tilts her head. But I'm genuinely curious what she means. I really do try my best to be honest, her lying game notwithstanding. "No," she eventually says. "I think you lie to yourself."

That gives me pause.

Because I do, in fact, occasionally say one thing when I feel or think the opposite. Especially when it comes to work and dealing with Mike. And the other day, with the orange juice at Anna-May and Graham's... I *hate* orange juice.

"I think you might be right, Princess," I say slowly, peering at her. Because it's also just occurring to me that, for all of those times that I've thought or felt one thing and said another, I've never done that with Lucy. Scratch that: she doesn't let me get away with it. "I also think you're the person I'm most honest with. Including myself."

Lucy smiles and looks out to the water again. And I follow her gaze towards the rippling ocean waves, the way they roll onto the shore lazily.

And all of a sudden, I start walking onto the sand away from her.

"Where are you going?" she calls out.

I strip off my shirt. "To the water."

"Right now?!"

Her voice is a little closer, so I know she's following me, and

177

I turn towards her, walking backwards towards the ocean. Her eyes drop from my face to my bare chest to my stomach, and her cheeks turn red. "Why not? Sun's out. Haven't been for a swim since I left LA. And I *did* agree that the water looks welcoming."

"You're nutty. It's gonna be freezing cold!"

"We don't know if we don't try."

I'm almost at the water now, and I kick off my shoes, stopping at the edge of the waves. This isn't the same kind of ocean as you get in LA, and a part of me missed these wild Washington waters. Frothy waves rimmed by dense forest, cold water that shocks your senses, sand pebbled with shells.

Lucy comes up next to me. "You're going to get hypothermia," she says matter-of-factly.

I was mostly kidding, but now, standing here in the sunshine, I feel... different. I feel lighter, more free. I feel younger than I've felt in years. I clasp my hands behind my head and turn my face to the sun, soaking up the rays. "I'll warm up."

Lucy's silent, and when I glance down at her, her eyes quickly meet mine from where they appeared to be lingering on my upper body. Her cheeks and chest are flushed even more red. My heart thumps hard.

"I haven't seen this side of you, Lachlan."

I let my gaze meet hers. "I can be full of surprises, too."

She bites her lower lip, and I get the almost irrepressible, totally inappropriate urge to do the biting instead. I force the feeling away and step one foot into the water. A shiver wracks through my body, but after a minute, I get used to it.

Lucy gasps. "You're not *actually* gonna do this."

"What did a wise person once tell me? It's good to be a little uncomfortable to appreciate being comfortable again?"

She smirks. "That sounds like some overly positive B.S. to me, Kent."

I give her a wink. And then, I run into the ocean full tilt, diving in headfirst.

The cold is a shock to my system. I come up to the surface for a breath and then slice forward through the water.

After a couple front strokes, I place my feet on the sandy bottom and turn back towards the shore, expecting to see Lucy's surprised expression.

But what I see surprises *me* instead. Because she's kicking off her shoes, her expression pinched as she glares at the waves. She pats down her body quickly, and then, with barely a moment's hesitation, she runs into the brackish water after me.

22

LUCY

Lachlan's kneeling in front of the wood stove in the living room. With only a towel around his waist.

Okay, fine. He's not *only* wearing a towel—he's got his running shorts underneath—but *holy,* I can hardly believe the expansive, perfectly defined planes of his upper body that are currently on display.

I'm sitting on a pillow on the hardwood floor, wrapped in a knit blanket. Honestly, I remember being cold—it's why I sat here, close to the stove and wrapped in this blanket, in the first place. But I don't feel cold right now.

Nope. I'm way too busy taking in the form of the beautiful man before me.

Because unlike when I saw him in that pink bathrobe, I'm not even *trying* to pretend that I can keep myself from looking at him.

Lachlan is all chiseled lines and sharp edges. He's an Adonis, a literal work of art. A testament to the dedicated hours he's clearly spent toning his body to perfection. From his broad, muscular chest, to his firm biceps, to the tops of the V dipping below his towel.

It's all I can do not to run my fingers over his warm skin that pulls taut over his arms and down the ridges of his back.

I ground my palms into the blanket to keep from reaching towards him.

Of all the ways I thought my attempts at running might go today, ending up here in the living room, soaking wet with ocean water and seated next to a shirtless Lachlan Chase was *not* on the list.

"Want some help?" I offer.

Lachlan doesn't even look at me, just lets out a chuckle that I understand to be a "no." Which is good, given that I know even less about lighting the old wood stove than I do about painting decks.

I was hyped up and distracted all day today, thinking back to last night's book club. The *look* Lachlan gave me before I followed Mabel into the kitchen, the times I caught him watching me throughout the night, the way he helped me, Jordy, and Celeste clean up at the end of the meeting. The way he politely took the hint and went to bed so that Jordy could vent about her latest dramas with Jake the Chad.

After a day filled with thoughts of him, I decided to take a page from his book and try running. So, I put on my cutest (read: rarely used for sweating) workout outfit and hit the road.

And as it turns out... the road hit me.

A couple blocks in, I was so winded that I ended up having a little lie down by a hedge. Which is where Lachlan found me.

Not embarrassing, in the least.

"Got it," he murmurs as a small fire lights. He throws in a couple pieces of wood and closes the door, allowing the fire to grow.

"Well done," I say, feeling almost shy as he sits on the pillow next to mine.

He looks at the fire proudly. "I wondered if I could still do that. I used to light fires all the time when I was younger."

181

"Accomplished arsonist, then?"

He lets out a chuckle that rumbles through his chest and that I feel in my core. "Obviously."

I smirk, letting silence fall between us. I'm not sure when it happened, but I've grown very comfortable in Lachlan's presence. It feels good being around him. On our walk by the coast today, it was so easy to spend time with him. We spoke about everything and anything, even laughed a few times.

It feels *so good* to hear Lachlan laugh. I wear it like a badge of honor.

I, Lucy Summers, inspired deep, rich, rumbling laughter from the most grouchy man on the planet.

Even if said laughter did come about due to my hedge-cuddling incident.

A sudden shiver rips through me. Without a word, Lachlan grasps the knit blanket and wraps it snug over my shoulders, facing me so he can rub his big hands up and down my arms. My breath catches at how close he is. That woodsy scent still lingers on his skin after a dip in the ocean.

"You're not cold?" I ask, my voice uneven.

"I'll be fine. Give it a minute, and the room will warm up."

He then grabs another log from the pile he must have placed to the side of the wood stove and throws it into the fire. Clearly sensing the question in my eyes, he says, "Chopped this out back from the wood in the shed. Hope that's cool."

"I'm sorry. *You* chopped that. By yourself."

He raises an eyebrow at me. "Surprised?"

Surprised at the thought of city-boy Lachlan chopping wood? Meh.

Surprised at how consumed I am by the mental images of him sexily wielding an ax? Yes, indeedy.

I hope he can't see the blush that's currently splotching on my chest as I nod. "How on earth did you find time for that between all the other things you've done around this house?"

182

"What can I say, I'm efficient."

I shake my head. "How am I ever going to repay you for all this?"

Lachlan is suddenly facing me again. His glacier blue gaze meets mine and then dips slightly above my eyeline. My breath is stuck in my throat as he presses the large pad of his thumb to the crease between my brows.

"Don't worry about a thing, Princess," he says quietly. "Your smile's enough for me."

I'm shattered by the tenderness in his tone, his unexpected words. He just gives me that special smile of his and sits back on the cushion. Like he hadn't just said one of the sweetest things anyone has ever said to me.

And it's *Lachlan*. The guy I've casually thought of as Grumpy Superman and told to his face that he was an a-hole.

"Besides," he goes on. "I'm happy to have something to do. I like to keep busy. And if I can't work, I might as well be doing something around this rickety pile of wood."

I chuckle. "Wow. You were being almost sweet there for a minute."

"Can't have you thinking I'm doing all this from the goodness of my heart or anything."

"Never." I shoot a glance his way. "You're going to be relieved when you get back to LA and have something better to do."

"Well, I did think I'd be back there by now..." he trails off, gazing around the room, and I realize he's looking for his phone.

"I'm sorry you're not," I say honestly. Because though I am comfortable in Lachlan's presence, and I do like having him around more than I should, I also find myself caring about his happiness. I can imagine he's excited to get back to his home.

"Maybe I'm not all that sorry."

My heart does a little leap at his words, and I have to look at him, examining his side profile as he examines the fire.

"Honestly, I didn't think I'd ever come back here. And I don't think I *would* have if it wasn't for this whole work mess in LA."

He scrubs a hand through his hair, and my curiosity is fully piqued. But I bite back all of my questions, giving him space.

"I told myself—told you—that I came back primarily to visit Beau. That's not the whole story. But maybe I'm happy I *have* been able to see him. It's been good to catch up with him a couple times. And I'm happy I visited my grandparents. Step-grandparents."

"You know, they call you their grandson," I say quietly. "Not step-grandson."

Some emotion steals across his features so quickly, I can't identify it. "I've always just kind of written my family off as too much. Too complicated."

"Show me a family that isn't complicated, and I'll show you some people lying."

"I suppose." His jaw ticks, and his expression turns thoughtful. "I always felt weird calling them my grandparents. My dad and I married into the Brighton family, and we took *their* name. A name which is still kind of a big deal in this area. Not to mention the money behind it." He grimaces. "I've never liked blurred lines, so I felt weird having the name when I'm not actually blood related to them. Still kind of do."

I'm a little taken aback by his confession, but at the same time, I'm not. For being so completely opposite to me, I feel like I get Lachlan. "Family can be complicated." I pause for a beat. "If I've learned anything over the years, though, it's that your family doesn't need to be the people you're related to by blood. You can choose your family, just as they choose you."

"Like how you chose Cascade?"

"Exactly. And there is *no* shortage of drama and complications with the people here." I chuckle dryly. "But at the end of the day, we help each other. We're here for each other. Gina's husband passed away unexpectedly a few years ago, so we're all parents to Jensen and Olivia. And when my mom got sick, everyone would bring us ready-made dinners so we didn't have to cook. And whenever your grandparents—"

I cut myself off, pressing my lips together.

Lachlan looks at me. "What? Whenever my grandparents what?"

"Nothing. They were just on my mind. It's not important."

He captures my wrist gently, circling his index and his thumb right around. "Please tell me, Lucy."

I grind my teeth, cursing my big mouth. "Well, whenever they would think one of you was coming to visit, they'd tell everyone in town. Get all excited. But then, something would inevitably come up, and you couldn't come, and so we would all band together to make sure they weren't too upset."

Lachlan's grip on my wrist tightens for a moment before he releases it. His lips press together as he looks at the fire again. It's roaring now, heating up the cottage, but I hardly notice.

"I'm sorry." I shake my head, wanting to console him somehow. "I don't want to guilt trip you or anything. I know you and your parents and youngest brother have a lot going on."

"We do." His voice sounds faraway.

I pick at my fingernails. *My stupid big mouth.*

But then, all of a sudden, his warm hand is around mine again. "Thank you for telling me, Lucy. Thank you for being honest. You're not scared of being honest with me," he says.

"It's ironic given how we met and the game we played that night. But no, I'm not scared of being honest, and I'm definitely not scared of you. I think you're sweet and thoughtful behind that intimidating, rough exterior."

His eyes sparkle. "Rough exterior, huh?"

His voice is a deep rumble—no longer like cement, but richer, smoother, softer. I let my fingers graze his right shoulder, brushing lightly across his skin. Not rough at all.

185

He then raises a hand and gently pushes my hair behind my ear. His eyes are hypnotically blue, focused on mine with such intensity.

"What're you thinking?" I ask, curiosity getting the best of me.

He shakes his head with a deep chuckle. "No comment."

"Not even a lie?"

He pauses for a beat, and then shakes his head. "I only want to tell you the truth, Luce. And I was thinking that I'm so glad I picked you up at that bus station."

23

LACHLAN

The following afternoon, I'm on a mission to pick up yet another container of almond milk.

Which would be a pretty straightforward task, if it weren't for the fact that this dreary, drizzly Friday is the day of the monthly Cascade Point Farmer's Market. It's taking place this afternoon and evening along Main Street, and therefore has created clutter to the extreme, with traffic cones, vendor carts, lopsided banners, wayward pedestrians *everywhere*.

I've had to take about sixteen detours since I left the cottage.

Now, my SUV is sandwiched between Tricia's coffee cart and a horde of animals that Agnes brought in from her farm.

I'm idly wondering if Louis will be as jovial today as he was the night of the book club—or whether he'll laugh in my face again—when there's a knock on my window.

Agnes is standing there, smiling at me. Her white braids hang down in front of her jean jacket, and her cowboy hat is slightly crooked on her head. She gestures for me to roll down the window.

"Quite the jam, eh, Lockie?"

"Lachlan," I correct automatically, but find I don't really

mind that the farmer called me by my shortened name. "And it sure is."

She peeks around the coffee cart with its red brake lights, and down the road ahead. "Looks like it might be awhile still. What've you got in there anyway?"

Before I can do anything, Agnes has her entire head inside my vehicle.

She swivels her neck around, looking for goodness knows what.

"Uh..." I'm simply trying to give her some space at this point.

She peers at me, her sideways eyes inquisitive. "What're you selling?" she clarifies. "*Ooh*, please tell me it's those white sweaters you wear. My husband Bert would just *love* one for shearing the sheep. They just get so antsy, but if Bert's wearing a fuzzy white sweater, it might put them at ease, you know?"

I *don't* know—also, the thought of one of my expensive cashmere sweaters being used for sheep shearing makes me queasy—but I paste on a smile. "No. Not selling any sweaters. Not selling anything actually."

Agnes's eyebrows pop. "Well, dear, you must've taken a wrong turn. This road is for marketplace vendors only. Tricia's going to be setting up her coffee cart around here soon, and I've got a little space just behind your car here for my llama-licious petting zoo."

I blink. Choose to bypass that one entirely. "Wait. You're saying I can't drive through here?"

Agnes nods towards Tricia's coffee cart, and as if on cue, the brake lights go off as she parks right in front of me. "Not unless you want to drive right through the bouncy castle down the way."

Would rather not.

She places her hands on her hips and looks behind us. "You

also can't go back as Bert's just arrived with our horses. Hey, baby!"

And with that, Agnes is off, jogging towards a heavily mustachioed man hopping off a huge black stallion, with three other horses in tow. It looks like a farmhouse behind my BMW, and as I'm watching, one of the horses proceeds to leave a little gift right on the road.

Looks like I won't be getting out of this mess anytime soon. So, I might as well walk.

After locking the car, I stroll down the street in the general direction of the grocery store. Unfortunately, this means that I have to cross Main Street. The market is already well underway here—the side street I parked on must be for overflow vendors—and the road is teeming with groups of people, vendor stalls and food trucks, and inflatables for children.

I'm standing next to a stall selling "Washington's Best Hot Sauce!" and am looking out across the market, so I don't notice the person sidling up behind me.

"Guess the farmer's market scene really *does* get to everyone eventually."

I turn around to face my brother, who's currently smirking at me beneath his shaggy beard.

"I wouldn't go that far." I chuckle. "I'm just here to see some llamas."

"Agnes brought them again, did she?" Beau asks, looking around with excitement in his eyes. "I'll have to tell Jordy. She's terrified of them."

"How on earth could you be scared of *llamas*?"

"Jordy would kill me if I told you the story."

I laugh. "I'm actually trying to get to the grocery store to buy more almond milk. I'm taking your advice. Playing nice with the locals."

"I am very wise." Beau nods oh so humbly.

189

I roll my eyes. "So, what about you? You usually spend your Friday afternoons strolling around a market?"

He snorts. "Not really. One of my favorite knife-makers has a stall here today. He does really good work, so I wanted to see if he's got anything new." He pauses for a moment. Narrows his eyes are me. "You seem like you'd be into knives. Would you want to check it out?"

"I can't say I'm big into knives, except kitchen ones. But, sure. I'll walk with you. Might even be on my way."

"It's not." Beau smiles. "But you've committed now, Lockie."

I give my half-brother a punch in the shoulder, and we do, in fact, get to strolling around the farmer's market. I'm surprised at how much more comfortable I feel around Beau compared to when I first arrived. Not totally comfortable, of course... but since having lunch with him, I feel like we've found some common ground.

"So." Beau sidesteps a couple of kids as they race past us. "Jordy told me that Benny's been hard at work on the ceiling leak at their rowhouse. How's it been for you, living with a literal ray of sunshine?"

I chuckle. "It's been good."

"Just *good*?" Beau waggles his eyebrows.

Of course he doesn't believe me. I wouldn't believe me either.

And at that moment, I think of what Lucy said to me before our swim yesterday—that I lie without meaning to.

I should put a stop to that. Be as honest with everyone—including myself—as I am with her.

So, I rectify my answer: "It's been pretty amazing actually," I admit. "*She's* amazing."

In fact, I wish I could capture last night in snapshots. The entire evening with her was sweet, but electric at the same time. I remember Lucy bravely diving into the ocean after me. The

190

way we swam, and she still looked so beautiful with her hair soaking wet. The way she shivered in front of the fireplace, and how I wanted to do anything I could to make her comfortable again.

The moment I pressed my thumb to the crease between her brows, it's like time stopped.

The woman is doing something to me. Making me lose control in the strangest ways. Part of me almost wanted to tell her last night about what's going on in LA—the media circus around me, SparksFly, and my job.

But then, how does a person tell someone they're inexplicably drawn to that their claim to fame is being a bad date?

"The way you're blushing, I'd say she's amazing."

I raise a hand to my face.

"Kidding." Beau laughs gleefully. "You look the same as ever. But that reaction tells me everything I need to know."

I roll my eyes at him, and then, in the vein of honesty, I add, "Seeing Anna-May and Graham was also really nice. I think I'd like to see them again before I go."

"Well, consider your wish granted."

Beau gestures behind me, where my step-grandparents are standing at a stall nearby selling Western wear. It's honestly hard *not* to notice them given Anna-May's towering top hat.

Before I can say anything—or prepare myself—Beau's waving at them. "Hey, Grandma! Gramps!"

Anna-May looks up, and her red lips form a perfect "O" of surprise, which quickly turns into a beaming smile. She swoops towards us, taking huge steps on the pot-holed road in impossibly high heels. The woman's balance is something else.

"Beau. Lachlan!" she sings. "Such a pleasure to see the two of you out on a stroll!"

She gives Beau a hug, which he easily returns. Then, she wraps me in just as tight of a squeeze. Surprised, it takes me a moment before I hug her back.

191

Graham, meanwhile, walks up just behind his wife. "Hey there, kids," he says jovially. "What brings you to the market?"

Beau explains his knife hunt, and soon, we're not a duo but a quartet. Anna-May and Graham fall into step between Beau and me, and the three of them get to chatting about this week's goings on.

It suddenly occurs to me just how bizarre this whole situation is. Here I am, strolling through a *farmer's market* in a small, rundown Washington town with *my family*.

If I woke up tomorrow in LA and this was all a fever dream, that would actually explain a lot.

What *doesn't* make any sense is the odd pang in my stomach at this thought. I ignore it.

"And what about you, Lachlan?" Anna-May asks, bringing me to the present. At some point during her conversation with Beau, she wrapped an arm through mine. Comfortably. Like she and I walk like this all the time.

"What about me?"

"How was your week?" she coaxes. "I heard you went to book club on Wednesday."

"And," Graham pipes in from Anna-May's other side, "I heard through the grapevine that you've been working with Darnell at the library. Is that true?"

"Ha." Beau bursts into laughter. "Would love to see Librarian Lockie."

I shoot my brother a glare (which he responds to with a wink). "No, I've been helping Darnell fix up the place."

"Oh, isn't that lovely?" Anna-May beams at me. "You were always so good at helping out around our house when you stayed during those summers."

I blink at her. "You noticed that?"

"'Course we did!" Graham says. "And we appreciated it. We actually had a plan to give you a gift, a token of apprecia-

192

tion, the next time you came to Cascade. But then, you moved to LA and... well, we didn't see you much after that."

There's a loaded pause. Anna-May drops her hand from my arm, no doubt feeling the tension of the moment. I'm reminded of what Lucy said last night, of how disappointed Anna-May and Graham were when my plans to visit fell through.

And so, I stop walking—splitting the flow of market-goers around us like a river—and I face our group. "I should have visited you guys more often. I'm sorry."

Beau gives a little smile, and Graham nods. Anna-May steps forward and wraps her arm back around my bicep. "Well, it's all water under the bridge, isn't it? Because you're here now."

With that, the four of us fall back into step, walking through the market all together. Just like a family.

As we move from stall to stall, conversation and laughter ebbing and flowing, I realize that this is... nice. There doesn't seem to be the undercurrent of negative emotion I always associated with my family, and the tension I usually carry in my shoulders has eased.

I'm actually quite happy that we all ran into each other.

"Ooh, knives!" Beau shouts before shooting through the crowd to a stall at the end of Main Street.

"Well." Anna-May tuts. "I'm not sure *who* decided that wearing heels today was a good idea, but I shall be quite cross with them."

It's only then that I realize that she's leaning her full weight against me. I'm practically carrying her, at this point. "We can walk to my SUV," I suggest. "I can drive you both home as soon as the llamas are gone."

Graham waves a hand. He's holding his wife's other arm. "No need. I've already arranged for a car to pick us up at the end of the market."

I tilt my head. "Cascade Point has a private car service?"

"Not officially. There are a couple kids here who like to

193

make an extra buck or two, so I have them drive us around when needed. Like on market days, when my beautiful wife here decides to wear wholly unstable footwear."

"At least I looked fabulous." Anna-May sighs dramatically.

"That, you did," Graham agrees.

Anna-May shifts her weight to hold onto Graham. "Go on and join Beau. We had best get home."

I gesture towards her. "I can at least help you to the car."

Anna-May purses her lips and then suddenly stands straight with a wink. "I'm fine, my boy, just love a touch of the dramatics. What is life without some ennui, hm?" She smiles wide. "We'll see you and your brother soon. Perhaps have a dinner on Saturday evening?"

"I'd love that."

I choose to ignore the fact that my vacation is *technically* over the following week, and I will likely be back in LA by Monday morning.

My step-grandparents head off towards a waiting car down the road, and I'm about to follow Beau to the knife stall when my phone rings. I take it out of my pocket, check the screen, and am shocked to see Mike's name on the display. My stomach turns over with anticipation.

"Mike," I answer the call. "How're things going over there?"

"Well, Chase." There's a sigh. "I have good news and bad news for you."

24

LUCY

"Can we get two number 9s, hold the jalapeños? One with fries and one with a side salad this time, please," Jordy says, handing our unopened menus (which haven't been updated since sometime in the 90s) back to Ace.

"Sure," he replies. "And two chocolate milkshakes?"

"I'll have chocolate." Jordy looks at me. "But this one is on a health kick."

I roll my eyes in a big way. "I told you, J. It was *one run* that turned into my getting very well acquainted with a hedge." I turn to Ace. "But actually, I'll do strawberry today."

"A strawberry milkshake *and* a side salad instead of fries? Who are you and what have you done with my Lucyloo."

"Your Lucyloo is still here. She just had a birthday cake at school today and OD'd on chocolate. Plus, we don't all have drills to do for work and can therefore justify eating a billion calories on a weekly basis."

"Excuses, excuses," Jordy says with a wink. "But for real, I'm happy we could grab dinner tonight. It's been *ages* since we caught up."

"We saw each other a couple nights ago for book club, you loon. And we text all the time."

195

"Still. Going from living with someone—and therefore sharing almost every waking minute with them—to only seeing them twice a week is *huge*. I was beginning to forget what you looked like."

I have to laugh. "Dramatic, much, J?"

Ace places our milkshakes on the table, and Jordy takes a big slurp of hers. "Have you heard from Benny, by the way?"

"Sounds like he's finally making headway on fixing the pipes."

"Yup. He thinks that we should be able to move back in next week." She blinks innocently. "Of course, if that's too soon for you, I could always ask him to push out his timeline. Maybe call in for a special delivery or something that will take him away for a day."

"You enjoying living at Celeste's that much?" I ask, just as innocently.

Jordy's smile turns into a grimace. "I love Cel, you know that. But her studio is *way* too small for my, and I quote, 'loud mouthed self.' We've been managing, but I will be very happy to return to my 9pm bedtimes with no light or music interruptions."

I take a long drink of my milkshake, but I feel Jordy staring at me.

"And?" she finally prods. "No complaints about *your* roommate?"

"No, it's been... really nice living with Lachlan." I smile. "We're getting along."

"You don't say. I saw you two the other night. You couldn't keep your eyes off each other."

My cheeks grow warm. They've been doing that a lot since Lachlan entered my life. "Okay yeah, there's chemistry," I admit. "But you've seen the guy—he could have chemistry with a toilet brush if he wanted to."

"That would be something. But no, Luce, this is something

196

else. Whatever's happening between you two is, like, electric. Charged. Celeste saw it, too. He looks at you differently. Looks at you like he can hardly believe what he's seeing."

Her words take my breath away. "Ha. Probably wondering how a person can be so messy."

"Yeah. Sure." Jordy laughs loudly. "But I will say, if Jake ever looked at me like that, I'd be wedding dress shopping STAT."

I purse my lips. "Well, chemistry or not, the fact of the matter is that nothing could ever happen with us. Aside from the fact that we're currently living together, Lachlan is going back to LA whenever his work stuff wraps up."

"What work stuff?"

"I actually don't know." I frown at my glass, remembering our conversation in front of the fire. "All he's ever said to me is that he's taking a break from work and that something happened in LA."

"And you haven't done any investigating?"

"What do you mean?"

Jordy looks appalled. "My dearest biffle, have I taught you nothing?" She yanks her phone out of her pocket. "Knowledge is power. And when it comes to men that you've firmly decided are your soulmate based on hours of chat on an app— or in your case, based on spending a night with them in a motel and then subsequently living with them—Google is your best friend."

Her fingers tap-tap on the screen as she pulls up a new search page. Ace places our cheeseburgers on the table, and I take a big bite of mine. As per usual, it's freaking delicious. The Beachside Diner never disappoints.

Have I thought about googling Lachlan? Of course I have. Many, many times since I met the guy. But something always stopped me—it felt like an invasion of his privacy or something.

Now that Jordy's doing it though, I'm torn. I'm practically

197

consumed with curiosity, but do I really want to know this information when he isn't willingly (knowingly) providing it?

I bite the inside of my cheek. "Jordy, I don't think—"

"Whoa."

I stop. "Whoa, what?"

She's clicked onto an obnoxiously too-bright, pop-uppy sort of webpage. "This really *is* a mess."

"What is?" Now, I can't help myself from taking Jordy's phone and looking at the article, which is titled "Loveless VP brings SparksFly to its knees."

I stare, fully confused, at a photo of Lachlan.

He's wearing a gray, tailored suit, the top button of his dress shirt undone to show a triangle of tanned chest. He appears to be looking right at the photographer with that classic skeptical one-eyebrow look of his, and his mouth is in a little sneer I recognize from when he's uncertain about something.

It's a candid. One of those trashy tabloid pics that must use a special type of unflattering lens. Of course, Lachlan still somehow looks like a freaking drop-dead beautiful specimen of a human. Sneer or not.

I scan the article quickly, noting the publication date of just two days ago. And between ads for wrinkle creams, celeb-endorsed coffee pods, and a new reality dating show, the article speaks of the big shot VP of the SparksFly dating app and website conglomerate who is, himself, a bad date.

At the bottom of the article, I see a photo of the woman he went on said date with.

And *ohmygosh*, this is why we don't Google dating prospects. Because the last woman Lachlan dated—success story or not—is Carly Braxton, a rising country music star who is at once cute and beautiful and seems so effortlessly *cool*.

"Whoa," I second Jordy's sentiment.

She takes her phone back, and after a few moments, she puts it down with a shrug.

198

"So he was a bad date one time," she says, taking a bite of her burger. "Geez. They oughta give him a break. I'd bet my left boob that the majority of my dates have been far, far worse."

"Wow. You must really mean it if you're throwing your boobs in the ring."

"Now there's a mental image I'd rather not dwell on. I'd love to know exactly what he did to constitute him being a terrible date." Jordy shoves a couple fries into her mouth. "Might have to listen to that tell-all podcast episode the article references."

"I don't think I will." I nod towards Jordy's phone, which is still lying article-up on the table. "That looks like meaningless gossip to me. But what's worse is that it's actually affected his job."

"So, you don't think it's true?"

I frown. Take a small bite of my salad and instantly wish I'd gotten fries instead. "No. From everything I know about Lachlan, I don't think he would be a bad date... assuming he wanted to be dating that person. I think there's more to the story than what we're seeing."

"Well, there's only one way to find out for sure: we need a guinea pig to go on a date with him." She points a fry at me. "You already said he'd have chemistry with a toilet brush. And you, sweet friend of mine, are mightily more attractive than a toilet brush."

"Thanks. I think."

"Just saying, you should *probably* go out with him. You know, for research purposes."

I roll my eyes with a laugh. "Jordy. Let it go."

"Fine, fine. Besides, you shouldn't date someone that you're living with."

"Nope."

"Even if you could *technically* no longer be living with him as of next week."

"When he will *technically* probably be back in LA." I

199

gesture at her phone. "Lachlan doesn't seem the type to let messes fester. I'm sure he's wanting to clean that up ASAP."

"Whatever you say." She then swiftly changes the subject to something Beau did at work yesterday.

I do my best to listen, but I'm lost in thought about Lachlan. About this bad date story and why on earth trashy gossip columns would be focusing on such a thing.

Don't get me wrong, we like gossip in this town, but we know when things go too far. We would never let it affect someone's actual daily life.

Even if a very small and unreasonable part of me is grateful that such an event landed Lachlan here in the first place.

Truth is, after everything that's happened with us, I wouldn't trade my time with him for anything. It's illogical, and it's stupid, and it's history repeating itself, but every time I see the guy, it's like he chips away at another part of my resolve to keep my heart away from him.

"Hey, isn't that our gorgeous friend?" Jordy asks.

My head whips up to where she's pointing through the window of the diner, and Lachlan is indeed, stepping out from his SUV. He's once again not wearing a suit but his black track pants and a hoodie. I don't know which look is more attractive on him—I'm here for it all.

He frowns up the front of the diner, clearly not seeing us through the window. His lips are pursed in a skeptical scowl that almost makes me laugh. He's just so predictable with his grumpiness.

Then, his eyes somehow find mine, and he gives me a small smile as he walks towards the diner.

"Ha. Toilet brush chemistry, my a—Hey, Lachlan!"

"Jordy." He gives her a nod and then looks at me in such a way that my toes tingle. "Hey, Princess."

Why, oh why, does that nickname make a trillion butterflies fly free in my stomach?

"Looking for some dinner?" Jordy asks him. "I'd recommend the Cascading Cheddar Cheeseburger and fries. Even better with a chocolate milkshake."

Lachlan grimaces. "No, thanks. Lactose intolerant."

"Say no more. I hate the toots."

Lachlan chokes while I roll my eyes at my best friend.

"I was hoping I'd find you, Luce." He scrubs a hand through his hair. "I'm headed to a homewares outlet outside of town to look for some tiles to replace the broken ones in your kitchen and thought you might want to come. But clearly, you're busy—"

"She's not!" Jordy practically shouts. "We're just meeting for dinner before my shift. And Cascade's always dead on a Friday night, so Lucy is *definitely* free!"

I give her a sizzling glare, which she smiles through innocently.

"And I'd really best be going. Chief will kill me if I'm late again. Lachlan, I'm once again leaving our girl in your capable, non-murdery hands."

"Thanks, Jordy," Lachlan says before turning to me. Only then do I notice that he's got a weird energy to him—he seems a little preoccupied. Like he's got something on his mind. "So, do you want to come? Fair warning, it's a drive away."

"I'm down for a road trip. Especially with someone who *hates* driving."

The tension buzzing around Lachlan seems to ease a little as he nods. "Driving is the *worst*."

Jordy's smile abruptly turns into a confused grimace. I give her a winky-blink before following Lachlan out of the diner.

201

25

LUCY

We're on the coastal road leaving Cascade Point when the rain starts up again. We're going at a pretty good clip through the oncoming downpour when I finally ask: "So, want to tell me why you're driving like someone's just told you your favorite dry cleaning place is closing down, and you have t-minus ten minutes to save your sweaters?"

Lachlan's hand, which is currently clenched into a fist on his lap, relaxes a little. "I'm sorry, Princess. I've got something on my mind."

"Want to talk about it?"

He places both hands on the steering wheel.

Hmm. This can't be good.

"Mike called this afternoon while I was at the farmer's market."

I look at Lachlan in shock. "You went to the farmer's market?! By yourself? Were you lost?"

Lachlan shoots me a glare.

"Sorry, I'll be serious. Who's Mike?"

His jaw clenches slightly. "My boss. The CEO at SparksFly."

Is it bad that my heart just threw itself against my ribcage at the thought that Lachlan's boss might have called him to come home? "And what'd he say?" I ask, my voice uneven.

"The long and short of it is I need to continue like I'm doing." He taps the steering wheel, but he seems more thoughtful than agitated. "According to Mike, the bad news is that things still aren't looking good, and the good news is that I get to take another week off."

I try to read his expression. I can't quite make out what he's thinking, what he's feeling. "And *is* that good news?"

He glances my way, and I swear there's a twitch in the corner of his lips that tells me that maybe he isn't *totally* unhappy with the news. "That depends. How do you feel about having a roommate for another week?"

Unlike Lachlan, I can't stop the smile that takes over my face, and I have to turn away from him. "I suppose I'll allow it. I *especially* don't mind if you keep helping out around the cottage like you have been," I tease him.

And myself. Because, obviously, that's not the *real* reason I'm happy for him to stay.

But if I say it enough, maybe I'll start to believe it.

"When I'm done with it, it's going to look good as new."

I notice his eyes dancing, the small smile on his lips. "You like this kinda thing, don't you?" I ask. "You like fixing things. The library, the cottage..."

"I used to." He frowns thoughtfully. "When I was younger, it was so satisfying to take something that was broken and make it better. It made me feel like I had some sort of control, even when everything else felt out of control." He tilts his head. "I don't get to fix things much these days. My place in LA is brand new, and we have an on-call maintenance team anyway."

"Must be nice."

"It is."

There's a sour taste in my mouth, but I distract myself by

203

turning up the radio. "I hate to break it to you, Kent, but I think you might be a country fan."

"It's looking that way."

I remember something from the tabloid article Jordy and I just read, and I blurt out, "That have anything to do with Carly Braxton?"

Lachlan goes quiet. "You've heard of her."

I hesitate, cursing my stupid mouth. But then... I stop. Because I *do* have something to say. And while Lachlan might not have volunteered the information that I read in the article this afternoon, I suddenly need him to know that I know. And that I don't believe a word of it. "I heard about the mess in LA. The whole 'VP of Love sucks at Love' stuff."

He winces a little, tightens his grip on the steering wheel, but says nothing.

"I just want you to know that I think it's stupid," I say firmly. "This whole thing is getting blown out of proportion. Your job at SparksFly has nothing to do with your relationship status. Or how you are as a date."

He's silent for a moment, and I sit back in my seat. I probably went too far. Put my nose where it didn't belong. As per usual, big-mouth Lucy puts her foot in it. Which probably explains why Jordy and I are such a good pair: our mouths are out of control.

"Thanks for saying that."

I peek over at Lachlan, notice that he's got a small, almost relieved smile as he looks at the road ahead. And I'm happy that I brought it up with him. Happy, for once, with my big mouth.

That's when I look out the window, and I realize where we are.

"Pull over."

Lachlan looks at me. "What?"

"Pull over!" I point to a small pullout off the side of the road. "There!"

Lachlan turns the wheel, and we skid a little in the mud, but the SUV turns obediently into the pullout.

I step out, zipping up my coat against the rain. Not that it's going to do much—ever since my Seattle adventure, this raincoat of mine seems to have a ten-minute limit on its waterproofness.

Lachlan steps out of the car as well. "Let me guess, Princess. This is where *you're* going to murder *me*, isn't it?" He sighs, pulling a jacket over his hoodie. "I knew it was a dangerous game spending time with a woman like you."

"You know me. Very dangerous."

"I'm shaking in my boots."

"You should be."

I wait for him to round the front of the car, and we walk to the wooden fence over a small overlook. The rain is coming down in sheets, but the air feels warm.

Or maybe it's just because I'm back here. With Lachlan, this time.

I press my hands into the wet wood, gazing out towards the rabid ocean waves. It's hard to believe that Lachlan and I went swimming in that water. My eyes trail the gray sand along the shore, the trees that look black in this lighting. And the sky—the clouds are like angry bursts and swirls above the ocean water.

It looks like a painting. Just as beautiful as it is in nice weather.

"So, we've stopped to... look at the view?" Lachlan pauses. "I assumed this was one of your famous pee breaks."

I let out a quick laugh. "Yeah. I probably will pee before we get back on the road."

Lachlan must hear something in my voice because he tilts his head. He's standing right next to me, so close that we're almost touching. "Why are we here, Luce?"

"This was my mom's favorite spot. When I was growing up, we used to go to the beach here. It was quieter than the one by

Cascade Point." I bite my lip. "This is where I spread her ashes after she died."

I close my eyes just as a gentle breeze blows, and I think of her smiling down on me.

"Hi, Tammy."

Lachlan's voice is flat and monotone as ever, but when I look at him, his eyes are shining.

"She'd say hi back." I grin. "Probably would also make comments about you being Clark Kent. Especially if you wore your glasses around her."

"From her, I'd take it as a compliment." He chuckles. "I would've liked to meet her."

"She would've liked you," I decide. "My mom was one of those people who spoke her mind every chance she got. She was blunt and open, and she laughed a lot and very loudly."

"Then I definitely would've liked her."

I can feel Lachlan's eyes on me. "She was the strongest person I've ever known. Kind to her core. Whenever I was sad or mad at my dad for leaving us, she always told me to keep my chin up. To feel what I was feeling, and let myself be angry and upset and scared, and then, to step out of it. To remember that I am deeply loved. And she did that. She never, ever let me forget that I was loved."

I feel a little breathless. I give my head a shake.

"Thanks for stopping. It's been awhile since I came to say hi to her."

Lachlan takes a loaded breath. "You're amazing to me, Lucy. You're able to be so vulnerable, so open, without any questions asked. You wear your heart entirely on your sleeve. It's very brave."

"That's one way to describe the fact that I have a big mouth and can't shut up for the life of me."

He laughs at that. A deep belly laugh that warms me from the inside out.

206

Though apparently it's not quite enough, because a huge shiver tears through me. My raincoat has officially stopped waterproofing, and coupled with the breeze, I'm chilled.

Lachlan steps closer to me, wrapping an arm around me and tugging me to his side so I'm suddenly flush against him. Stealing his body heat.

"Want to get back in the car?" he asks.

I shake my head, a little overcome by his woodsy scent, his proximity. "This is fine."

His glacial eyes meet mine, and he smiles. "This reminds me of something."

"What?"

"We were basically this close in the motel that night." His eyes dance across my face. "When you were trying to spoon me."

"*No way* was I trying to spoon you."

He laughs. "You definitely did. But honestly, I was at fault, too."

"I knew it. You're a secret spooner."

He shakes his head. "I tried to stay on my side of the bed, turned away from you. But at some point in the night... we met in the middle."

Dang it. Curse my unconscious self for not being awake to remember this!

"Truth is," he continues. "I can't sleep most nights, but that night, I slept. And now, sometimes I can't sleep thinking about it."

My breath catches. And even though I know I shouldn't, even though I know we have really only gained an additional week on what is a temporary arrangement, all I can think is that I want to kiss him. Feel his mouth on mine.

Then, his eyes drop to my lips. And my mind shuts up.

"Are you going to kiss me?" I whisper.

He places a finger under my chin, tilting my face towards

him. "Thinking about it." He makes this low, guttural noise in his throat that makes my body flood with warmth. "I said it before, Luce, you're dangerous. But maybe I'm dangerous, too."

"I've said *this* before: I'm not scared of you."

His hands are moving into my hair, locking into the strands behind my neck. My heart is racing. All I know is that I want his lips on mine.

His eyes, which to this point, have been on my mouth, now rise to meet mine. His pupils are dark and dilated, but there's something more there. Something reverent and hungry. "What am I going to do with you?"

"You're going to kiss me," I whisper brazenly.

A smile breaks on his lips, just for a moment, before he ducks his head down towards me. My arms rush up his sides and lock behind his neck, and right as our lips are about to touch...

A siren blares behind us.

We jump apart as a fire truck stops in the pullout behind Lachlan's SUV. And hanging out of the side of the truck is his brother Beau.

"Lockie, there you are!" His eyes widen a fraction when he sees me, but he shakes his head. "Lockie, you guys have to come with me."

"Where?" Lachlan asks.

"The hospital." Beau's jaw clenches. "Graham collapsed."

208

26

LACHLAN

The North Pacific Regional Hospital is a bright, boxy little place with a wall of windows at the entrance that reflect the gray sky. The lights inside are a stark, fluorescent white that makes you forget, makes you totally *unaware* of, the time of day.

It reeks of antiseptic and cleaning products and is almost eerily silent due to the fact that it's mainly an emergency department, and apparently, there haven't been many emergencies since we arrived here eight hours ago.

"You've got to stop that," Beau grumbles from where he's sitting on one of the sinfully uncomfortable chairs in the waiting room.

I pause my pacing. "Stop what?"

"Walking around like that. Or, if you have to do it, the least you can do is walk yourself to the cafeteria and get me something to eat."

I narrow my eyes at my younger brother and am about to retort when Anna-May speaks up. "Boys, please!" She shakes her head. "Now is neither the time nor the place for your fraternal frivolities!"

I exchange a regretful look with Beau. "Sorry, Anna-May," we mutter in unison.

I fall into a chair next to Beau, wincing at the hard plastic.

It's been a long night of sitting here at the hospital, waiting anxiously for updates on Graham's condition, and we're all a little fried and sleep deprived at this point.

But the good news is, according to Dr. Khalifa's latest update, Graham is going to be just fine.

Apparently, yesterday evening, he passed out in the cheese aisle of the Cascade Market. Louis called the fire station, and so it was Beau and Jordy who assisted Graham and called the ambulance to take him to North Pacific—about a half hour drive away from Cascade—before they went to alert Anna-May and me (and Lucy).

According to Dr. Khalifa, Graham had a "heart event." Thankfully, she assured us that it wasn't anything too concerning—was mostly brought on by dehydration. He's been sleeping through the night, hooked up to an IV, and we're waiting to see him when he wakes up.

I'm brought back to the present by a series of *dings* coming from Beau's phone.

"What *is* that?" I ask.

"Duolingo."

"Like, the language app?"

He nods. "I'm learning Italian."

"Why?"

"So I can understand Jordy when she bad-mouths me to her family." He holds up his fingers in a pinching motion, like the really bad TV chefs do. "*Sei fuori di testa!*"

I squint at him.

"Means you're out of your mind. She says that a lot. Pretty sure she's telling her mom that *I'm* out of my mind, so I want to learn the perfect Italian retort for when she says it next."

I nod towards his phone. "Is she coming back here later?"

"Yup. Chief couldn't have us both miss our shifts, so she'll come whenever she's done at the fire station."

210

"She looks out for you."

"She does."

The *ding*s continue, loud and strong. Jordy stayed with us at the hospital last night until Anna-May arrived.

I'm happy that my brother has someone here. Someone he can count on, someone he's close to. He and Jordy seem to have a solid friendship... if a little too playful and jokey for my tastes.

As for Lucy? She stayed the whole night, propped up beside me on one of these uncomfortable chairs. She's gone home now to freshen up and grab me my glasses and a change of clothes. Which, of course, prompted a fairly impressive line-up of Clark Kent/Superman references before she went out the door.

It's a Saturday, so she has the whole day off—and would no doubt normally be spending it outside of a too-bright, too-quiet hospital—but she told me that she'd be back and would wait with me as long as it takes.

There are no words to describe what that means to me. What *she* means to me.

During the doctor's most recent update, I didn't even realize I was holding onto Lucy's hand until she placed her other hand on top of our clasped ones. At that moment, I knew just how grateful I was to have her there.

It makes me wonder how anyone could consider leaving Lucy. How a person could look at her, and *know* her, and not think that they want her in their life, in any capacity. How *could* her dad have walked out and never looked back?

The jerk has no idea what he's missed.

There's another *ding* from Beau's phone, and I look over to where my brother's slumped down in his chair. He missed his shift last night and hasn't slept. Across the way, Anna-May is sitting primly with a book on her lap, though she hasn't turned the page all night.

It occurs to me that *I* am the jerk.

I think back to when I first arrived in town. I was stomping around in my designer clothes, demanding different things from this community—demanding dry cleaning, better food delivery, a high-end barbershop, or whatever else. What an idiot.

Now, I can see everything that I've missed: years of time with my step-grandparents, seeing my brother Beau grow into the man he is now, a chance to have a family, in some way.

And the fact is, I would've continued missing out had everything in LA stayed exactly the same.

"Anna-May Brighton?"

Dr. Khalifa's voice snaps us all to attention.

"Yes, doctor?" she asks breathlessly, rising to a graceful stand. "Is he awake?"

"He's awake, and he's stable." The doctor nods, scanning her clipboard. "You should be able to visit him in just a few minutes, but first, I want to speak with you about his heart health. It seems that..."

She goes on to drop several medical terms that I'm not able to process at the moment and then describes a few small changes that Graham can make to help with his health.

Meanwhile, I'm filled with relief knowing that he's going to be okay.

Dr. Khalifa takes Anna-May to see him first. Beau and I stand in the waiting room, watching them disappear down the sterile hallway towards the patient's rooms.

"Was that the doctor again?"

Lucy's back. She's standing behind Beau and me, wearing a happy, bright blue sweater and jeans, but her face is drawn with worry. Her eyes skate over my features quickly. "Is Graham still okay?"

"He's fine. Anna-May's just gone in to see him."

She lets out an exhale. "That's great news."

"It is," I agree.

And then, I step forward and wrap my arms tight around

212

her, burying my face in her hair. It takes only a moment before her arms lock behind my back, and she curls herself into me.

In this moment, full of relief and exhaustion, I realize with startling clarity that Lucy isn't just a random girl I picked up from a bus station in Seattle anymore. She's not just my roommate. Not just a friend.

With every day, she becomes a little more of everything. She's the woman I can't get out of my head. The woman I crave to see every moment she's not with me. The woman I'm so stupidly attracted to, the feeling can't simply be described as physical.

I'm attracted to her mind, her humor, her smile, her love of life.

If a simple list could contain all of the things I like about Lucy Summers, I'd write it. But that list grows impossibly longer with each day that I know her.

I feel my heart rate start to slow as Lucy trails her fingers up and down my back. She smells like sea breeze and honey shampoo and...

Bacon?

I pull back from her. "Why do you smell like smoked meat?"

Her eyes are still a bit glassy as she lifts a paper bag I hadn't noticed she brought with her. "Got us some breakfast sandwiches from Earth's End in case you guys were hungry. There are two chicken superfood and two bacon-and-egg."

"Bacon and egg for me!" Beau swoops in to grab the bag. "Thanks, Luce."

I smile down at her, tuck her hair behind her ear tenderly. "Thank you, Princess."

She beams up at me, her cheeks turning pink, when the door to the patient rooms suddenly slams open dramatically.

Anna-May is striding towards us. "Gray's looking well!" she chirps. "Perhaps a little pale, which I did mention to him. But he's going to be just fine."

213

Lucy runs up to wrap my grandmother in a hug. "I'm so glad to hear that, Anna-May. Graham's so strong."

"He is, though of course I'd never tell him such a thing. That man has a big enough head as it is." She laughs, but her relief is clear as day. She grasps Lucy's hands. "Thank you for being here, my dear."

Lucy waves a hand. "I'm happy to be here with you all. With Graham."

I walk up next to her and slide my hand around hers, feeling at once grounded and lifted by her small palm against mine. Anna-May smiles, and her eyes dart first to our interlocked hands and then up to me. She gives a knowing little nod.

"Well," she says. "The doctor said we could visit Gray one at a time."

I'd love to get in there and see my grandfather. Lucy must sense this because she says, "Go on in and see him. I'm sure they're only allowing family in at this point."

"You *are* family," I say immediately, noticing Anna-May's smile get wider out of the corner of my eye. "Beau can go first, and we'll wait here. Maybe we can go in together after."

Lucy's green eyes dance when they meet mine. "I'm here for it all."

27

LUCY

Monday is the start of Snowflake week.

Of course, with everything that happened over the weekend and the trips back and forth to the hospital to see Graham, I forgot about this little fact.

And boy, oh boy, my kids are *not* letting me live it down.

"Miss *Summers*," Olivia whines, pointing at the whiteboard. "Why is Shawn's lantern still on the board? And the penguin you made? And River's stupid Aquaman drawing?!"

"He's *not* stupid!" River squawks indignantly. "He's a *hero* of the *ocean,* and he has an underwater summer cabin close to here!"

So, Aquaman summers in Washington State. Who knew?

"Olivia's right," Beth, Olivia's best friend, pipes up. "It's almost time to leave, and we haven't been able to draw our snowflakes *all day!*"

"I'm sorry, kiddos, you're totally right!" I hop to a stand before this argument can escalate. Olivia and River are two of my more outspoken students, and they each have their friend groups who rally behind them, so things can get real noisy, real fast. "I had a very busy weekend, and it slipped my mind to get the board ready for you all this morning. "

"It's okay, Miss Summers," says Margaret, the shyest, quietest girl in my glass. "We forgive you."

"Have you tried a white claw?" Olivia suddenly asks.

I almost drop the whiteboard eraser.

"What's a white claw?" Shawn's voice is laden with curiosity.

How do I explain this?

But Olivia's got it covered. "I'm pretty sure it's a donut. My mommy just says she needs them when Jens and Ace are practicing for their band."

"It's *not* a donut." Zachary, our tiny resident know-it-all, sighs loudly. "It's a *juice*. My daddy has them on his golf trips."

I peek over my shoulder. "Are these... morning golf trips?"

"Usually afternoon or nighttime." The boy frowns. "Sometimes he has them in the morning if it's his birthday or if he's mad because of his fantasy hockey game."

I smile, letting out a quiet *phew* under my breath.

The final bell rings, and there's a shuffle and scuffle as my kids start to pack away their things.

"That's it for today, everyone! But I promise we'll have an *extra long* drawing session tomorrow, okay?"

"Yayyyy!" Beth and Olivia say in unison as they gather their sparkling pink and purple backpacks.

By the time I've said goodbye to the kids, chatted briefly with parents, and sent everyone home, it's been a half an hour. I turn my focus to deep-cleaning the whiteboard—seems someone used something slightly more *permanent* than whiteboard marker during last week's themed drawings.

Only when the board is sparkling do I check my phone—which I've tried (and mostly succeeded at) *not* doing all day.

Because my busy weekend wasn't the only thing distracting me. My thoughts of Lachlan were above everything else, at every turn. Whenever my mind was at rest, I thought of him. Of his family.

216

You are family.

That's what Lachlan said to me at the hospital, and I've never in my life felt anything like what I felt after he said those words. Tingles from my hairline down to my toes. Because I know that Lachlan Chase Brighton does not *do* family or community, so if he considers me to be in that category...

Well, I'm touched.

But I already called Lachlan out once for sometimes saying things he doesn't mean.

And while I certainly want to believe that he meant it, the truth is, I have no idea where Lachlan and I stand at this point. We've spent time together as co-sleepers, roommates, friends. We've established that one (or both) of us will be moving out sometime soon. And now, we've almost kissed.

Needless to say, I'm a little lost.

It doesn't help that I haven't hadn't a chance to speak to Lachlan alone. Even this morning, he was gone before I got up, leaving a note that he was at the hospital, prepping for Graham to be discharged.

He seems to like communicating in handwritten notes when we can't speak face-to-face. Which is so charming and swoony, it makes me feel like the heroine in one of Jane Austen's romances.

At that moment, there's a knock on the door of my class-room. "Hey, Princess."

That deep, rumbling voice feels like a physical caress on my skin.

Although, it's regrettably cut short by my squawk of surprise.

I'm on the ground, where I've been hoarding colorful blocks in front of me like a rabid chipmunk entering winter, and there he is.

Lachlan is standing in the doorway of my classroom with the cutest smirk. He's wearing a white button-down work shirt and gray slacks. I wonder if he decided to dress a little nicer today for the occasion of bringing Graham home. The thought is at once so disarming and sweet, and I all of a sudden know for a fact that that's just what he did.

He also seems incredibly amused by the unfortunate noise that just left my mouth.

"Am I interrupting something?"

"Nothing! Not at all. Just cleaning up," I say cheerily. Too cheerily. Like I wasn't actually pretending to put blocks away while lost in a full-scale daydream about him.

"You don't say."

I pick up my block pile proudly and drop it into a bin. "Yup. You know, doing my part to make things a little less messy."

"You, Lucy Summers, trying *not* to be messy? Color me shocked."

"I told you I can be full of surprises." I stand, giving him my signature winky-blink seeing as I can't actually wink.

"You've certainly surprised me more than a few times, Princess." He gives me a proper wink in return. "Surprised me in the best way."

My cheeks heat. For someone who doesn't like to use his words, Lachlan sure wracks up points on the "sweet compliments" scale.

"Let me give you a hand," he says before moving to the side of the classroom, where he kneels down on the rainbow floor mats in his slacks and rolls up the sleeves of his dress shirt.

He starts to gather blocks and baby dolls, placing them in their plastic bins.

He looks every bit the businessman doubling as a caring father. My entire heart melts into a puddle.

Before I can do something stupid (like drool or jump on him), I scurry over to my desk. "How's Graham doing?"

"We got him home and settled in his favorite chair. When I left, Anna-May was brewing him a coffee. Dr. Khalifa recommended switching to decaf, so I hope my granddad can stick to it."

"Your granddad, huh? Losing the 'step?'"

Lachlan looks up from his task of gathering dolls in his big hands. "Yeah. I'm proud to be Graham's grandson, biological or not. Lucky to be."

"He's your family."

There's a ripple of something in Lachlan's expression, and he puts the last doll away before standing.

His eyes lock on mine as he walks towards me, heat melting the glacier blue of his irises.

I find myself leaning back instinctively onto my desk.

In just a few steps, he's towering over me. But he doesn't feel intimidating. Not at all. He feels strong. Stable. Safe.

I want to run my palms flat along the planes of his muscular chest and down his arms. I imagine the feeling of his shirt beneath my fingers, the feeling of his bare skin the other night...

Nope. We're not going there, Luce!

"I wanted to thank you."

My mind returns, and I peer up at him. "Thank me for what?"

"For lots of things." He tosses a hand through his hair. "For encouraging me to see my grandparents, for reminding me how important family is, for what you said yesterday about the mess in LA."

I shrug a shoulder. "Those people clearly don't know you."

"No. But *you* know me. And you make me want to be better." He takes a breath. "You know, two weeks ago—frick, even a week ago—I might not have cared less about any of this. Don't get me wrong, I would've been concerned for Graham, but I wouldn't have worried like I did."

Lachlan's jaw sets, and his eyes harden for a brief moment.

"This place has done something to me. *You* have done something to me."

His hand reaches out towards mine, one finger coming close to grazing my skin, before he drops it back to his side. I almost wonder if he did this without realizing it.

So I close the distance, clasping my hand around his warm, firm one. It feels easy, comfortable. Almost *too* easy and comfortable. Once again, I'm reminded that Lachlan and I haven't established what's actually going on between us.

I let his hand fall and lean away, putting space between us.

His eyes search my face. "What's on your mind?"

I blink, looking away from him. "Nothing."

"You're lying."

I pause. "No comment."

"Not even a lie?"

Lachlan repeats the words I once said to him. And so, I repeat his response, meaning every word. "I only want to tell you the truth, but I..." I trail off, wondering how to phrase this. "It's been a pretty intense couple of days, hasn't it?"

"It has."

"And maybe we both said some stuff we didn't mean."

He frowns. "Like what?"

I bite my lip, then roll my eyes. "You're really gonna make me say it?"

"Not if you don't want to," he replies. "But, yeah. I'd love to know."

"You called me your family."

"I know. And I meant what I said." He stares at me. "Have I not made that clear?"

I blink, for once totally and completely lost for words. "But that's... I mean, that's really..."

He seems amused at my ramblings. He pushes a strand of hair behind my ear, letting his fingertips graze the skin of my neck and pulling a hot shiver out of me. "You *are* like family to me, Luce." He pauses, his eyes sparking. "And I hope you meant what *you* said at the pullout."

220

His fingers have left a trail of fire on my skin. "What part?" I croak.

"The part where you said I was going to kiss you." His eyes drop to my lips. "Because I can't believe how extremely attracted I am to you. Pretty sure I've wanted to kiss you since I picked you up at that bus station with your sad excuse for a bike."

My breath catches with the intensity of his gaze, the way his hand hovers next to my hip. I let out a laugh that's more of a wheeze. "Well, Kent, I meant what I said, too."

At my words, a daring smile crosses his lips, and I get the sense that I'm about to see a new side of Lachlan. One I suddenly can't wait to meet.

His eyes bore into mine, intense and dark and simmering once more, but with something much more potent that makes my heart slam against my ribcage.

My knees start to give out, and I let them, leaning back onto my desk. In one smooth motion, Lachlan places his big hands on either side of my hips and lifts me, placing me gently on the surface of the desk.

He leans back to look at me, looking like he might devour me whole. My entire body feels lit from within as he comes in close and presses the smallest, lightest kiss on the corner of my mouth. Then, another on my upper lip.

Little teases. I might melt into a puddle right here.

I lock my arms behind his neck, wanting to keep him close, wanting him to stop teasing me.

But he's not done yet. He places his mouth mere inches from mine, so close that I can feel his breath on my lower lip. He secures his hand at the back of my neck, tangling his fingers in my hair and locking me in close.

"Do you believe me?"

"Believe what?" I gasp.

"That I'm telling you the truth. That you mean *so freaking much* to me."

"I believe you." And of course I do. Of course I believe this man with his unexpected heart of gold.

All I can hear is my heartbeat pounding in my ears, all I can feel is the warmth of Lachlan's body. So, so close to me...

And then, finally, his lips are on mine. It's like a sweet tidal wave taking me under.

He kisses me hungrily, passionately, his lips brushing against mine at a feverish pace as he cradles my head. Firmly but gently. Always firmly but gently.

He nips at my lower lip, and I tilt my head back to deepen the kiss. He's at once satiating me and also making me want more. I lock my arms tight around him, and he responds in kind, moving me forward so our bodies are flush.

I've never been kissed like this in my entire life. Never wanted anyone or anything like I want to be in this moment, his lips on mine. Everything about this just feels *right*.

But what happens next?

The voice in the back of my mind is quiet but clear. Clear enough that I place a palm gently on Lachlan's chest.

He must sense something because he releases me and steps away.

"Sorry, Luce, I kinda forgot where we were for a moment." His breath is ragged, and his blue eyes are dark and hazy as he looks at me.

Why did I stop that kiss again?!

"It's fine. I was right there with you." I give my head a shake to clear my desire-soaked thoughts, feeling a little discombobulated. The last thing I ever thought would happen today was for me to have the living daylights kissed out of me on my desk by Superman.

When I look up, Lachlan 's smiling at me.

"What?"

222

"You look cute."

"Wow. That has to be the fastest anyone has ever gone from 'extremely attractive' to 'cute.'"

He laughs, the sound rich and melodic. "You can be both things at once. You're everything."

28

LACHLAN

I wake up the next morning with the memory of her lips on mine.

Because Lucy doesn't just embody sunshine. She *tastes* like sunshine. Honey and sugar and cinnamon. Warm, sweet, and just a little bit fiery.

I'm craving her, wanting more than anything to kiss her again. To see her again later today.

I get out of bed and throw on my running clothes. Lucy has an assembly this morning and left bright and early, and I make a firm resolution to put her out of my mind.

I barely make it to the kitchen.

After a drizzly run down the coast, I head to the library, where Darnell and I are putting together some new bookshelves.

He and I have become fast friends while working together over the course of the last week. I find I really enjoy his quiet, stoic, totally deadpan company.

Together, we've painted the library an eggshell white and put in carpeting that Darnell ordered awhile back and never got around to asking Benny to install. We've also designated a couple of walls by the entrance to be painted by local Cascade Point artists.

When I walk into the library, I'm surprised to see that one of the artists has already come and gone: the wall to the right of the entrance is now sporting a beautiful mural of a girl curled up on a blanket reading a book.

I raise my brows at Darnell, who's currently staring at an IKEA-level-confusing instruction manual. "Wow. When did *that* happen?"

He frowns at me. "I assumed *you* let the artist in here."

"Wasn't me." We both stare at the mural. I'm not artfully inclined in the least, but even I can appreciate the careful strokes of the paintbrush, the blend of colors. "Did anyone else have access to the library last night?"

"It's been closed since we painted last week, and you and I have the only sets of keys. So..."

"Someone broke in."

Darnell looks fully alarmed, and he peers around the library. "Nothing's been taken, far as I can tell. I checked the office this morning, as I always do, and we don't seem to be missing any money or anything." He gazes back at the mural. "So, all they did was paint."

"Gotta be Cascade's Banksy."

Darnell snorts with laughter. "Never a dull moment around here, I swear. Just wait 'til the Seattleites hear about this. They'll be coming in droves."

I laugh along with him, and the two of us get to work.

By the afternoon, Darnell and I have assembled all of the bookshelves and placed them around the library. We still have some work to do with the reception area, and we have plans to put in a couple of reading nooks, but the space is looking much better.

Darnell smacks me on the back before we both head out.

Which is timely, as I'm itching to get home to Lucy.

225

When I went by her classroom yesterday, I wasn't necessarily planning on kissing her. I just wanted to see her. And when she asked me if I meant it when I called her my family, I was almost shocked.

This woman—who has been living rent-free in my mind, who has been making me feel things since the moment I met her—didn't realize how important she is to me.

That kiss on her desk confirmed it: I'm crazy about her.

It's a dreary afternoon, and as soon as I get back to the cottage, I get a fire going in the wood stove. Lucy isn't back yet, but I turn on the kettle for her in case she wants a hot drink.

Finally, the front door slams.

"Honey, I'm home!!!"

I stand up straight. "In the kitchen!"

It's such a domestic exchange. I kind of love it.

Lucy skips into the kitchen carrying what looks like one of those metal head scratchers, but with... pompoms on the ends of the branches?

I frown as she places the monstrosity on the counter. "What's that?"

"What's what?" she asks, and I nod at the bizarre spidery thing. "Oh. My solar system."

I stare at her blankly.

She bursts into laughter, pointing right at my face. "I love when you do that."

"Do what?"

"When your eyebrow pops like that, and you look at once offended and uncertain."

I put my fingers to my brow, and Lucy walks towards me, grazing my other hand with hers.

"It's my favorite," she says. "Like my own private inside joke."

"With my face."

226

"Your face and I have inside jokes." She blinks at me innocently. "Does that bother you?"

I shake my head, wrapping my arms around her and pulling her close. "You could never bother me."

Lucy places her tiny, cool palms flat on my chest as her green eyes meet mine. Once again, I can't believe how into her I am. She could tell me to rub butter on my head and dance around the kitchen, and I would do it.

"Is that a challenge, Kent?" she asks in a low, threatening voice.

"Maybe it is, Princess."

She removes her palms from my chest... and pokes me aggressively in the side. Luckily, I saw it coming and managed to steel myself right before her index finger jabbed in below my ribcage. She winces a little as she pulls her finger back.

"Is that all you got?" I ask.

A fire lights in her eyes. I love to see it. Love this fiery, sparky side to her. "You have *no* idea what you're in for."

"I think I want to find out." I grasp my wrists behind her back, essentially locking her in. She struggles for a brief moment before relaxing against me. "I'm kind of crazy about you, Lucy."

Her eyes widen for just a second, and I get the sudden sense that she's considering something. But before she can answer, there's a knock at the front door and she leaps out of my arms.

"Hellooooo!" a familiar voice calls from the entry.

"Jordy!" Lucy dashes out of the kitchen. Squeaks as she gets to the hallway. "And Celeste? What's going on?!"

"Didn't you see my text?!" Footsteps are coming down the hall. "We're having book club here again tonight 'cuz the community center is still out of commission. Hi, Lachlan!" Jordy says this all in one breath as she drops bags of chips on the counter.

"Hey, Jordy." I frown. "Hang on, it's Tuesday, not Wednesday."

"We bumped up the book club to a day earlier this week because the high school's putting on *Hamilton* tomorrow night." She pauses for a minute, looking me up and down. "My, my. Looking more like a Cascadian by the day, aren't we?"

I roll my eyes, even as her words do, surprisingly, mean something to me. I gesture down at my casual sweatshirt and cozy chinos. "Because I'm dressed down, you mean?" I fire back.

"Hey, we like to be comfortable 'round these parts. None of that neat and tidy LA crap. There are too many poop-happy seagulls here to justify it."

With that lovely image, Jordy skips out of the kitchen, and Celeste walks in. I haven't spoken to Celeste much, but I know she's a close friend of Lucy's.

I walk over to help her place her groceries on the counter.

"Thanks," she says shyly, blinking up at me with almond-shaped, dark brown eyes. She's a few years younger than me, has wild, thick black hair, and is wearing a necklace with a gold bow on it.

"No problem. We haven't officially met. I'm Lachlan."

"I know. You're Beau and Marcus's half-brother."

My eyebrows rise at the mention of my other brother. "You know Marcus?"

Her cheeks turn pink. "I used to."

She takes off down the hallway towards the front door before I can ask what she means by that. Not for the first time, I wonder how my youngest brother is doing. And where he's at these days.

I begin to unpack the groceries, and soon enough, other voices fill the cottage. Laughter and conversation spill into the kitchen from the living room, and I find myself smiling.

It feels good to be in a loud house like this, even if these are unexpected visitors. It's the kind of thing I would *hate* to happen in LA, but here, it feels almost normal.

In Cascade Point, the abnormal *is* normal.

228

I greet people as they mill through the kitchen, filling mugs with coffee or tea, and glasses with wine or juice. Some people head to the porch, but most gather in the living room due to the bad weather. Lucy, meanwhile, spins through the kitchen, making sure everyone has everything they need. She's a fantastic hostess.

"Dang it," Jordy grumbles from next to my right shoulder.

"What's up?" I ask her.

"I *knew* we should've checked our list once more, but Celeste just *had* to get to the arts and crafts shop before closing."

"Is everything okay?" Lucy is suddenly standing right next to us. It takes everything in me not to wrap an arm casually around her waist.

"We forgot the cookies."

I frown. "Well, we've got brownies, cupcakes, cinnamon rolls. All kinds of sweet treats."

"No, Lachlan." Jordy turns to me very seriously. "The cookies are *key*. You have no idea how much this town loves cookies. There will be a riot."

I look at Lucy, fully expecting her to roll her eyes and tell Jordy she's being dramatic or something. Instead, her green eyes are just as wide and panicked.

Which, of course, is completely unacceptable.

"I'll go to the store," I volunteer.

"Really?" Lucy asks. "Because you know Cascade Market's closed right now, so you'll—"

"Have to go to the store in Pacific Beach, yeah. And I'll make sure to grab some gluten free cookies—"

"For Mabel. And when you're back, we can pop them in the oven—"

"So they make the house smell like baking," I finish for her. "Great idea."

Lucy's smile is sweet and grateful. I have to smile back at her.

229

And then, Jordy utters: "Geez. Get a room, you two." She pauses. "Or I guess you already have, the first night you met. And you can also currently get one at any time. Uh... ignore me."

Lucy's cheeks go apple red, and I take this as my cue to kiss the top of her head and step out of the kitchen.

As I leave the house, pulling up the hood of my raincoat, it hits me that I'm driving out of my way to a small-town grocery store to pick up cookies for virtual strangers. People I didn't know, or care about, just two weeks ago.

I've barely thought of Mike or SparksFly or my work in days. Which has to be a personal record, surely.

I barely recognize the person I am right now.

The person who will also make sure to buy freaking gluten-free chocolate chip cookies for freaking Mabel, not just because I know that's what she likes best, but because I *care* about what she likes best.

I suppose this is what a proper vacation is supposed to be like—a break from regular life. A break from reality.

So, why is being here, and doing this, and spending time with these people almost beginning to feel like what's actually real?

29

LUCY

"So, that's when Jake and I decided that our relationship has run its course." Jordy sighs, fingering the tassel on the throw pillow she's sitting on.

I continue to rub her back while Celeste looks on from the couch, chin in her palms. All around us, book club is well underway, with various groups catching up on gossip seeing as we've already discussed last week's reading material: *A Midsummer Night's Dream*, ironically chosen by Celeste during midwinter.

I'm sad for my friend and the dissolution of her relationship with Jake the Chad, but I'd be lying if I didn't say I wasn't at least a little relieved. The guy has absolutely nothing on my brilliant, hilarious, ridiculous best friend.

"Maybe this is for the best?" I say gently.

"Maybe. Because I'm definitely not moving with him to Seattle to pursue his gym-fluencing. I did tell him that was a dealbreaker for me."

I wrap my arms around her and hug her tight. "I'm glad you won't be moving, J."

"Me too. And Jake really did have his odd little quirks. Like his superstition that the Kraken would win the Stanley Cup if he didn't cut his toenails." She purses her lips. "Thank goodness it's not beach season."

Celeste and I both grimace.

"There are plenty of fish in the sea," Celeste says soothingly. "Fish with nicely clipped toenails."

"Yeah," Jordy replies. "Though half of those fish are the scary, deep-sea ones that have no business seeing the light of day."

Cel and I snort with laughter, and thankfully, Jordy laughs too.

"Besides, it's so easy for you to say, Cel. You've been with Derek how long now?"

Celeste smiles, though it doesn't reach her eyes. "Three years, as of a couple months ago. I think."

We all look towards the side of the room, where Beau, Derek and the guys from the basketball team are gathered together, eating and drinking and being merry. Derek and Celeste are one of those couples that you almost forget are a couple. They've been together for ages and are so comfortable around one another, it's like they're really, really good friends.

"And what about you, Miss Lucyloo?" Jordy asks. "Looks like you've found a good fish, too."

The three of us all now return our attentions towards the kitchen, where Lachlan is standing in front of the stove with a spatula, talking to Darnell. He took off his sweatshirt and is now sporting my mom's lacy pink apron over his polo and chinos.

The apron—like the bathrobe—is comically small on his large frame, barely grazing his shoulders and upper thighs.

As we watch, Lachlan laughs at something Darnell says. I have to smile along with him, wondering what they're talking about. Almost wishing I was there too...

"You are just *smitten*." Jordy giggles.

"I mean," I sputter, my cheeks warming. "So, what if I am?"

"Well," Celeste says reasonably. "He seems really into you,

too. More than anyone else you've introduced us to. No offense."

"But, isn't he leaving soon?" Jordy asks quietly.

"That's the plan. He's only here for one more week." I clench my eyes shut. "I know he loves LA, his stay in Cascade was always going to be temporary. But for some reason, my heart wants so badly to skip over that fact and fall for him anyway."

It isn't helped by the fact that Lachlan keeps saying (and doing) all the right things.

Case in point: being all sweet with me, and kissing the living daylights out of me, and saying he's crazy for me, and running off to the store, unbidden, to get cookies for everyone.

It's been almost *too* easy to fall for him. And I'm not sure I can keep living in denial of what these incredible words and admissions and actions are doing to me and my heart. This grumpy, beautiful man's cinnamon center is completely melting down my walls and defenses.

It's enough to fully confuse a girl. Make her want something that she knows she can't have.

Just look what happened to my mom after she fell in love with someone who wasn't happy living in Cascade. She was left all alone.

The three of us watch Lachlan as he chats with Wyatt for a moment and then goes on to take another batch of chocolate chip cookies out of the oven. He sets them aside except for one for himself, over which he sprinkles some cinnamon. Which is so fitting, I have to smile.

"There's no denying it," I admit. "I'm definitely falling for him. Which is terrifying because I know he can't stay here. And I can't leave. This is my home."

"The classic conundrum." Jordy lets out a breath next to me. "Can I give you some advice on the heels of my breakup?"

"Shoot."

"Maybe it's worth taking the risk. Our friend Billy the Bard here said it best: 'The course of true love never did run smooth.'" She taps the cover of her (SparkNotes) copy of *A Midsummer Night's Dream*. "Maybe it's okay to fall for someone who treats you well. Who seems to see you and *get* you."

Celeste agrees. "And to quote Shakespeare again: 'To be wise and love, exceeds man's might.'"

Jordy frowns and begins to leaf frantically through her booklet.

"That one's from *Troilus and Cressida*." Celeste rolls her eyes.

"Bill sure had a lot to stay about love, didn't he? But just as in..." Jordy screws up her face. "Troy and Cleopatra, or whatever... isn't that what love's about? You can't logic yourself into or out of it. At the end of the day, you can't help who you fall for."

Jordy's no longer looking at the kitchen now, but instead towards the group of basketball players. I frown, wondering what that's about, but she sighs before I can say anything.

"Moral of the story is that you and Lachlan have some sort of a real, genuine connection, and I don't know about you, Luce, but I don't think that happens often. Maybe you have more to gain than you have to lose. And no one knows how the story's going to end. So you might as well hold on tight for the ride."

At that moment, the subject of our conversation looks directly at us.

AKA directly at our three heads bobbing over the couch like a pack of creeping lurkers.

Jordy, Celeste, and I immediately dive down, landing in a heap.

"Whoa, whoa, whoa!" Louis, seated on a chair nearby, pops to a stand as someone's leg almost whacks his teacup right out of his hand. "What's all this about?!"

"Sorry, Louis," we say in unison as we untangle ourselves.

234

He harrumphs, sits back down, and takes a begrudging bite of cookie.

As we all get cozy in our seats again, I can't help but think about Jordy and Celeste's advice.

I knew, from the start, that it would be stupid and foolish to let myself fall for Lachlan Chase.

But when I look towards the kitchen, and my eyes meet his, and he gives me that special smile, it occurs to me that it's too late.

I've already fallen for him. And I'm not sure I want to go back.

30

LUCY

By the time the book club winds down, we've gone through four bags of chips, three bottles of wine, two meat and cheese plates, and approximately one billion cookies.

Wish I could say I was exaggerating, but I'm sure Lachlan will agree with that number.

He was amazing tonight. Between heating and reheating cookies, pop tarts, cinnamon buns and anything else, he managed to keep an eye on people's drinks. And he did it all with barely a word. Positively stoic in his lacy pink apron.

And his thoughtfulness wasn't lost on anyone. Gina and Mabel even pointed out that he was a consummate host.

I just can't believe how comfortable this domestic life feels with him. Turns out that I love living with Lachlan. I love that he takes charge when he notices something that needs to be done, love that he treats this house almost as if it were his own. He might be the best roommate I've had.

Don't tell Jordy.

And times like tonight, I can almost believe that he's enjoying being here. That he might actually *like* Cascade Point. I no longer see the grouchy stranger who stomped into Cascade Point complaining about everything it lacks. He's become respectful of our town and its weird, sometimes old-fashioned ways.

As we say goodnight to our last guest, all I can think is that we're finally alone.

At last.

Lachlan's eyes meet mine and the air between us feels charged and fizzy with electricity. We've been dancing around each other all night, moving in tandem from a distance as we floated around our guests. But now, it's just us in this big, silent house.

"We did it," he murmurs. "We managed to avoid a cookie riot."

"Thank goodness for that. Things can get pretty ugly 'round here if there's not enough treats."

"Well, people have only just started to accept me, so here's hoping I scored myself some brownie points tonight."

"*Cookie* points, you mean?"

Lachlan groans, throwing his head back. "You and your dad jokes, Luce." He then steps forward and finally closes the distance between us, wrapping his arms behind my back. I love how he does this like it's second nature.

I place my palms on his chest, playing with the apron's hem. "This look suits you."

Lachlan looks down, and his eyes widen in shock. Like he forgot that he's spent the entire evening wearing a pink, frilly apron with a whisk pattern and *"Cook by the Ocean"* (inspired by Mom's love of DNCE) printed on the front. Complete with hearts where the O's should be.

He grasps my fingers gently. "Not as well as your One Night Stance hoodie suits you."

"Maybe we should trade. I wear the apron, you wear the hoodie."

"Well, if you think this apron doesn't fit me... Pretty sure the hoodie might burst at the seams."

237

"Hmm. Not worth the risk." I sigh, winding my hands up behind his neck and playing with his hair. "That hoodie is *far* too precious to me to be torn up."

He pulls me closer. "Just the hoodie, huh?"

I don't respond. I love the way his eyes skate over my face like he's memorizing me. Or memorizing this moment. I could spend literal hours, months, in Lachlan's arms, just like this.

Because Jordy made a good point. Maybe *it's okay* to fall for such a good, decent man.

And the truth is, I'm tired of fighting what I'm feeling for Lachlan. Tired of pretending that I'm not falling for him, just as he seems (incredibly) to be falling for me.

Too soon, he releases his hands to lightly tap my hips. "Let's clean up. Then, I have something to show you."

"Another best-selling apron look, I hope?"

The eyebrow pop he gives me makes me laugh. "Full of surprises, Luce."

So together, Lachlan and I clean the house. We clear the living room of plates and glasses, replace the napkins in the drawer next to the stove, stack dishes in the dishwasher. Lachlan must've done something to it as it properly *cleans* now, instead of half-heartedly sanitizes.

The man is an absolute wizard with fixing things, and I know that I'm going to miss this (among many, many other things) when our time together comes to an end.

I push away those thoughts for now, just trying to enjoy the moment and this amazing man.

Once everything is put away, Lachlan walks into the kitchen with a folded piece of gray fabric.

"Is this the surprise?"

He gives me a mysterious little smirk. "Take it and go to the porch."

"Uhm, it's freezing outside tonight."

"Hence the blanket." He walks up close to me. Close

enough that he's almost touching me, but not quite close enough. "Just trust me."

I scan his face. His expression is wide open, his mouth twitching with amusement, and I remember being at the motel with him, when he told me to take another folded piece of fabric and head to the bathroom.

So, just as I did that night, I oblige, wrapping my arms around the blanket and heading for the back porch.

The night air is cold and damp, and I shiver. I quickly unfurl the blanket and wrap it around my shoulders, turning on the porch light and wondering what on earth Lachlan expects me to do out here.

Then, I see it.

I let out an audible gasp as I walk over to the swing hanging at the far end of the porch. The white bench with an adorable heart carved into the back of it used to hang from chains in this very spot, but the chains broke a few years back. I never bothered fixing it, and so I set the bench into the garden, hoping people wouldn't think much of it.

And yeah, it wasn't perfect—the bench has no legs and therefore required you to kind of fold yourself down into it via yogi squat.

But hey, some people are into that type of thing.

I run my fingers along the bench, now properly secured and hanging as a porch swing should.

With a little squeal, I hop onto it and rock myself back and forth. My mom and I used to sit out here in the summer when the weather was nice. We'd watch the ocean (because you could actually see it back then), and she would drink her coffee while I drank my hot cocoa. It was our favorite spot to read and hang out.

I close my eyes now and let the happy memories fill me up.

"Room for one more?"

Lachlan is standing right in front me, the frilly apron gone. He's carrying two steaming mugs.

I shuffle to one side of the bench. "Guess we'll have to try it out."

It's a small seat—my mom and I were squished sitting here together when I was a teen. And Lachlan is, at best, a few sizes bigger than my mother was.

He frowns at the bench for a moment, that skeptical brow I love so much gathered up near his hairline. Then, he puts the mugs down and loops an arm beneath my knees.

"What're you—?" I squeak as he lifts me, just to sit and place me squarely on his lap.

He hands me one of the steaming mugs and keeps the other for himself.

"Perfect," he says and takes a swig of his hot drink. I watch his Adam's apple bob as he swallows, the tendons of his neck... And I'm not at all cold anymore.

I hold my own mug to my face. Take a deep inhale of the sweet, rich scent. "Hot cocoa?"

"Of course."

"I never would have guessed you'd be a hot cocoa lover."

"I'm not. This is coffee."

"Coffee at 10pm? I think I'm figuring out why you have trouble sleeping."

He lets out a laugh. "Decaf. Anna-May insisted I take some home with me. Honestly, I think I like not being as caffeinated. Feel like it might be improving my mood. Though maybe that's just who I've been spending my time with."

He takes another drink of his coffee. I lick my lips, feeling my heartbeat in my temples.

"About what you said earlier..." I start.

"What part?"

"You know, that you were crazy about me?"

He looks at me, his expression totally uncomprehending. I

240

suddenly wonder if I somehow misunderstood or misheard something. Maybe I imagined it? He did say those words, didn't he?!

"I *am* crazy about you," he corrects.

"Right." I smile, blushing. "Well I want you to know that I... I'm falling for you, too. As well. Currently."

I trail off. For a teacher, I'm surprisingly ineloquent at times.

Or maybe the term is non-verbal. Because my mouth is hinging open and shut like I might say something else.

But Lachlan smiles, and my mouth—verbal or otherwise—shuts up. It's that special smile I've only ever seen him give *me*, the one that's soft and genuine and tender.

"I know."

I lean back. "You *know*?!"

"'Course I do. I know, from my own experience, that what I feel for you isn't something I've felt, ever. And I know for a fact, from everything I've seen and learned while working at Sparks-Fly, that what's going on between us doesn't happen often, to anyone."

It's almost word for word what Jordy said. But it doesn't quite quell the questions still nagging at me—the *what happens next* for us. What happens when he goes back to the city, where he belongs, and I stay here, where I belong.

I raise a hand to twist my fingers into his hair, pressing my forehead to his cheek.

"We're in trouble," I whisper.

He pulls back to look at me. His blue eyes sweep across my face as he pushes a lock of my hair behind my ear. "What's on your mind, Princess?"

I smile humorlessly. "No comment?"

He simply shakes his head.

I hesitate. It would be easy to brush this off, to sweep it under the rug, but I know that Lachlan won't let me get away

241

with it. And I don't want to do that with him. Never want to do that with him again.

"I've never felt like this about anyone before either. But I love Cascade Point. The people here are my family. I don't think I could ever move away."

Lachlan takes my hand and kisses my palm. "No one's asking you to," he says gently. "I get it now. This town, with all its quirks and funny people, is a part of you. It's never been an option in my mind that you would leave this place."

His words soothe me. Because Lachlan Chase Brighton really does see me. Really does *get* me. And that's what makes this next part so scary.

"But I can't ask you to leave your life in LA either." I suck in a breath. "I know how much your job means to you, how much you love your city things. I want you to be happy, Lachlan."

"*You* make me happy," he responds immediately. But he looks out into the dark, and his jaw clenches as he thinks. "I'll just have to work something out."

Hope threatens to blossom in my stomach, but I try not to let it take hold. Not yet. Not before I'm very sure of what I *think* Lachlan is saying.

"What do you mean?"

"I want to be with you, Luce. And I'll find a way to make it happen."

I press a kiss to his lips, and he responds in kind, cradling my face as a veritable shower of fireworks goes off behind my eyelids. Because yes, as corny and cheesy and clichéd as that sounds, it's the only way to describe what happens when Lachlan kisses me.

He goes on to lay soft kisses along the line of my jaw and down the side of my neck, sending shivers across my skin. I turn my head to meet his lips again, but we feel almost too disconnected. I want to be closer to him.

I turn on his lap so I'm facing him, wrapping my arms

242

behind his neck so our bodies are flush together. One big hand finds its place on my hip, and the other cradles the back of my head. I pull him ever closer, deepening the kiss, loving the feel of his stubble on my skin.

This kiss is somehow better than all the ones before.

Because this one feels like a promise. A giving of myself to him. A want to show him that I'll always try to make him feel as happy and safe as he makes me feel.

He kisses me back as though to make the same promise.

It's enough to fill me with so much care and emotion, I feel breathless.

Lachlan kisses me tenderly, passionately, *thoroughly* before he breaks away, releasing my lips to press another kiss on my throat. I lay my forehead against his, and he massages one hand against the back of my neck.

"Jordy told me tonight that our house is fixed."

Lachlan doesn't stop his gentle caress. "Yeah?"

"She's moving back in tonight. I probably should, too."

"If that's what you want."

I pull back to look at him. "I don't necessarily *want* to," I say slowly. "I've loved having you as a roommate. But I think it might be the best idea. If we're going to try to be together for real, we probably shouldn't start out living together."

"Agreed." Lachlan laughs. "Imagine what Louis would have to say to me about that one. Want me to help you pack?"

"Maybe. Yes." I frown. "Turns out I brought over a *lot* of stuff."

Lachlan laughs. "Why does that not surprise me?"

And so, while Lachlan gathers the stuff I left in the living room, I head upstairs and get to packing my clothes, shoes, and various school art projects. Soon enough, he's upstairs with me, helping me shove everything into bags, all the while muttering about *clutter* and *mess* and *chaos* with a grumpy little smile on his face.

Sometime around midnight, the last bag is packed and Lachlan collapses across my bed. I can't help but fall down next to him.

"How do you have so much stuff?" Lachlan mutters tiredly.

I yawn. "It's not 'stuff'. It's prized possessions and valuables."

"So, that weird spider head scratcher thing is a *valuable* now."

"You mean my solar system? It absolutely is valuable." I'm tracing my fingers down his arm when I notice something. "Hey," I say softly. "You got your watch back."

I feel him smile against my hair. "Wyatt gave it back to me tonight. It's working like a dream. So, I guess it *is* possible to get what you want here."

"Imagine that."

His chest rises and falls beneath my cheek as he laughs. Then, he winds his arms up around me and squeezes me against him. "I'm glad I'm here," he whispers, so quietly at first that I don't know if he meant for me to hear it.

"I am, too," I reply anyway, my eyelids growing heavy. "But I should really get going."

"Mmm. I'll drive you."

And there and then, we fall asleep, cuddled up with each other, just as we unknowingly did a couple weeks ago at The Last Stance Motel.

31

LACHLAN

The day after Lucy and I have another totally unexpected one-bed sleepover, I drop her (and her things) at her rowhouse nice and early, promising to pick her up after her school day.

Then, I'm off to the library again, where Darnell and I work through the morning, putting the finishing touches on the space. The library looks great, if I do say so myself—cozy and quiet and welcoming, with a (partially soundproofed) play area for younger kids and several little reading nooks.

But even as we're working, I'm consumed with thoughts of Lucy Mary-Ann Summers and the absolute spell she has me under. A spell I very much never want to break.

Because if she's Princess Belle, I want to be the Beast.

Though, ideally, the Beast at the end of the movie with significantly less body hair and claws and the like.

Lunchtime rolls around, and the reason I know this is because I have my wristwatch back. Wyatt gave it to me at book club last night, totally fixed. It's kind of amazing how people here just... make do with what they can.

There's definitely a lot more to this town than meets the eye. A lot more than I ever expected.

I head to the fire station to have lunch with Beau. We've had

245

lunch a couple times lately, and I find I quite like spending time with my younger brother.

Today is the first time we're having lunch at the fire station, and as I walk into the brick building, I'm totally blown away.

Because the Cascade Point Fire Hall looks less like a workspace and more like a compulsive hoarding house.

It's *chaotic*. There's paperwork scattered on every surface, trinkets and random tools and parts of machinery lying on chairs and worn couches and across the floor. There's an (empty, I hope?) birdcage hung above a table with a towering stack of donut boxes (also empty, I hope), and the fire trucks barely squeeze into the garage in a row.

"Hey, Lockie!" Beau shouts from somewhere I can't even see. Maybe behind the towering stack of boxes?

"Beau, this place is a mess."

My brother laughs a booming laugh, and I finally see him approaching me from the direction of the fire trucks. He's undone the top of his coveralls and wrapped the arms around his waist, and is wearing only a tank top base layer. Which is fitting seeing as the inside of the fire station is toasty.

Like, *really* toasty.

"Yeah, it's been better in here. Doesn't help that the furnace is broken, so we're all sweating our faces off. Chief's trying to get ahold of Benny to fix it now."

"Benny's in high demand around here," I mutter as I take off my jacket and my sweater, placing them on the back of one of the chairs that isn't totally buried beneath a mountain of crap. "Can I take a look?"

Beau's eyebrows pop. "At the furnace? Knock yourself out."

He leads me down a hallway to a boiler room and points out the furnace. After a couple minutes spent examining the machine, I figure out what the problem is, and Beau obediently hands me tools as I get to work fixing it.

Within minutes, there's a distinctive clunk as the furnace shuts down.

In the far, far distance, a chorus of whoops and cheers and hollers erupts.

By the time we arrive back in the main room, there's a crowd of firefighters gathered together, talking amongst themselves. A familiar tiny woman with her coveralls undone over a navy t-shirt blasts towards my brother and me.

Well, "flip-flops" more like.

Surely it's a safety hazard for firefighters to wear rainbow flip-flops on shift?!

"Was that you guys?" Jordy looks between us, her blonde ponytail whipping back and forth. "You shut off the heat?"

"That was Lockie."

"And not a moment too soon." Jordy shakes her head before elbowing my brother in the side. "This one was mere *moments* away from stripping his shirt off, and trust me, no one wants to see that."

"That is a bold-faced lie, Jo," my brother shoots back. "And no need to hate on me just 'cuz I've been keeping up with our pushup challenge while you've been flagging."

"Have not."

"Have *so* been."

Jordy rolls her eyes. "Okay, fine. I *might* have fallen behind a little last week. But between having to sleep straight as a board on Celeste's tiny air mattress, and having Jake end things with me, I haven't been feeling my best."

"Psh. You should be sleeping plenty soundly now that that tool is out of your life."

Jordy gives my brother the flattest glare ever.

"What?" he asks. "He was a loser, and you deserve much better."

"Thanks. I think."

Beau wraps her in a headlock. "My best friend deserves the

247

best. After all, she spends most of her time with *me*. Can't have you taking a step down." Within seconds, Jordy expertly maneuvers out of the headlock and twists Beau's arm behind his back. He raises a hand, wiggles out of her grasp, and kisses his bicep. "See, Jo? Your loss."

Jordy turns red and opens her mouth to retort when a firefighter I vaguely recognize from book club (thankfully) walks up to us and interrupts. Brett, I believe his name was.

"*You're* the one who turned the heat off?" Maybe-Brett pats me on the back.

"No way!" A firefighter I don't know steps up out of nowhere. "The guy from LA? Thanks, dude."

"Beau, you gotta invite this guy to Stu's party," someone else says.

Soon enough, Beau and I are engulfed in a sea of firefighters thanking us for stopping them from melting.

It takes a few minutes for us to break away so we can finally have lunch, and I take a relieved seat at the table in the break room, clearing space for the burgers I got from the diner.

"Well, you just earned yourself more brownie points." Beau smirks. "You're really starting to fit in 'round here, city boy."

I roll my eyes. "Ha, ha."

Beau opens the wrapping around his burger and takes a sniff. Even from where I'm sitting, I can smell the melting cheddar. "It's nice to have you here, Lockie. You'll be missed when you go back to LA."

He takes a ginormous bite of his burger, and I flash back to the conversation Lucy and I had on the porch swing last night.

Truth is, I hadn't really considered the fact that I'm meant to be leaving this town soon—and how that will impact Lucy—until she brought it up last night.

But of course, it's something I need to consider. *We* need to consider.

"What if I don't go back?" I say slowly.

248

Beau stops mid-bite and stares at me with his brows raised. "You're thinking of staying?"

I purse my lips. "I have to see if I can figure something out with work."

Beau's eyes twinkling. "I guess I have Lucy to thank for this change of heart?"

I think back to last night, sleeping with Lucy in my arms. *Properly* sleeping, because for the first time in a long, long time, I didn't wake up at all during the night. I loved her rhythmic breathing, the way she snuffled, her occasional snore. Loved the way her sleeping face was so peaceful, eyelashes brushing her cheeks...

"She's a big part of it, sure," I say with a nod. "But honestly, this town is kinda growing on me. And Graham and Anna-May are getting older. Their house could definitely use some work, and you don't seem like the handy type."

"Nope. A handyman, I am not." Beau shakes his head. "But you're really thinking of keeping your job *and* being here? Bit of a commute to make every day. Not great for the environment." He takes another huge bite of burger. "You work at a tech company. Don't you have a fancy 'work from away' setup or something?"

"Remote working, you mean. Some people at my company do that." *Including Dee.* "One of my best employees works from Mirror Valley, actually."

"Small world. Well, why don't *you* do it?"

"I wish it were that simple." I frown. "My boss likes having the ability to call me into his office on a whim."

"Duh. I'm sure there's teleconferencing or hologramming or whatever."

I have to chuckle, but I realize he's right. Zoom exists for this exact reason. "That *does* seem like the best option right now. The best way to keep my job *and* be here with Lucy. She's good for me, and I think I'm good for her. She's changed my life."

249

I trail off into silence, and Beau smirks. "Dang, dude. You've got it *bad*."

I eye my younger brother carefully. "And what about you? I know you said you and Jordy are just friends, but nothing's ever happened between you two?"

Holy. Look at me. Asking for *gossip* about other peoples' *love lives*.

Can't help but be curious, though.

In answer to my question, Beau abruptly chokes on his food and then lets out a loud bark of a laugh.

"Alright," I say with a roll of my eyes. "Point taken."

Beau wipes his hands on a napkin. "Well, Graham and Anna-May will be happy to hear that you're thinking of staying here. And I guess I'm kinda happy about it as well. I know we weren't exactly close growing up, but I guess I've missed having you around."

"Same." I nod at my brother, then smirk humorlessly. "I know it wasn't exactly easy to be close to me. In retrospect, I think I kept you all at arm's length."

"Why?"

"I felt like the black sheep of the family, the odd one out..." My brow furrows as I try to vocalize it. I've never said these words out loud, have barely allowed myself to think them. "Not only because of our age difference, but because Darla's not my biological mom."

Beau looks perplexed. "And?"

"Well, I wasn't *born* a Brighton." I sweep a hand through my hair. "And I guess I felt like an imposter. Felt I didn't earn or deserve the Brighton name."

My brother looks like he wants to say something, but I shake my head. "It felt like Graham and Anna-May knew it, too. It was the only explanation I could think of for the way we all grew apart."

"What happened between our parents and grandparents

250

wasn't because of you, dumb-dumb."

I blink, lost for words given his statement, but also because of that wildly immature and uncalled for nickname he just bestowed upon me. "Well, I know the drama wasn't *entirely* about Dad and me, but—"

"No." Beau shakes his head. "It was about Mom."

"*Darla?*"

Beau nods, swirling the bottle of Coke I got for him and making bubbles rise to the surface. "Anna-May and Graham got drunk off some mulled wine a couple Christmases ago and gave me the full story." He sighs. "Basically, when Mom was back in town for that brief visit and she started dating Dad, Anna-May and Graham initially didn't think much of it. But then, they met Dad, and they met *you,* and they fell in love with you."

He glances at me with a brow raised. "Which I still can't understand to this day."

I whack my brother in the arm, and he laughs.

"They didn't trust Mom. They knew how flighty she was. So, that's why they pressured her to end things sooner rather than later. Tried to stop her from breaking yours and Dad's— and I guess, *their*—hearts."

My brows rise as I take in this information.

"Of course," Beau continues, "Mom married Dad and stayed committed to her family, and ended up having Marcus and me—you're welcome, world—but the damage was done. Mom was hurt that her parents thought so little of her, and that never ended up going away. And so, we moved to Colorado, and Anna-May and Graham had to fight to see us."

There's a rearranging of sorts happening in my brain as puzzle pieces fall into place. A different place. "So, it wasn't about me not belonging in the family."

"Nope. It's 'cuz Mom was such a wild child." He snorts. "*Mom.* Can you imagine?"

"Marcus had to get it from somewhere."

251

"True. Anyway, that's the full story, not that you asked for it or wanted it—"

"I did." I cut him off quickly. "I just... can't believe it. Can't believe I never saw it that way."

I continue circling my own drink around the bottle. Beau's explanation of the past does make more sense than my own long-held assumptions, given my history with Anna-May and Graham. The way they always seemed so accepting of me, though I was quick to brush it off. The way they called me "grandson" and not "step-grandson."

The way, on this short visit, they never once made me feel like I wasn't welcome.

My heart swells with some sort of emotion. Not bad, but not good either.

"Well. That was touchy-feely enough for one week," Beau says chirpily, rising to a stand. "You good, bro?"

"I'm good. Thanks."

He shrugs. "I'd say anytime, but I think the heat in here is just making me extra sappy."

I laugh and pat Beau on the shoulder as we leave the break room. In the weeks that I've been here, I've gained a new respect and appreciation for my brother. I have to admire his strength and honesty. I'm looking forward to getting to know him again.

"So, tell me about Stu's party," I say.

"Oh, yeah. It's happening this weekend and most of the town will be here."

"Dancing around all the crap, I presume?"

Beau laughs. "No, we're going to try and clean up as much as we can before the party."

"You're gonna need all the help you can get," I mutter as we step into the main room. Frick, did it get even messier in here since we went for lunch? "I've finished up at the library, so I can give you guys a hand."

"Thanks, man, that'd be awesome. It's Stu's retirement

252

party—he's leaving the force after fifty years of service. Can you believe that? *Fifty*. That's about as many pushups as I can do in one sitting."

I roll my eyes tiredly. "Jordy's not here to hear your humble-brag, dude."

Beau laughs. "Good point. Where is that little monstrosity anyway?"

He marches off in the direction of the fire trucks, and I'm about to leave the fire hall when my phone dings with a voice message.

From *Dee*, of all people.

I haven't heard from her since getting to Cascade Point, barring a few check-in messages when I first arrived. Dee hasn't reached out to me once—was probably trying to give me my vacation.

"Hey, Lachlan." Dee's voice is at once so familiar and so foreign. It feels like a lifetime ago that I last spoke with her. A different life. "I hope you're enjoying Cascade Point. It's been a week since I heard from you so I'm thinking that maybe something's going well and you're actually *enjoying* your time off?! A girl can dream, can't she?" She lets out a quick laugh. "Anyway, I didn't want to bother you, but I thought you should know that Mike called me just now."

Mike called *Dee*?

That's odd. My boss normally only communicates directly with me or the other VPs.

The message continues: "He said that he's been working on a project lately and wants me to touch base with him about some stats ASAP. Any idea what that might be about?" She hurriedly adds, "If not, no worries and please enjoy the rest of your vacation. KByeeeeee."

I frown at my darkened phone screen, my gut churning a little.

The optimistic part of me—which, conveniently, sounds like

253

Lucy—says that he's just respecting my time off. Deferring to Dee while I'm on my vacation.

But Mike tends to loop me into all of his projects, whether they have something to do with me (and my teams) or not. And I know, for a fact, that there isn't anything we're working on that would require stats at the moment.

What project could he possibly be working on?

After a moment, I brush off the questions and put my phone back in my pocket.

Mike's been my boss for a decade. We've been through thick and thin with this company, and I trust him implicitly. He had to have a good reason to call Dee.

He'll touch base with me, loop me in, whenever he needs to.

32

LUCY

The final bell rings, and for the first time ever, I've packed up faster than my students.

Olivia clearly notices this because, on her way out of my classroom to meet her big brother Jensen, her backpack sparkling under fluorescent lights, she says, "Going to meet your man-friend, Miss Summers?"

Beth appears out of nowhere, similar backpack in hand. "Uhm, isn't he Miss Summers's *boyfriend*?" she asks.

Olivia shakes her head, the obvious authority on such matters. "My mommy says that the word 'boyfriend' sounds like high school, so she always talks about Miss Summers and her man-friend."

This little debate over my relationship status catches the attention of River and Shawn, and the boys are looking over with curiosity as well.

Great. My classroom of five-year-olds is now debating whether I have a "boyfriend" or a "*man-friend*."

"He is *too* her man-friend," Olivia insists. "And yesterday, Mommy said it's about time that Miss Summers found someone 'cuz she was starting to look like a real cat lady."

Thanks, Gina.

But I mean, I *do* love my knits. And I like cats.

"Mommy also says he must be a good man-friend because he always orders her favorite drink at the cafe."

Ah-ha!!

Thank you, Olivia, for spilling the beans on the fact that Lachlan Chase Brighton really *does* love a cinnamon mocha. Which I happen to know is Gina's favorite drink.

I'll have to pick one up for him at some point. Surprise him.

Now that he's said he wants to stay here in Cascade, I feel like we have *time*.

As soon as the last child has been gathered up by her father, I practically run out of the school, bursting through the front doors.

And there he is, at the end of the sidewalk.

Lachlan's standing just outside of his car, as promised, and is speaking with Gabby. Well, it looks like Gabby is speaking *at* him and Lachlan's wearing a "do tell" expression that I can see, from here, is taking some effort on his part.

I can't help but stop and stare for a few moments, noticing the easy way Lachlan smiles. The tension that's released in his shoulders sometime during his stay in Cascade.

My grumpy Superman.

My gorgeous, grouchy man with a gooey cinnamon center.

And he looks *so good* here. He's My Lachlan, and I almost can't remember City Lachlan anymore.

I approach them, and Lachlan and I say our goodbyes to Gabby and get into his SUV. The rain is constant but light today —the wind is the real problem. Especially seeing as I stupidly chose to wear a skirt.

"Thanks for picking me up." I turn to Lachlan as we drive out of the parking lot. "I spent the entire outdoor recess time with my arms plastered at my sides, moving around in a very sexy, teeter-tottery crab walk. Didn't really want to have to do that all the way home."

256

Lachlan glances at me, his eyes dazed. "What?"

"Because of my skirt," I explain and then add, "Okay, I *am* wearing fleece-lined tights so it's not like I'd fully flash anyone. But still, it's the thought that counts."

"Thought that counts."

I peer at him. His jaw's clenched, his brow dark, like he's deep in thought. "What's on your mind?" I ask.

He gives his head a shake. Seems to return to the present moment. "Sorry, Princess. It's nothing important." He corrects himself. "I mean, it *isn't* important, but it *is* on my mind."

"Do you want to talk about it?"

His brow darkens for a brief moment, jaw clenching. But then, he looks at me, and all at once, his expression softens. Relaxes.

"No. Because right now, there's something else I want to do. Somewhere I want to take you."

"Hey, I'm just your Passenger Princess. I'll go wherever you want to go."

Lachlan takes my hand and kisses my palm, and we get on the road outside of town. To my surprise, we're headed inland, this time.

"Where are we going?" I ask.

"It's a surprise."

I laugh. "Another one? You're constantly surprising me, Lachlan."

"Good." He flashes me a smile. "Can't have you thinking I'm predictable."

"I would never dare."

The road takes us uphill through a forest of dense evergreens. It occurs to me that I've never been out this way. Country music plays quietly through the car's sound system as Lachlan and I chat, his hand wrapped around mine.

We reach some sort of summit, and Lachlan pulls the car

into a lot off the side of the road. The rain's stopped, though the sky's still shaded and gray.

Lachlan heads to the trunk, where he grabs a blanket and a canvas bag, and then comes around to open my door for me.

"I wanted to try out the whole dating thing again." He takes my hand. "This time, with a woman I *really* want to take out."

"Lachlan Chase... is this a date?"

"It absolutely is."

I can't stop the smile that breaks across my face as I hop out. Together, we walk down a dirt trail bordered with trees leading away from the parking lot. The dense brush eventually opens up to reveal a viewing platform.

"Wow," I say under my breath as a beautiful vista unfolds before us.

We're at the top of a hill overlooking the ocean and the islands just north of Cascade Point. Whitish-gray clouds hang between points of land, draping low over the ocean, and the sky is so perfectly reflected on the surface of the water, the entire scene feels moody and ethereal.

"I've never brought anyone here before."

Lachlan's voice is quiet, and I turn to see him looking straight at me. His eyes are hooded and vulnerable, and they light a fire deep in my core.

"Those summers that I'd visit Graham and Anna-May, I'd come here when things were becoming too much. For some reason, this place was always deserted, so I'd come when I wanted to think. And for the quiet. You have *no idea* how noisy Beau and Marcus could be."

He lays out the blanket across the platform. We haven't talked much about his family or his childhood, and I'd be lying if I said I wasn't curious. So curious to know everything about this man.

"Did you have to come here a lot?" I ask quietly.

258

"Pretty often. There was a lot I had to think about. A lot I wanted to get away from."

He sets down a couple pillows I recognize from the porch furniture, and I sit down. He hands me a Thermos, keeping one for himself, and I sip at my hot cocoa. He then pulls some of my favorite foods out of his canvas bag—cookies, chips, a burger from the Beachside Diner... items I can't even remember telling him I loved.

This man, I tell you.

We settle in, and I want to ask him more about his past, but he says, "I had a really interesting chat with Beau earlier today."

"Yeah? About what?" I grab my favorite bag of chips and tear open the top.

"Well, I asked about he and Jordy."

My eyes widen. "And?!"

"Nothing. He laughed in my face."

I roll my eyes, crunching into a chip. "I get the same reaction whenever I bug Jordy about it."

Lachlan shakes his head with a chuckle, but then goes quiet again. He's staring out at the view with his brows drawn together. "Remember that photo I left for you?"

"Has Jordy been giving Beau a hard time about it?"

Lachlan gives me an amused glance. "Jordy saw it?"

I shrug bashfully. "I put it in my favorite handy-dandy hiding place, but I should've known that she'd know to check the flour jar."

Lachlan laughs. "Well, that photo was taken here in Cascade Point during one of my visits in the summer." A small smile touches his lips. "It was one of the only days I remember being genuinely happy here. Maybe that's why I kept the photo all these years."

I bite the inside of my cheek. "I should give it back to you. Give you the memory back."

"No, I'm glad you have it. Especially now that I've recon-

259

nected with my grandparents—we can create some new memories." He takes a breath in. "I'm assuming you know that my parents and grandparents don't get along."

I nod.

"I always thought it had something to do with me and my dad. Obviously, you know that my dad married Darla Brighton, and so we became a part of the Brighton family, even though I'm not biologically related to Graham and Anna-May."

"I know," I say gently, wondering where he's going with this.

"Well. That weighed on me a lot growing up."

My eyebrows raise. "Did Graham and Anna-May make you feel—"

"No," he says quickly. "They seemed to accept me so easily, so readily. But you know as well as I do that people lie." A humorless smirk appears on his lips. "I used to think it was fake. A front. When I got older, I went to the only place I could think to go."

I frown. "LA...?"

"I had it in my mind that I could make something of myself there. I dropped my last name, telling myself it was because 'Lachlan Chase' looked better, but I think, deep down, it was because I didn't want to be tied to anyone or anything. I wanted to build a life for myself, by myself. Build up my *own* name. Stop feeling like... I'd taken something that wasn't mine."

He glares out at the scenery, but I can see the pain behind his eyes. It's everything I can do not to wrap my arms around him.

"So, I made a name for myself," he continues, "was successful all on my own. I worked, and worked, and tried, and sacrificed, and kept myself entirely on one track. And I did it. All by myself."

I catch my breath. My heart feels so much for this big, strong man with his tough exterior. Beneath it, he's one of the

260

sweetest humans I've ever known. Selfless, helpful, communicative and kind.

And there he was, feeling unseen and undeserving. Feeling like he had to do this life alone.

"I thought I did it, thought I had the life I wanted... until I came back here." His jaw clenches. "Now, being in Cascade again, seeing Graham and Anna-May and Beau, I feel like one of them. Feel like I belong. I thought being away from my family was the only way I could be my best self, but I think I might actually be my best self here. With you, and with them."

"I get it," I say quietly, thinking of my mother. Of my own chosen family in this town.

"I held onto the assumption for so long that I was the problem, that my inclusion caused the rift in my family. I was blinded to what was actually happening: Anna-May and Graham *do* see me as one of their own. And I've been a fool not to let them into my life sooner..."

He trails off.

And now, I can't help but reach over and take his big hand in both of mine, giving it a gentle squeeze. "You are *not* a fool, Lachlan," I say passionately. "Not at all. You are one of the most incredible people I've ever met. I'm sorry that you felt alone, felt like an outsider and an imposter in your own family." I shake my head sadly. "I can't imagine how painful that must have been."

He doesn't respond, just stares out to the horizon.

"Did I ever tell you what happened when my dad left?"

Lachlan gives his head a shake.

"My dad was from Cascade Point. He grew up here but never seemed all that happy here. I guess he often spoke about wanting to move elsewhere, but just... never did. And then, he met Mom, and they got married, they had me. But then, they started fighting. A lot. Constantly. And Dad left. Said that he felt stuck here. Felt stuck with..." I catch a breath. "Felt stuck with *us*."

261

He looks at me, anger in his eyes, but I turn away.

"Mom didn't tell me this until years later, of course, after I practically forced it out of her. I always wondered why my dad never came to visit and why he went off to Portland to start a new family." I bite down on my lower lip. "I was so upset. So hurt."

Lachlan's arm is suddenly around my waist, pulling me closer to his side.

"I always believed that people can't change, can't be someone they aren't, but you broke that rule, and continue to break it. You surprise me so much, every day, revealing a new part of yourself that I can't help but fall for." Tears begin to gather behind my eyes. "And *that's* why you're incredible to me, Lachlan. You're constantly doing something I thought was impossible."

He lets out a deep chuckle. "And here I was thinking that *you're* incredible because you can go through all that with your parents and come out like... well, like *you*." I meet his eyes. "Lucy, I can't even describe what you've done to me. You've pushed me to see that I want a *life* versus just living. Does that make sense?"

I cuddle into his side, letting his words wash over me. His words, and also his actions. Lachlan isn't just the guy who seems cheery and optimistic and "perfect" on a dating app. He's the man who sticks with me, who tells me the truth, and who I want to tell the truth to. Forever.

"What're you doing this weekend?" Lachlan asks gently, his deep voice a rumble.

"Hm?"

"It's Stu's retirement party at the fire station. And seeing as, according to nearly everyone in this town, you are my *woman-friend*, I think it's of vital importance that we make an appearance."

I sit up to look at him. "*Woman-friend?*"

262

"Well, I'm not going to call you my girlfriend. We're not fifteen and drawing hearts on each others' desks in homeroom."

"I *guess* this was a pretty good date," I say slowly, teasing him. "Actually, this might be the best date I've ever been on. So yes, I would very much like to come to the party as your girl-friend. Woman-friend. Whatever."

He smiles and then traces his nose down my cheek, sending an electric thrill down my spine. "How about you just stay my princess?"

His words melt my insides. "Yup," I manage on a croak. "That works fine for me."

He finally presses his lips to mine, his hands tenderly cupping my face. I get lost in those fireworks behind my eyelids again for a moment, before I pull back. "Hang on. Do you even know Stu?"

"Sure I do. Great guy. Been working as a firefighter for the past fifty years. Pretty tall—"

"Like, 5'6"."

"—with glasses—"

"Nope."

"—has a long, braided goatee."

I snort with laughter at that. "Well. I'd love to meet *this* Stu you're talking about."

Lachlan tugs me back towards him so I'm toppled against his chest again. "You will, Princess. We have all the time in the world."

33

LACHLAN

The day of Stu's retirement party is a day like any other, except for one very big important thing.

The sun's shining.

And I mean, *really* shining. Like, the clouds are fewer and farther between (they pass over every two minutes as opposed to the usual twenty seconds), and the sidewalk and roads are starting to dry, creating a patchwork of dark and light cement.

It's a day fit for celebration. All the more because I'm entering the party with my girl by my side.

Now, I squeeze Lucy's hand, and she smiles up at me. Her aquatic eyes sparkle in the sunlight. "You ready?" I ask her.

"Ready for what?"

"Our grand debut as a couple."

"Oh, honey," she says, adjusting the collar of my shirt. Her fingers graze the skin at the base of my neck, and it's all I can do not to wrap my arms around her and tug her closer. "You can't honestly think that *this* is our grand debut? From what Jordy's told me, people were pairing us up as early as the first book club."

She places her palms flat on my chest and gives me the cutest little blink that I think is meant to be a wink.

I let my eyes drop down her body again, taking her in. She's wearing an orange knit shirt with a white trim and buttons down the front, along with blue jeans that hug her curves and are kind of driving me wild. And she's got her orange bandana tied up in her hair.

I give the bandana a little tug. "I just want to make sure that everyone knows you're mine."

Her eyes spark, and I take her hand again.

Together, we step into the fire station, entering what feels like a pressure cooker of heat and conversation and loud music and food smells.

I spent the last few days helping Beau and the other firefighters clean up the place. Okay, it was more of a frantic "shove everything into any available closet" kind of thing. I'd love to see this place get a proper deep clean one day, but that certainly wasn't going to happen before the party.

"Yoohoo! Lachlan, Lucy!"

I look to see none other than my grandmother charging at us through the crowd, her red spectacles balanced on her nose. She's wearing a long polka-dot dress with sleeves (more of a robe, actually) and a feathered headband.

"You're looking lovely this evening, Anna-May," Lucy says with a smile.

"Thank you, dear. I was looking for my silver pashmina to complete the outfit, but it seems it was having a bit of a tete-a-tete with a beaded scarf that will require some detangling." Anna-May tuts before her eyes zero in on Lucy taking my hand.

I pull her closer—making it obvious where we stand (AKA together)—and Anna-May's head swivels up towards me. "It's about time!"

I look down at Lucy. "What can I say, Anna-May? You were right."

"Psh. I saw this coming from a mile away. And am I ever happy to see it finally come to fruition. For *both* of you."

265

I'm not quite sure what possesses me to do what I do next—maybe the emotionality of the last couple days, or seeing my own family "mess" in a whole new light—but I step forward and wrap Anna-May in a hug.

She seems surprised at first, and then relaxes into my arms.

When we step away, she clears her throat. "Now, I just need to find your grandfather." She swivels around on her heels. "Graham! Graham? Where are you, silly man?"

"Over here, love!" comes the answer from somewhere in the direction of the food tables.

"Grandpa's here as well?" I ask.

"The man's made a rather speedy recovery." Anna-May smiles. "Though it might have been partially hastened due to the fact that I've stopped stocking the house with various sugared items, and he saw this afternoon as an opportunity, of sorts."

"It did sound like he was over by the cakes," Lucy confirms with a nod.

"My goodness." Anna-May sighs with despair. "It's just one thing after another, I tell you!"

With that, she swoops her robe (dress?) around herself and marches off in the direction of the offending cakes.

Lucy and I turn back towards the festivities, which are currently in full swing. I got to know a few of the firefighters while helping clean the place, and I wave to the guys now. Stu's in the center of their group, a bejeweled crown perched on his bald head as he booms out a laugh.

There's a tap on my shoulder, and I turn to face Cascade's Benny of all trades... currently dressed in a full three-piece suit with his hair slicked back.

"Ben, you're looking sharp!" Lucy tells him.

"Even I'm impressed." I give him a wink.

"Have to look good for potential clients," Benny announces

266

boisterously, waving a hand before taking a sip of his beer. "So, I hear I have *you* to thank for saving the day."

He's staring right at me, and I'm drawing a blank. I glance at Lucy, and she looks as lost as I feel.

Benny then offers a gap-toothed smile. "You fixed the furnace here the other day."

"Oh, yes. Tried to." I shrug. "It's been awhile since I worked with furnaces, but it seemed to do the trick."

"Sure did. It was actually an impressive job. And you got it done quickly." Benny's eyes dance. "And I heard you helped Darnell with the touch-ups at the library and have fixed parts of Lucy's cottage. It seems that Lachlan Brighton might have some skill and talent in repairs and home improvement."

"He sure does," Lucy pipes in before I can say anything, grasping my bicep. "He could be the secret third brother on that *Property Brothers* show, I swear. He's seriously good at all that fixing and repairing and maintaining and renovating stuff. A wunderkind, if you will."

I have to laugh. "That's a little much, Luce."

But Benny isn't laughing. Instead, he peers up at me. "Well, I could certainly use skills like yours around here. If you're planning on sticking around..."

I smile at Lucy. "I am."

"Great. In that case, give me a call sometime tomorrow. But not after 5pm, as I'll be running to Seattle for a delivery. And not before 3pm, seeing as I promised Agnes I'd help her out with the llamas. So, really, anytime between that."

"I'm not really looking for a job, Ben."

"Well. Offer's open anyway."

The man disappears into the crowd, and I'm about to take Lucy's hand again when my phone goes off in my pocket.

I check the screen.

It's... *Mike*.

267

Maybe he's finally looping me in on whatever he called Dee about.

"What's up?" Lucy asks, peering over my shoulder. She deflates a little. "Oh."

I reject the call.

Because, honestly, I don't really care what the new project is. Whatever it is, it can wait.

I put my phone back in my pocket and look at Lucy, who's staring at me with her eyebrows raised. "What?" I ask her.

"You're ignoring a call from your boss?"

"I'd rather be here right now with you, enjoying this party."

Such words would have never left my mouth a couple weeks ago. I also never would've declined Mike's call a couple weeks ago.

Guess Lucy was right. Certain things *can* change. Or maybe, it's not so much that I changed, but that I came back to myself and who I truly am. Because that's what being in Cascade has done to me.

Who could've guessed that I'd find myself again—the best version of myself—in a tiny, rundown cottage in middle-of-nowhere Washington State?

My phone rings again, and I ignore it. I'll call Mike back later. Because after he fills me in on his news, I need to tell him *my* news and pitch the whole "remote working" thing to him. And I'm certainly not going to get into that conversation right now.

I turn to take both of Lucy's hands in mine. "Where do you want to start, Princess? Food, drinks, dancing, catching up with our good friend Stu?"

"I'll grab us a snack, and then maybe we can find Jordy." Lucy gets up on her tiptoes to scope out the firefighters. "She's probably lost deep in that group somewhere."

I press a kiss to the top of her head. "I'll be here."

As Lucy makes her way through the bustling crowd, I look

around the room. I spot Louis and Mabel and all the usual book club attendees, along with some other people I've met in passing. Everyone's mingling, laughing, having a good time. Ajay catches my eye and gives me a wave, which I return.

It's only just occurring to me that I'm happy.

Happy like I was the day we took that childhood photo I gave Lucy. Happy in a way I never was in LA, where I thought —firmly believed—that I *was* happy. But whatever I'm feeling now, whatever Cascade has done to me, it's on an entirely different level.

There's a tap on my shoulder, and I smirk, already knowing that it has to be my brother. He's the only one I haven't seen in this crowd.

"Hey, B..."

My voice dies in my throat as I turn to face someone who is very much *not* Beau.

It's my boss. CEO of SparksFly.

Mike Niles.

34

LACHLAN

Mike looks me up and down, dark eyes pausing on my casual jeans and polo shirt.

"Lachlan. What's this place *done* to you?"

I can't speak past the shock that's blocking my throat.

And all of a sudden, Mike is laughing. "Well, seems my surprise was pretty effective. I was hoping to start this off with a phone call, but *someone* screened my calls and ruined the plan." He frowns pensively. "I suppose it's fair enough to ignore your boss's calls while on vacation, even though I do pay you a generous bonus each year with the hope that you'd pick up."

He smacks me on the shoulder, and that's all I need to come back to life.

"Mike," I choke out. "What... what're you doing here?"

"In this unfortunate excuse for a fire station?" He taps his chin as he looks around. "Seems that there's some sort of party or celebration happening here, and I thought I'd check it out."

"No. What are you doing in Cascade Point?"

"*That* is an excellent question. I have some exciting developments I can finally share with you, Chase, but it's all very hush-hush. Is there anywhere we can speak alone? Somewhere quiet and less chaotic?"

270

He grimaces as Jensen and Ace run by, each precariously balancing plates of cakes and brownies and cookies. Mike's grimace turns into a full scowl when Ace drops a plate and a small dollop of icing lands on his sports jacket.

He scrubs at it furiously, swearing under his breath.

Meanwhile, I'm glad for the boys' distraction, because this is taking me a minute to process. It feels weird—almost wrong—to see my boss here, in my town.

And on that...

I peek my head above the crowd, looking for Lucy. I don't see her. Not by the food, not by the firefighters, not on the dance floor.

"Chase," Mike barks, apparently no longer amused. "Where can we go to talk?"

I look for Lucy once more before ushering Mike outside into the warm sunshine. It's significantly less noisy on the sidewalk.

"Much better," Mike mutters. "Though the sun's a weak little thing here, isn't it? The rain's finally let up in LA, and the beaches are packed. You'll love it when you get back."

How do I tell him?

"Listen, Mike. It's great that you came all this way, but—"

"Did you figure it out? Please tell me you figured it out."

Only then do I realize that Mike is vibrating. Practically bouncing and fidgeting with this weird, gleeful, but almost nervous, energy. Like he's had three too many cups of coffee.

I frown at him. "Figure *what* out?"

"How it all went down." He calms down a little as he peers at me. Seems almost disappointed. "After the news came out a couple days ago, I assumed you'd put two and two together."

"What news?"

Mike gives me and my blank expression a funny look. "Surely you've read about it by now, no?"

I shake my head.

"Guess that explains why you didn't call me. I figured you

271

were waiting for an explanation in person, which is why I came all the way out here." He raises a dark brow, looking around us. "Of course, I wasn't sure exactly *where* you were in this tiny town seeing as you ignored my calls, but I heard the festivities and figured I'd come check this out."

"Okay. You found me," I say, getting impatient. "So, what's going on?"

"SparksFly officially announced their new reality TV dating show."

I blink. "SparksFly is doing a *dating* show?! Since when?"

Mike's strange fidgety energy is back. "It's a new development. One that I'm *very* excited about."

I'm trying to catch up. No, trying to *understand* what in blue blazes my boss is talking about.

Is *this* the project Mike called Dee about? Because if it's something as big as a freaking dating show, as one of the VPs, I should have known about it when the first inkling of an idea was being thrown around.

Not now. Not when it's already been announced.

"So, you see, it all makes sense now," he says gleefully. "It was me."

"What was you?"

Mike rocks back on his heels, dark eyes glittering. "I contacted the podcast. I told them about your bad date with Carly and encouraged them to feature it."

My heart literally stops.

"*You* sent in the story?!" I manage to croak.

"I did. And I gave them more than enough snappy taglines to catch the attention of the broader media. Of course, it also took some extra funding to keep the story at the forefront, but it will be worth it."

I'm completely thrown. "How did you even *know* about my date with Carly?" I ask, wracking my brain for a time when I would have told him about it.

Nothing. Total blank.

Like I said, I don't mix personal and professional.

"I ran into her at that coffee shop you love not long after your date. Sweet girl. Chatty. She was more than happy to tell me all about it. Of course, in exchange for her effusiveness, I insisted that the podcast hosts mention her social media handles and upcoming single."

I shake my head, still not understanding. "But SparksFly was dragged through the mud. We looked like a complete farce."

Mike frowns, and I see the first sign of regret in his features. "That *was* difficult. Those negative, disparaging comments were hard to see, but it had to be done. Burning the forest to grow something new, so to speak. And all press is good press, am I right?"

None of this is making sense, and my frustration is steadily growing. "But why do all this? What does this have to do with a dating show?"

Now, Mike seems almost upset. "This is not the reaction I was expecting from you, Chase. I figured you, of all people, would understand."

"Why would *I* understand you throwing me into the spotlight without my permission? Without any warning or explanation? And it wasn't a good spotlight either."

"Well, in my defense, I didn't think you'd care. You're just like me, Chase. Work is your *life*. You know what your priorities are."

I don't even know how to respond to that. Though it could be because... *he's right.*

Work *was* my life. *Was* my priority.

"You know SparksFly's growth has slowed in recent years," he continues. "We had to get creative. And when I heard about your date, the stars aligned. An idea was born based around someone at *our* company—with its entire portfolio of dating apps and websites—being a bad date himself."

273

He's leaning close to me now. So close that I'm hit with the strong smell of his cologne, and I have to hold back a grimace.

"This scenario was even *more* perfect seeing as you don't date much. There was no risk of anyone coming out of the woodwork and calling B.S. on the whole thing. I couldn't have planned it better if I'd tried."

"Planned what?" My voice is caked with frustration. I'm sick of Mike's freaking riddles. "What on earth are you talking about?!"

He simply smiles at my agitation. "We want to *you* to be the star of the show."

"Excuse me?"

"We want you to be the first male candidate. I have the best hook for it—"

"Wait." I cut off my boss. "You want *me* to participate in a *reality dating show*."

"Star in the first season. Yes."

This is so unhinged, all I can utter is: "Wow."

"Isn't it great? It all came together so perfectly. I've thought of each intricate detail. Because, Chase, you've had your fifteen minutes of fame now with this bad date story. So, when the show is announced and that *you'll* be featured in it, front and center, people will go nuts. It's brilliant marketing."

With those words, I see everything with startling clarity. The puzzle pieces fall into place.

Mike Niles is the type of guy to do cutthroat things for the sake of his company. Even throw his employees—throw *me*— under the bus. Upend my entire life for the sake of... a reality dating show.

And I want to be nothing like him.

In fact, the thought of steamrolling people for the sake of your career—or your company—is now pretty appalling.

I know what I have to do.

What I *want* to do.

274

"Absolutely not." My voice rings out loud and clear.

Mike literally startles at my response, his smile wiped right off his face. "What did you say?"

"I said no. In fact, in what world do you think I would say *yes* to such a thing?"

"I assumed you'd say yes because I believed you were a smart man who could sense a fantastic opportunity." Mike's voice is low. Threatening. But I'm not scared of Mike Niles.

"What, you thought you were doing me a favor?" I shake my head. "Never. I would never be in a dating show. You could not pay me enough money, could not give me enough bonuses. Actually, I should tell you—"

"Chase, let me walk you through it." Mike sounds fully annoyed now. "This is a way for you to gain recognition and visibility on a global scale, you understand?"

Yup. Mike is speaking to me like I'm a child.

"Not to mention, with the way I set everything up with the media, the show *will* be a success. Which, of course, means *you'll* be even more successful. Think of this as a promotion. Plus, I know that you're too busy working to date—which, as your employer, I have to commend you for—so this way, you can date as a *part* of your work. How does that sound?"

Like a wildly messy HR nightmare, but Mike isn't known for considering those types of things.

Nope. That used to fall on me.

"I know how hard you work, how dedicated you are to this company, Chase. I know how much you *want* to succeed. How much you crave it. Can't sleep for thinking of it. This is a once in a lifetime opportunity to push SparksFly to new heights. An advancement for the company, and for you. And I don't have to tell you that it means getting you out of this dump." He grunts. "Come on. You don't want to be stuck in this tiny town with the horrible roads and the old buildings and the rogue, cake-slinging children, do you?"

275

He's saying all the right things, all the right words, for someone who isn't me. Because I'm not that guy anymore.

And, quite frankly, I can't believe I ever *was* that guy.

"Nope. I'm gonna pass," I say firmly. "Because even aside from the fact that what you did is seriously shady—and probably actionable—I could never be on your dating show because I've already met someone incredible. I'm completely, head over heels, out of my mind crazy for her. And honestly, I'm crazy about this tiny town, too."

Mike's mouth drops in shock. But he recovers enough to snort. "I don't really know how to take this, Chase. But I will tell you that you're making a huge mistake. And I hope you understand that I might not be as willing to look in your direction when future promotion opportunities arise."

"Oh, that's no problem at all, Mike." I give him my best smile. A Lucy-level beaming smile, full of sunshine. "Because in case it wasn't obvious, I quit."

35

LUCY

I'm over by the cookies when I hear about the man in the blue sports jacket.

"He just strolled in here, but no one knows who he is," Mabel's saying to Tricia. They're a few paces away from me, standing at the dessert table.

Ears piqued, I pause from sprinkling cinnamon over my plate of chocolate chip cookies and turn towards the two women. "Who's this?"

"A man walked into the fire station a few minutes ago, but I've been asking around and no one's ever seen him before. He hasn't talked to anyone, but he didn't look lost or anything." Mabel shrugs, stacking another gluten-free cookie onto her plate. "Probably just an out-of-towner on his way to Pacific Beach or something. He'll figure himself out soon enough."

"So, no one's asked him what he's doing here at Stu's party?" Tricia asks.

"Not that I'm aware of." Mabel nods at her. "But, take a look. He was standing near the front doors."

Tricia—who is easily the tallest of the three of us—stands on tiptoe and pops her head above the crowd. "He's talking to Lachlan."

277

I frown. "What?"

"Yeah." Tricia shakes her head with a laugh. "Of all the people the guy could have approached in here, of course he went for the newbie. Hopefully he doesn't need directions."

Mabel and Tricia both giggle, and I roll my eyes at them. "Come on, ladies. Lachlan wouldn't be the worst one to ask; he knows the area pretty well. A few days ago, he even brought *me* somewhere new."

"He can bring me anywhere he wants," Tricia practically swoons, before giving me a sheepish look. "Sorry, Luce. I'll stop drooling over your guy now."

I laugh. "It simply wouldn't be right if you weren't fawning over the hot people coming through this town."

She stands on tiptoe again. "I mean, sports jacket guy is pretty nice looking, too. A touch on the older side. Whenever he's done with Lachlan, I might go over there and see if I can be of any assistance." She puts her plate down on the table. "Best I nip to the restrooms and freshen up the lipstick first!"

With that, Tricia trots off, and Mabel lets out a sigh. "Lucy, why don't you get on back to Lachlan? He may actually need help giving pointers to the man; we certainly don't want him to send the poor guy towards Sinkhole Road."

Mabel shudders, and I shiver along with her.

Sinkhole Road is exactly how it sounds—a stretch of road just south of Cascade that's fallen into a spontaneous and highly unusual sinkhole. The area's been roped off for ages, but Maps can sometimes accidentally take you that way, which is a touch alarming.

I take Mabel's advice and hurriedly make my way through the crowd towards where I left Lachlan. Of course, at that very moment, the "Macarena" comes on, and a dance party erupts in the center of the room. Needless to say, it takes me a few minutes to cross.

By the time I get there, Lachlan's gone. There's also no sign of a man in a blue sports jacket.

I frown, looking around with my plate of cookies. Lachlan has disappeared into thin air, which is quite impressive.

That's when I notice that one of the doors is slightly ajar. I approach, intending to close it, but then, I hear voices on the sidewalk just outside.

"I know how hard you work, how dedicated you are to this company, Chase."

Chase? The man must be speaking to Lachlan. He's definitely not from Cascade Point, or he would have referred to him as "Lachlan" or "Lockie."

And he said "this company"... Could this be Lachlan's boss?

Is the man in the blue sports jacket *Mike*?

"I know how much you *want* to succeed. How much you crave it. Can't sleep for thinking of it. This is a once in a lifetime opportunity to push SparksFly to new heights. An advancement for the company, and for you."

There's a pause. I feel strange as his words sink in.

"And I don't have to tell you that it means getting you out of this dump. Come on. You don't want to be stuck in this tiny town with the horrible roads and the old buildings and the rogue, cake-slinging children, do you?"

I can't listen to any more of this.

I step away from the door and place the plate of cookies on a table nearby. My gut is churning uncomfortably as I head back towards the party. There's laughter and dancing and music all around me, but I'm very much no longer in a celebratory mood.

Because this man—Lachlan's boss—is offering him a once in a lifetime opportunity. A way to advance and take a step forward in his career, and I know how much time and effort Lachlan has invested into his work...

My mom always said that you can't force someone to be something they're not. I believed that Lachlan was breaking that rule. He said and did all the right things: mended bridges with his grandparents and with Beau, softened towards our town, even started to fit in.

I started to imagine the life we could create here. Together.

Because it might all be true. Lachlan might, indeed, want to stay here.

But the thing is, even if he *has* changed and he *does* love this town, can I really let him miss out on something spectacular— the level of success that he spent years and years dreaming about, and working towards, and sacrificing so much for?

This opportunity might lead to everything he ever wanted. He'd be making a name for himself. And if it isn't at his fingertips now, with *this* opportunity... well, maybe someday it will be.

I want nothing more than for Lachlan to be happy. I don't want him to ever feel *stuck*. Like my dad did.

But then, something dawns on me. Because this *isn't* the same situation. It's not history repeating itself, like I feared.

My dad *was* stuck here. He spent his whole life in Cascade Point wanting to get out, wanting to leave, but he couldn't.

Lachlan already *has* a life elsewhere. He has the choice to leave or to stay.

And so do I.

So, maybe the kindest, most selfless thing I can do for him is to make *his* choice easier.

I grab my coat and dash out the back door of the fire station.

36

LACHLAN

Sometime after the third "You can't be serious!" and the fifth derisive snort, Mike is finally on his way.

But as he gets into his rented Mustang convertible without a glance back, all I feel is... relief. Immense relief. Like I've just pulled a splinter from my finger. A splinter I didn't even realize was there, aching.

Now, I walk to the fire station without a single glance back. I'm only looking forward to seeing my girl and celebrating firefighter Stu's retirement with my friends and family.

Friends and family I almost can't believe I have now.

In the span of a couple of weeks, Cascade Point has firmly and irreversibly established itself as my home. This quirky, gossipy, dilapidated little town crept right into my heart, and I can't imagine leaving this place, or the people here.

I especially can't imagine a life without Lucy by my side, and I've been working on something special for her. I'm planning on showing her this evening.

I can't wait to see the look on her face, the smile that lights up her eyes.

I just need to find her first. And break the news that I'm unemployed.

The party is still going in the fire station. Ramping up, if anything. The center of the room is a mess of bodies as people dance to a country song. A Taylor Swift original.

I walk around, looking for her in the crowd, but I don't see her and/or her orange bandana anywhere. Only then do I spot a plate of cookies balanced on a table close to the doors. The chocolate chip cookies are topped with cinnamon (my favorite).

Did Lucy make that plate for me, and then just... walk away?

"Hey, Lockie."

Tricia's come up next to me and is smiling at me with *very* magenta lips. "Where's that hottie in the sports jacket you were speaking to?"

I press my lips together. "He's long gone."

Tricia literally droops. "Shame. I was going to see if he needed directions. Maybe take him up on an offer to drive around in that Mustang Louis said that he was driving. Guess you gave him what he needed."

"I guess I did," I say with a smile.

Mabel appears at my other side like a white-haired, wine-buzzed phantom. "Oh! Was Lucy any help? I mentioned to her that she should go over and make sure you weren't sending the poor soul towards Sinkhole Road."

I blink. "I'm sorry. Sink-*what* road?!"

But Tricia frowns at Mabel. "That's weird, Lucy just ran past me out the back of the building. She seemed in a hurry. Maybe she noticed Sports Jacket was leaving and decided to try and chase him down." I raise a brow at her, and she gives me a sheepish grin. "Sorry, Lockie."

I tilt my head at her. "So, Lucy left?"

"Yup. A few minutes ago. She raced right out the door like she had a fire under her butt." Tricia purses her lips. "She didn't tell you she was going?"

I shake my head, my stomach churning.

282

Lucy *raced out* of the building... after coming to find Mike and me?

Could she have found us outside and overheard our conversation? Not that that's a bad thing—she would've heard me reject Mike's whole dating show racket. She would've heard me quit. But why didn't she stick around?

Unless something upset her.

I think back over my entire conversation with Mike, filtering through his words and my own. And then, I remember the awful way Mike described this town. Remember that he referred to me being *stuck here*.

Uh oh.

I excuse myself from Tricia and Mabel, grab my jacket and head out to my SUV.

I make my way slowly—oh, so slowly—through town towards Lucy and Jordy's rowhouse. I don't know what I was thinking, insisting that I pick Lucy up at her house and drive her to the fire station. It's a painfully slow alternative to just walking, given the awful roads and potholes.

As the newest resident of Cascade Point, I will be taking this complaint to the town council STAT.

When I finally arrive outside the rowhouse, it's clear that no one's home. So, I head to the next logical spot—Lucy's cottage.

The sun's setting when I pull up outside the cottage, and the sky is streaked with pinks, purples and oranges. I run up the path to the cottage, but the windows inside are dark. There's no one waiting out front.

Where could Lucy possibly be?

Maybe I have it all wrong. Maybe she's back at the fire station. Maybe I went off on a wild tangent of assumptions and ended up here, while Lucy is partying it up with Stu & friends.

Feeling like an idiot, I'm about to walk back to my car when I hear an odd squeaking sound.

It's soon followed by a very faint "Wait!"

I peer down the rapidly darkening street towards town, and that's when I see her.

Lucy Summers is *trying* to run towards me.

And she's pulling a child's creaky red wagon.

I cover the distance between us in a few strides, coming right up to her and her bizarre cargo—the red wagon is hauling an aloe vera plant, a cardboard box with a scribbled "wool" on the front, and her blue teaching binder.

Her white heels are dangling from her wrist, and I can see that she's instead wearing Jordy's rainbow flip-flops.

Lucy—with no small amount of dramatism—pushes the handle of the wagon into my hand and collapses against my chest. Her hair is a bit of a rat's nest mess, and she's stripped off her coat and is only wearing her tank top. It occurs to me that she must've dragged that wagon all the way from her rowhouse.

I place a hand on her hair, cradling the back of her head. "Hi, Lucy. Whatcha doing?"

"I went for a run," she wheezes.

I drop the handle of the wagon to wrap both hands around her, propping her against me. "Wearing flip-flops?"

"Well, I certainly wasn't going to run in heels, was I? I don't have *that* much of a death wish."

I smile against her hair. "You left the party."

"I did. I had to go home and collect this stuff."

She steps out of my arms and gestures at her little wagon. I frown at her. "You collected your... aloe vera plant? Why?"

She squares up to me, placing her hands on her hips. Her cheeks are flushed from the exertion, and her hair is falling out of her bandanna, and her shirt is lopsided, and she looks so freaking beautiful, it's all I can do not to carry her into the house right now and lock the door behind us.

"I've started packing."

That's not what I expected to hear.

"Packing for what?" I ask her.

284

"To move with you to LA. Or wherever Sports Jacket man wants you to go." She narrows her eyes. "I'm assuming that was your boss, right?"

"Yeah. That was Mike."

"He offered you a big promotion in LA. And I want to come with you."

"You want to move somewhere new," I clarify, glancing at her wagon. "And you're only bringing a plant, some wool, and a binder."

She shrugs sheepishly. "Well. This is more of a gesture than anything. I have *way* too much stuff to actually pack it all and haul it over here. But I want you to see how serious I am."

She takes a breath, pushing damp tendrils of hair behind her ear.

"I want to be with *you*, wherever that takes us. Lachlan, you said that I make you happy and you can't imagine taking me away from this town, right? Well, as much as I love Cascade and everyone here, you're my family now, too." She nods decisively. "So, if LA is where you need to be right now, I will go with you."

I look at Lucy. Look at the beautiful, amazing, slightly unhinged woman in front of me. I don't think I've ever loved her more than I do in this very moment.

"I'm not going to LA, Princess."

"Yes, you are," she responds firmly, crossing her arms in front of her chest. "I won't take no for an answer. You can't let this opportunity pass you by."

"Sure I can." I smile. "Because I quit."

Lucy's arms fall to her sides. "You quit your job at SparksFly?"

"I'm officially jobless. Penniless. You might need to support us both for a while."

Lucy snorts, but her frown quickly returns. "And this is what you... want?"

285

"*You're* what I want. Living here is what I want. Spending time with my family is what I want."

"But we're not perfect here. Cascade doesn't have any big corporate tech companies for you to work with. We don't have everything you could want or need, at the drop of a hat."

"'Course you do," I say quietly.

But her frown only deepens. "What about everything you've worked hard for? " She bites the inside of her cheek. "You're not really going to give all that up?"

"I am, and I'm happy to. I have new priorities now. I meant what I said, Luce: you make me want to have a life, and I want to do it here. And..." I smile. "I can show you how serious I am about that."

I take Lucy's hand in mine, and I bring her and her wagon towards the cottage. We climb the front steps, but I stop before we can walk through the door.

"You ready?" I ask her, just as I did earlier today.

"Ready for what?"

I smile, and then open the front door.

Lucy's jaw drops.

"There's a lot to be done still, obviously," I say as I lead her into the cottage. "There's only so much I can get at the hardware store, so I've got a list going for a trip to a bigger store in Seattle, and I want you to come with me. I want you with me every step of the way."

Lucy looks around the foyer, where the walls are freshly painted. I've also polished the hardwood floors, and I bought a blue and white area rug that reminds me of ocean spray.

We step into the living room next, where I haven't made many adjustments, save painting the wall by the door and hanging a few photos from Lucy's childhood that I found in the boxes beneath the stairs. Her eyes shine as she looks at the photo of herself and her mother at what appears to be her middle school graduation.

"I was thinking that we could knock down that far wall to create an open living and dining room setup, if you want," I tell her. "That way, it's an easy space to move through for when we have people over. Or host book clubs."

In the bedroom upstairs, I've started removing some of the carpet, revealing the wood floors underneath. I explain the other changes I'd like to make to the room, including building a large custom cupboard for all of Lucy's knit-fluencer projects.

Back in the kitchen, I tell Lucy that I've ordered a new stove and fridge online, and I've started replacing a couple of the smaller cabinets and cupboards. Including...

"The sticky drawer!" she squeals.

"Yeah. That section was a mess."

She whirls around to face me, her eyes glowing. "Lachlan, how did you manage to *do* all this?"

"I told you I'm efficient. And this is just the start. I want to fix up this cottage to *your* standards. Whatever makes you happy, Lucy."

"You make me happy," she says immediately, wrapping her arms around me. "And I want to do this with you. Together."

She stands on tiptoe and presses her lips to mine. Her clean, sea breeze scent fills my senses, and I can't stop myself from placing my hands on her waist and tugging her closer, deepening the kiss.

After a moment, I step away to lead her to the last room: the master bedroom.

I push open the door and stand behind her, wrapping my arms around her so that her back is to my front. "I haven't made any changes here yet, but I have plans for this room, Princess. I want us to sleep here together someday. When we're married."

She freezes, fingers mid-stroke down my sleeve. When she turns to face me, her green eyes lock on mine. "*When* we're married?"

"Does that scare you?"

287

"Not at all. Except of course, if you plan on booking the honeymoon suite at the Last Stance Motel." She laughs. "But this might be my favorite room in the whole house."

I put my hands on her hips and turn her quickly so her back is now flush with the doorframe. I place an arm above her head, leaning in close. "It'll be my favorite room, too," I say quietly, and her eyes darken.

I trace a finger down her cheek and let that hand rest on her hip. "Lucy, I want you to know that the Lachlan who lived in LA and worked at SparksFly... I'm not him anymore. You brought me back to life, back to who I am, back to my family. What I see ahead of us is a new and fresh start."

Lucy smiles up at me, her cheeks pink. "I'm so happy to hear that. So happy that you're happy here. Because I love you, Lachlan Chase Brighton."

Her fingers tighten behind my back, and I press my forehead to hers. "I love you too, Lucy Mary-Ann Summers. Love you with everything I have and all that I am. I can't wait to spend our lives together here, in this town, with these people. After all, I'm *fairly certain* that's what you want, too?"

Lucy tilts her head back to look at me. She's so freaking beautiful, with her hair a mess, and her shirt lopsided, and her lips in a gorgeous smile that I want to see every day for the rest of my life.

Her eyes sparkle as she says, "No comment."

EPILOGUE
LUCY

Six months later

There was a time when I believed that a date shouldn't end with a person left stranded, soaking wet and alone, on the side of a road...

Guess the joke's on me.

Actually, the joke's on Jordy.

"Hey, girl!" I call through the cracked open window of the Jeep. "Need a lift?"

My best friend and roommate looks up from where she's seated at a bus stop by Pacific Beach, the hood of her raincoat pulled right up to shield her face from the downpour. Her bow lips are turned down in a pout, but her face brightens the minute she sees that it's only me heckling her from the driver's seat of an SUV.

"Lucyloo!" She bounds towards me. "Took you long enough!"

I laugh as she rips off her coat, folds it into the plastic bag I give her, and then hurries herself onto the passenger seat. "Brr!" she says, turning all the heat registers towards her. "Blast it!"

So I do. It might be mid-June, but these summer thunderstorms are something else.

"So, what happened, J?" I ask as I pull back onto the road. "The guy was a dud?"

"He was a *stinker*. The type of guy who hates sweet treats. And it's not that he's healthy and simply chooses not to eat sugar. No, no, I can totally respect that. What I *can't* respect is a man looking down his nose at me and making comments about his Atkins-diet-loving ex while I'm just trying to enjoy one tiny slice of chocolate cake."

I gasp. "How dare he."

"Right? I don't need that energy in my life." Jordy tuts. "Plus, you know, he believes that wildfires are a conspiracy theory made up by aliens."

I snort. "Wait. That was serious?"

"Yup. Turns out that part of his dating profile was entirely accurate. The rest of it? Not so much." She shudders. "Anyway, all's well that ends well. And thanks for picking me up."

"No problem. I was in Pacific Beach anyway to pick up those cute lace curtains I liked. And for some reason, Lachlan practically insisted I take the Jeep and do it today. He practically threw me into the driver's seat and started the engine for me."

"That explains it." Jordy laughs. "I was wondering why you were driving."

"Pretty good, huh?" I say, proudly. Because I *am* proud. I haven't had many opportunities to drive in my life, and when Lachlan bought this Jeep, I asked him to teach me. He's been a surprisingly patient and forgiving teacher. Especially when I almost hit that pack of seagulls last week.

In my defense, they *did* fly away in time. But not before leaving some gifts on the windshield, of course.

"Isn't it your six month anniversary today?"

I look over at my best friend in surprise. "Yeah, six months since our first date. How on earth did you remember that?"

"I remember everything, remember?" I could swear there's an odd tug in the corner of her lips, but she shakes her head and changes the subject.

Jordy regales me with more details about her date all the way back to our rowhouse, and by the time I pull up out front, I'm in stitches from laughing so hard.

I'm about to get the curtains out of the trunk when Jordy stops me. "I got it," she says, with a weird little smile on her face.

"That's okay, J. It's just curtains."

Her smile becomes even more strange. "I'll meet you inside, Lucyloo."

I frown at her. "Jordana... What's going on?"

"Nothing."

She's a terrible liar.

After giving her one more highly suspicious, narrowed-eye look (which she fully ignores as she puts all of her focus into opening the trunk), I walk up the front steps to our little rowhouse by the port.

And that's when I notice a folded piece of paper tacked to our door. I turn to point it out to Jordy, but she's still riffling away in the trunk of the Jeep.

I grab the paper and flip it open to see that there's writing inside. Distinctive blocked lettering.

Princess. I once wondered if a simple list could contain all the things I love about you. Now, six months later, I know for certain that such a list could never be simple. Because how I feel for you is not and will never be simple.

I've got a little adventure planned for you today. Come to the cottage. And don't worry about the car. Jordy, Beau, and I have that one covered.

I love you

—L

Tears prick my eyes as I hold Lachlan's beautiful note to my chest.

Jordy's now ambling down the sidewalk, carrying rolls of lace curtain. Behind her, Beau has appeared and is getting into the Jeep. He started shaving his beard a few weeks back—with only stubble covering his strong jaw—so I can clearly see the mysterious smile he gives me before driving off.

"Jo?" I croak to my best friend, holding up the note. "What is this?"

She shrugs, but I notice her cheeks are pink. "You should probably go see what he wants."

So I do. I run (jog) the entire way to the cottage, hardly aware of the burn in my legs. Because no, I'm still very much *not* a runner.

When I finally reach it, the Jeep is parked outside. I bolt up the front steps, taking them two at a time, and burst into the foyer.

"Lachlan, I got your note!"

There's no response, and I begin to walk through the empty house, wondering where he could be. Wondering why he wanted me to come here. Wondering what "adventure" he has in store for me today.

That's one thing that hasn't changed in the time that we've been together: Lachlan is still constantly surprising me. Every day. In the best ways possible.

Over the last six months, we've only gone from strength to strength as a couple. He's my closest friend, my confidant. The one I talk to about every mundane school day, every struggle and challenge, and every blessing and piece of fortune. In turn, he shares his life with me. Giving so much of himself that it's hard to imagine that our relationship started with him sharing nothing, except lies.

I walk into the living room, where my body instinctively floods with warmth. Lachlan and I have been hard at work

292

fixing up the cottage. It was tough to get that wall knocked down between the kitchen and living room, and there've been more than a few complications, but we've taken them all in our stride.

And now, I couldn't be happier with the end result.

The living room, kitchen and dining room are now open-plan, and the bay window at the front floods the entire space with bright light, no matter the weather. The hardwood floors feature shaggy navy blue carpets beneath the new cream sofa and wooden coffee table. Lachlan also bought a gorgeous teak wood dining table from a friend of his down the bay. The kitchen has all new appliances, but we kept the look of the wood cupboards. For nostalgia's sake.

It feels like... *home*. Reminds me of when I shared this cottage with my mother, and it makes me excited for the life Lachlan and I will create here.

And I can't wait to someday move back in, with him.

That's when I spot a familiar maroon item folded on the sofa.

My One Night Stance hoodie. Which I definitely don't remember leaving here.

Frowning, I pick up the hoodie, and as I do, a piece of paper falls from it. I pick it up and find that there's yet another note.

Hey, Princess. This might surprise you, but this hoodie is my favorite item of clothing that you own. Because it represents the start of everything... The first night we met. The first night we shared a bed, and I got to hold you in my arms. The first time I started to wonder about the strange, mud-drenched girl with the orange bandana and bright green eyes.

I'll never forget that motel (for many reasons, including that horrific couch), but it will always have a special place in my heart.

Put this hoodie into the canvas bag I left you and bring it with you upstairs.

So, the game begins.

293

—L

"What is going on?" I mutter, holding this note and the last one against my chest before tucking both of them into the back pocket of my jeans.

Because Lachlan still leaves me handwritten notes, and I've kept every single one. From the most boring, grocery-list-level ones, to the sweet, romantic ones that make my toes curl.

I bound up the stairs to the second bedroom. Our current renovation project.

The walls are half-painted, the hardwood floors have yet to be polished... But at the end of the room is the custom cupboard that Lachlan built for my knitting things.

For some reason, I find myself drawn to the cupboard, and I open the doors to see a new set of knitting needles wrapped up in some creamy white wool. I run my fingers along the wool, and catch sight of another slip of paper.

This note is shorter but written in the same familiar block lettering.

Here you are, Princess. You mentioned awhile ago that you wanted this particular type of wool to create a new dress for yourself. Well, the other dresses you knit for yourself drive me freaking wild, so of course, I had to indulge you. Seriously, who would've thought I'd be so attracted to a girl wearing knits? Definitely not me.

Place this into the canvas bag with the hoodie. You're headed to your classroom next.

—L

My heartbeat's in my ears as I skip down the stairs and out of the cottage. I'm about to run down the sidewalk towards school when I stop myself short.

The school is a blocks away, and I'm going to need much more work-out friendly attire than the jeans and knit tank top I'm currently sporting. Is this "adventure" some backwards way

294

for Lachlan to try and get me to enjoy running and the great outdoors again?!

At that moment, a familiar face appears from around the Jeep. "You want a ride?"

I beam at Beau. "Sure do!"

I hop into the passenger side of the Jeep, and Beau and I get on the road towards the elementary school. Of course, I can't stop myself from shooting him rapid-fire questions.

"What's all this about, Beau? What's Lachlan up to? Why has he sent me on this scavenger hunt?"

Beau doesn't answer any of them. Doesn't even flinch. Which shouldn't surprise me—the guy can be pretty stubborn. Not unlike his brother, actually.

As he pulls up outside of the elementary school, he speaks his first and only words: "I'll wait for you here, but don't take long. I got stuff to do."

I give him a flat look but obediently hop out of the Jeep.

It's a Saturday evening, so I use my keys to unlock the doors and head to my classroom.

The fluorescent lights flood the room, and I look eagerly around the pods of tiny desks, the colorful mats on the ground, the stacked bins full of toys, crafts, textbooks, and everything else a five-year-old could need at school.

Summer break starts this week, and as excited as I am to have a couple months off, I already know that I'm going to miss my kids. It's hard to believe how much they've grown in the span of a year. That might be one of my favorite things about teaching kindergarten—watching these tiny humans grow and develop into their unique personalities.

I'm excited to one day have my own little kiddos with Lachlan. I already know that he's going to be a great father—the perfect blend of disciplined and wise, patient and kind. He and sassy Olivia, in particular, have formed a unique bond that makes my ovaries ache whenever I see them together.

And that's when I see it. On my teacher's desk.

I dash over and find the knitted duck stuffed animal I got from the breakfast place near the Last Stance Motel. The one I've kept in my classroom for my kids ever since. And there's a note pinned to it.

I have a feeling you might see where this is going, Princess. Because yes, this classroom—this desk in particular—is another favorite place of mine. The exact spot where I first kissed you, where I first gave into what I was feeling for you...

Turns out, those feelings were substantial. And now, here we are.

I know this duck belongs to your class, but maybe, for now, you can borrow it. Tuck it into your canvas bag. The next stop is back at the cottage again. Come and find me out back.

P.S. Beau had better be driving you. He owes me one. If not, you have my full permission to call him and give him a piece of your (and my) mind. Better yet, sic Jordy on him.

—L

I giggle at his last words, at the thought of Jordy ripping Beau a new one when he's a full foot taller than her. She'd do it, though. I've seen it happen.

As I tuck the note alongside the others and place the duck in the bag, my mind snags on one word in particular. *Borrow.*

Lachlan has left me three things now: a hoodie I've had for months. New knitting needles. And now, this borrowed stuffed animal.

Oh, my gosh.

By the time Beau and I are pulling up in front of the cottage again, the car completely silent this time, I'm totally lost in my thoughts. Because I have an inkling of an idea where this is going, why Lachlan's sent me on this wild goose chase...

"We're here, Luce." Beau's voice startles me back to the present. "You gettin' out?"

I don't make a move to exit the Jeep. Instead, I look out the

296

passenger window at the cottage. "Hey, Beau? You know what this is all about, don't you."

He doesn't respond. When I look at him, he simply nods.

"And you think it's a good idea?"

Beau frowns then, averting his gaze to look out the window ahead of us.

I'd like to think that I've grown even closer with Beau—and with Graham and Anna-May—since Lachlan and I have been together. We often see them at book club, and we have bi-weekly family dinners arranged at their grandparents' house on the outskirts of town. We've spent countless evenings together, laughing, talking, catching up.

Over the last months, I've watched Lachlan fit seamlessly back into his family. And I'd like to think I fit with them, too.

But the way Beau pauses, I start to worry.

And then: "No, it's not a good idea. It's a great one."

I reach across the car to wrap my arms tight around Beau. He chuckles gruffly and pats me on the back.

I get out of the Jeep and find myself on the sidewalk yet again, canvas bag hanging from my arm. It's pretty full, but if I'm right—and what I think is happening is *actually* happening —there's only one more thing I'd put in here.

I stride down the sidewalk and up the porch steps. Walk through the house and out to the back porch.

And there, I find the love of my life staring out towards the orange sun peeking from beneath gray clouds as it sets. We ended up removing the hedge out back, so our view is entirely unobstructed, and the sunsets can be pretty spectacular. As is the one tonight.

Lachlan's facing away from me, his arms crossed, and I don't think he heard me arrive so I take a minute to catch my breath, here in silence.

Doesn't hurt that he looks *good* from the back like this, in his charcoal chinos and black tee which stretches over the broad

297

planes of his muscular back. I've run my fingers down his back so many times at this point, but I'll never get enough of it. Never get enough of *him*.

"Hi," I say quietly.

Lachlan doesn't flinch, but he turns his head so I see the silhouette of his side profile—his strong nose and even stronger jaw. He's grown his hair out a little since living in Cascade, and I love the way it curls at the end. Love the way it feels between my fingers.

"Hey, Princess. You got through that pretty quick."

"What can I say, I love surprises."

Lachlan chuckles, and now, he turns to face me fully, leaning back against the porch railing. He gives me that smile that makes my heart skip a beat, and his glacier blue eyes lock on mine. "Good thing I love surprising you."

"You're good at it, too." I shake my head, trying to catch my breath.

We've been together for months, but every time he looks at me like he is now, it's like the first time all over again. The butterflies, the warmth spreading through my extremities, the skipping heartbeat...

I hold out the canvas bag. "I have all your notes and the things you wanted me to collect."

"I *was* wondering if the note on your desk would still be there. Not sure if wayward children or geckos might be roaming the school on a weekend."

My laugh sounds breathy. "So. What's all this about?"

Lachlan's blue eyes twinkle as he gestures towards the porch swing. "Let's sit."

I wait for him to take a seat on the swing before curling up on his lap, just as I've done so many nights before. He rocks us gently back and forth, and presses a kiss to the top of my head.

"Remember six months ago, when you offered to move with me to LA?"

I blink, slightly taken aback. I wasn't expecting him to bring *that* up right now. "Yeah?"

"And remember how you said that you wanted to be with me, no matter where that takes us. Because we're family."

I nod slowly, replaying those hazy words in my mind. I meant them, of course, but I was quite caught up in the heat of the moment.

I mean, I hauled my favorite aloe vera plant all the way here in a child's wagon.

"These months have been the best of my life. Seeing you every day, going for strolls with my grandparents, hanging out with Beau and the boys, working hard doing repairs and renos in town now that Benny's handed all those projects over to me... I've never felt happier, more fulfilled."

His chest rises and falls against my cheek as he hugs me closer.

"You once asked me, during a lying game, whether I had a special someone, a girlfriend or was married. Back then, I thought the entire notion was ludicrous. And so, I lied and responded that I was deeply in love."

I swallow thickly around the ball in my throat. I might've been drunk off my rocker that night, but that part of our conversation is crystal clear in my mind. "I remember," I say quietly.

"I had no idea then that I was meeting and getting to know someone who would check those boxes off for me, one by one. Because you changed my life, Lucy Summers. I would go to the depths of the ocean to make you as happy as you make me. And if it wasn't obvious, I'm deeply, inescapably, irrevocably in love with you. And I fall in love with you more every single day."

I close my eyes against the tears that well at his sweet words. "I love you, too, Lachlan. So, so much. More than I could ever imagine."

He places a finger beneath my chin and gently tilts my head up. He wipes at the dampness beneath my eyes as his gaze locks on mine. His beautiful eyes that draw me in, that capture me, and I am very much a willing captive.

"I'm yours, Lucy. My heart is yours, forever and always. So, all those months ago, when you told me I was your family, well... you already know you're mine, too. And now, I want to make it official."

He begins to shift. Begins to move so one hand locks beneath my thighs, and the other wraps around my back. Before I can say or do anything, Lachlan is standing with me cradled in his arms.

He places me carefully on the porch swing.

And then, he kneels on one knee.

Takes out a little blue box.

"Lachlan," I gasp as he pops it open, revealing a sparkling, beautiful yet understated diamond ring.

"Lucy Mary-Ann Summers... Marry me?"

He barely finishes what he's saying before I'm diving off the swing and into his arms. "Yes, yes! Ohmygosh, yes, Lachlan. A thousand times over!"

I'm kissing him and kissing him, and he's smiling against my lips as he holds onto me tight. Tears are fully trickling down my face now, but I don't care. My heart is so full, I think it might burst.

When we pull away, Lachlan gently places the ring on my finger. It fits like a dream, and I watch it sparkle and glitter in the light of the setting sun.

"Wow," I whisper. "Lachlan, it's gorgeous."

"Suits you well, too. It's my grandmother's."

"This ring belonged to Anna-May?"

"The very one Graham gave her. She passed it on to me as soon as she heard that I'd quit my job in LA and was staying in Cascade Point. She knew, as well as I did, that I was going to marry you." He chuckles. "Graham joked that the ring wasn't quite flashy enough for Anna-May's tastes these days, but he agreed that it would suit you perfectly."

The knowledge that we have the blessing of Lachlan's grandparents, along with Beau's, fills me with even more joy, and I have to place a hand over my heart. I'm so elated that they're happy to accept me as one of their own. To also become my family, officially.

Lachlan places his hands on my hips and moves me around so he can sit on the porch swing again and place me back in his lap. I press a kiss to his hair, his cheek, his neck, inhaling his aftershave and the smell of his warm skin.

And there, curled up together on the porch swing, watching the sunset, I know for certain that I've never experienced a moment so perfect. But I also know that more moments like this are to come. Again and again and again.

Because that's what Lachlan and I are together: perfect.

We're perfect opposites. Perfectly different. Perfect for each other. Like two puzzle pieces that look nothing alike, and yet fall into place, side by side.

He's everything I could've ever wanted, and everything I never knew I needed. The man I'll always choose to fight for, and try for, and be honest with.

And it all started with a lying game.

THANK YOU FOR READING!

Thank you so much for picking up Lachlan and Lucy's love story. I hope you enjoyed getting to know these two characters... and the lovely, quirky coastal town of Cascade Point.

If you enjoyed this book, please do leave me a review. As an indie author, reviews mean the *world* to me. I appreciate each and every one of them!

www.ingramcontent.com/pod-product-compliance
Lightning Source LLC
Chambersburg PA
CBHW030422180626
46812CB00005B/2141